Laelia

Laelia

A NOVEL

Ruth-Miriam Garnett

ATRIA BOOKS

New York   London   Toronto   Sydney   Singapore

ATRIA BOOKS

1230 Avenue of the Americas
New York, NY 10020

ISBN: 0-7434-6630-6

First Atria Books hardcover edition January 2004

ATRIA BOOKS is a trademark of Simon & Schuster, Inc.

Manufactured in the United States of America

*To Irene and Freeman, my profound and exquisite parents,
in deep gratitude for their blueprint.*

Acknowledgments

I would like to thank with great emphasis my editor and friend, Malaika Adero, whose meticulous brilliance greatly increased the joys of this labor. I could not budge without my sister Olivia, who reads whatever I ask whenever I ask, and who is there unfailingly when solitude overwhelms. I write for her, for my brothers Freeman and Stephen, the two pillars of Rome, and for each of their sons, my nine nephews. Sharon Bowie and Natalia Kanem were early readers. Adrienne Ingrum encouraged me to write fiction years ago; I finally heard her. My poet cadre, Mervyn Taylor, Dawad Philip, Peggy Tartt, Gary Johnston, Sekou Sundiata, and Jacqueline Johnson, are indispensable to my mojo. Susan Christine Mullen and Crystal King have guided me through much opacity and always let me whine. Thanks to my extended tribe, the Garnett, Honesty, Kinchelow, and Thomas clans. You are the best people I know.

Let your women keep silence in the churches; for it is not permitted unto them to speak; for they are commanded to be under obedience, as also saith the law.

—I Corinthians, 14:34

Prologue

LYDIA WRINKLED HER small nose, her black oval-shaped sunglasses shifting upward, then down again, uncomfortable against her flattish cheeks. She knew the glasses would leave reddish half-circles under her eyes after she took them off, an annoying temporary scarification on her easily irritated skin, but she always felt more confident wearing them. She realized also just then that she had rubbed a blister on her right foot. The new leather of her moccasin started fighting the skin of her instep as she walked up the long driveway leading to the Cates mansion. She felt this was not a good sign, and that maybe she shouldn't have come. Now, standing in front of the oak double doors framed in beveled glass, she shivered slightly. Her body felt cold, though she sweated, and her jet black hair, curly and parted in the middle, was moist from the scalp to the ends that rested teasingly against her neck.

"I can't," she said aloud, as if making an apology to herself. "Today, I can't."

No one seemed to be home, she reasoned, but then reason gave way to a feeling that she should not be where she was, that there was no way she would be welcome here. The huge house, the groomed yard, the long driveway were aloof, unaware of her presence, and she felt totally out of place. Lydia hated that feeling, familiar to her for much of her life, that no warmth awaited her, no hope, no possibility. The feeling that she was not privy, didn't belong, enveloped her. She thought she heard footsteps approaching in the hallway beyond the door.

"I can't do this," she repeated.

Turning away, she started the trek back down the driveway to her car parked on the street in front. She halted, thinking she needed to do something, not just run away. Her whole life she had had to fight. When she was afraid, she fought harder.

Lydia turned herself around and began to walk toward the back of the house. She wasn't yet ready to leave, but she didn't want to be seen by anyone. As she walked to the rear of the estate, looking at the tailored hedges that ran all the way up the drive like an endless beard, she almost forgot how scared she was and how badly her foot hurt. A third of the way down the backyard, she saw a greenhouse. She knew Rebecca Cates grew orchids, that she had great success crossbreeding varieties from all over the world. She knew that Rebecca, her sisters, and their spouses lived together in the mansion. That was all she knew about Rebecca. She thought these were probably the least important things to know about the woman whose help she so needed.

Lydia, limping, approached the greenhouse, her chaos resolving itself gradually into curiosity, then amazement, once she looked inside. The order and stillness of the long space soothed her, and she forgot her discomfort of a few minutes earlier. She gazed at the rows of plants mounted on long tables, tools hanging from wall racks, beneath them some watering cans, and shelves full of beakers of various sizes, flawlessly arranged. The flowers, incredibly vibrant pink, yellow, orange, purplish, and stark white, dazzled her.

"So beautiful in here," she spoke to herself softly. "This is a good person."

Lydia walked through the long building warmed by the sunlight streaming through the glass panels, which were its ceiling and the upper half of its walls. She stopped to look at a square thermostat in the middle of the large room. It was numbered in both Fahrenheit and centigrade measures. On the back wall of the greenhouse, a half dozen of what looked like butchers' aprons hung on a row of hooks. The stiff shapes of the canvas fabric looked to Lydia like a group of uncles watching protectively over the plants and implements underneath them. The flower smell grew stronger as Lydia walked the length of the room. Mingled with this fragrance was another, more delicate smell, that of freshly dug soil. Her senses overwhelmed, Lydia began to cry, and now with mascara melting, reddened cheeks, and blistered foot, she knew she would have to come back when she was composed and presentable, and wearing different shoes.

Exiting slowly from the greenhouse and crossing the brief distance from the yard, Lydia walked the length of the driveway once again, feeling somewhat lighter than when she approached the house and grounds the first time.

A few minutes into her five-mile drive to the highway, down a neighborhood street, pleasant, but with smaller homes than the one she had just visited, she saw three women walking in her direction. Instinctively, Lydia knew they were the Cates sisters. She watched them until her car, heading down the opposite side of the road, outstripped them. Before the gathering distance shrunk them, she formed a quick impression of the trio. They seemed lighthearted and suitably elegant to be the inhabitants of their mansion. That was all Lydia could tell about them from her brief inspection. But inside her she knew the spirits of the flowers and the charmed glass place would bless her when she returned.

I

IT WAS TECHNICALLY still spring, the end of May, and the residents of Peoria, Illinois, were experiencing the first hint of what was usually a stiflingly hot summer. The three Cates sisters walked the mile and back to Sunday church services for as long as the weather was mild and the spring flowers remained in bloom. This morning, as usual, they did not walk exactly abreast. Rebecca, the eldest, led by a few paces. A large, light-skinned woman, she strode vigorously enough for her legs to make a swishing sound against the stiff fabric of her skirt, strands of gray-streaked hair escaping from the bun wound loosely under her wide-brimmed hat. Her fitted jacket outlined her large bosom, defined a surprising waist and the fertility-goddess dimensions of her hips.

Claudia, the middle sister, walked crisply but without the advantage of Rebecca's low-heeled pumps. She artfully placed one yellow-heeled foot in front of the other, in the manner of catwalk models. Her shoes matched precisely the color of her shantung suit. Slender, erect, and regal with an amazing instinct for style, she followed slightly behind Rebecca, her veiled cloche not quite concealing her strong, interesting features. Her veil, falling over her wide-set black eyes under thick arched brows and just beneath her slightly hooked nose, provided her with intended mystery. Sensing beads of moisture on her nose, Claudia removed a jewel-encrusted compact from her purse, powdered precisely, and returned it.

Rebecca, observing from the corner of her eye, smiled, then shifted her glance to Gracelyn, the youngest Cates sister. Round and sensual, Gracelyn at fifty had an ebony cherub's face with smooth bark-colored skin. Sauntering unevenly in a loose-fitting royal blue jersey dress, a matching sweater tied at her neck, she took in the landscape and good-naturedly stopped to hail a non-churchgoing neighbor bending over her garden.

Their community knew them as Reuben and Mattie Cates's daughters, female scions of the utterly respectable and monied Cates patriarch. Reuben had held his own with the nearby white businesses, putting in innumerable hours poring over catalogues and stocking his small department store with high quality, yet affordable brands. Mattie Cates had had an eye for what ladies wanted: thread, lampshades, a variety of colored stockings. The couple's astute synergy had resulted in stable profit margins year after year.

That morning, the women sat in their usual place, the sixth pew back at the First Baptist Church in Peoria, the church they had grown up in. As children, they had filed in in front of their parents, who sat together next to the aisle. The seating arrangement never varied. It was always Rebecca, then Claudia, then Gracelyn, the intractable birth order they preserved in their various rituals as adult women.

Rebecca Cates, the spitting image of Reuben in her coloring and girth, listened carefully to what was coming from the pulpit. Reverend Wilson and his wife, Julia, had come to Peoria four years back when the previous pastor, Reverend Simmons, died from a massive heart attack. The girls had grown up with the elegant, erudite Reverend Simmons. His sermons were metaphysical, uplifting, and not overlong. However, Reverend Wilson was long-winded and a relentless purveyor of moralistic instruction. His bent these days was to remind women of their submissive role in the church and in the home. Rebecca surmised that this effort followed a scandal involving the leader of the national church organization. The man was discovered to have a mistress, upon whom he lavished considerable church money, including bestowing upon this woman a waterfront cottage. The situation was kept hush-hush until the man's wife discovered the infidelity, traveled to the resort cottage on Lake Michigan, and set it afire. Both the black press and the white press went wild, following the case. Congregations could not look the other way; women condemned this and other ubiquitous male behavior in a louder voice than at any time before in the history of the church.

To move things back to normal, Wilson offered a steady procession of wicked and wily women chronicled in the Bible. The preacher intoned: ". . . Job remained faithful to God against all odds. Even his wife encouraged him to curse God. But Job said to her, 'Are you crazy?' "

In previous weeks it had been Jezebel, Delilah, the deceitful Tamar, and Timothy's railings against women whose sole purpose was to corrupt as many men as possible.

Rebecca wondered if she was the only one in the congregation observing the pastor's wife, Julia, while all this was happening. Julia piqued her curiosity, because more than once Rebecca had found the small woman staring at her. The first time this happened, Reverend Wilson had praised his wife from the pulpit, calling her soft-spoken. Julia's eyes darted to where Rebecca was sitting, searching her face confusedly. The second time Julia's gaze fell on Rebecca, Wilson spoke fervently about keeping the marriage vows in sickness and in health, and until the parting imposed by death. Rebecca wasn't sure at first whether Julia was friend or foe, but her overriding instinct told her the somewhat nervous woman was seeking her approval. She was in any case non-threatening, not that there was any way she could have threatened Rebecca. Julia was never present at the male-dominated meetings of the trustees and financial committees of the church to which Rebecca was customarily invited, along with her large checkbook. But Rebecca did encounter Julia at church dinners, socials, and concerts often enough to assess her. When Rebecca and her sisters attended these functions, Julia went out of her way to speak to them. Rebecca observed that when this happened, Wilson, whose eyes were frequently upon his wife, frowned noticeably. The Cates sisters thought Julia friendly and naturally pretty, though they described her in their chat as regrettably unadorned, with lifeless hair, scant makeup, and the most minimal pedestrian jewelry. She seemed a part of the background, much like the obsolete piano kept in the church basement's dining hall. Julia, Rebecca concluded, acquiesced to her husband in every way, was loyal to him, and content to be the wife of the pastor. Other than that, there did not seem to be too much bubbling underneath her surface.

After the scandal in the national church organization subsided, for the most part the women of the church were again sanguine, playing their roles as cooks, choir members, and ushers and doing most of the busywork of the church. None protested when Reverend Wilson urged his women parishioners to triple their fund-raising efforts by increasing their bake sales, flea markets, choir concerts, and special-occasion teas. When he announced he would table a proposal for a church day-care center until the following fiscal year, the women complied with his stated priorities. They deferred to and fussed over a succession of young male seminary students assigned to First Baptist at Wilson's request. They accepted the authority of these men half their age whose tenure at the church would be only temporary, and they paraded their unmarried daughters before them. A young woman seminarian was assigned to the church shortly after Reverend Wilson became pastor, but she left without explanation after only a few months into her appointment. From the pulpit, Wilson decried what he called a lack of tenacity in some young people.

Rebecca listened halfheartedly to Wilson's Sunday morning tirades, footnoting what might be done to rid the church of his leadership. But for now, the Cates women had more pressing matters to address and they had to be pragmatic. Wilson would have to be neutralized in their current scenario.

Each of the Cates sisters had felt for a time that her husband should be put away where others could take care of him. The sisters had married men only slightly older than themselves, but these men, who had been no match for their wives in their unusual vigor, strong constitutions, and mental energy, were all in decline. Rebecca's husband, Jake, suffering from brain damage and forgetting the tasks appropriate to daylight, burned toast in the middle of the night. Claudia's intemperate husband, Timothy, stopped work on a modest pension, was awake for half days only, and when not drinking, shaking. Gracelyn's Bernard was bedridden with a sinister bone cancer and moaning constantly.

Lucy Sims, a nurse attendant, was on hand every weekend from Saturday morning to dusk Sunday to tend to the sisters' ailing spouses. She made rounds at intervals, opening the door to each bedroom, bathing and feeding Bernard and checking Jake's elimination, then locking the doors behind her. She made certain Timothy ate something when sober, and when not sober, removed his clothes, cleaned up any vomit, and sponged him down with a wet cloth. She left copies of the *Peoria Call, Jet Magazine,* and *National Geographic* in the men's rooms. Afterward, she locked each one's door again and headed downstairs for the next meal preparation.

Lucy was a good nurse—kind, efficient, and able to control each of her charges. When Timothy was not shaking too badly, Lucy steered him and Jake down the back stairs, holding each man's arms carefully, and took them out into the backyard to sit for an hour in the sun. She read short stories to poor Bernard when his moaning lessened and allowed him to concentrate.

After Lucy exited the Cates mansion Monday morning of each week, Rebecca, Claudia, and Gracelyn threw themselves into the care of their men. Following Rebecca's lead, Claudia and Gracelyn gritted their teeth and did their allotted tasks superlatively, one sister taking over for another when burnout resulted from the grueling round-the-clock duties. Visitors to their home were impressed with their work ethic, how busy they were during daylight hours. On a typical day, Gracelyn prepared meals for the invalids, Rebecca scheduled doctors' appointments and computed insurance deductibles, and Claudia went to the pharmacy for medications and ran other errands. Visitors who were themselves caretakers knew especially what the sisters faced daily. They understood the endless planning and work required in a situation that would mean life or death at any moment a mistake was made. They understood the discipline and dedication that must underlie a commitment to sick persons, maintained despite the sameness and unpleasantness of the work from day to day. They understood the danger to the well of exhaustion, frustration, and despair should they sense their utmost efforts were unable to thwart the persistent deterioration of their charges. They knew what it took to cherish the sanctity of life enough to wrestle with the gravity of life eroding.

As their husbands' health worsened, the Cates women vacated the second-story bedrooms they had shared with them. Rebecca and Claudia dispersed themselves to the third story of the large house and Gracelyn occupied the attic, which she had begun to imagine vividly as her writer's garret. Throughout the day, the ministering of multiple medications kept the women rotating their trips up and down the stairs to Jake's and Timothy's rooms. Timothy was invariably hung over and frequently passed out. Only in the evening did he summon enough sobriety and strength to exit the house. At any hour of the night also, the sisters might hear Jake wandering downstairs, or Bernard's moans. Though usually awakened, they did not always bestir themselves. Only the smell of something left burning on the stove or a draft from the front door hastily closed and now swept open in a gust of wind would bring Rebecca or Claudia to her feet to investigate. Gracelyn would answer Bernard's muffled moaning and go downstairs from her attic space to adjust his pillows or see that he had enough blankets. Though the disruptions were frequent, the sisters decided against Lucy's method of locking the men in to prevent them from harming themselves.

"Jake knows this house like the palm of his hand," Rebecca told her sisters. "If he wants to wander around, he'll be safe enough. And if he lights the stove, the smell will hit me. I don't think we should lose a good night's sleep over it. Dr. Turner can't give Bernard any more morphine than that drip allows, so we just have to let him holler. Gracelyn, I wouldn't even disturb him; just try and rest your mind until that pain passes."

"It's hard to lie there and hear him suffer."

"I know it is, honey child."

"But I'm just so tired at the end of the day."

"Of course you are. You need your sleep. You can't do a thing for him rest-broken, and he most likely doesn't know if you're there or not, he's so far gone."

Gracelyn nodded weakly.

"Timothy is going to get to town and find some liquor whether we lock his door or not," Rebecca continued. "That skinny man is spry, and I don't put it past him to go out the window and climb down the trellis. Other than that, it's no use having him bang on the door in the middle of the night causing a commotion. We have to get our rest for our own sake, as well as for the menfolks'. We can't do everything round the clock, day in and day out. And what we can't do, the Lord will." As always, Rebecca's dictum was followed by her sisters.

The Cates women maintained a pristine order in the house, enabling the sick and the well to coexist. When Lucy returned on Saturday morning to relieve the sisters, she never found anything amiss in the men's cleanliness, nor were their pharmaceuticals ever in short supply. She commented often to her neighbors how circumspect the Cates women were as caretakers, and mused along with them how difficult it must be to care for chronically ill menfolk.

With Lucy in charge of their men, Sunday after church for the Cates sisters was long and pleasurable. Once home, they enacted their weekly ritual of cooking a massive dinner and talking up a storm while eating it. Immediately following the second course of their meal, they collected baskets of threads, yarns, and fabric scraps and removed themselves to the sprawling front porch of the mansion, where sunlight filtered like quicksilver through the railings. Seated in wicker fan chairs painted a spring green, they worked studiously on crochet, needlepoint, and piecework and continued the conversation begun at the dining table.

Today, Rebecca, eyes steeled and staring straight ahead, paused from probing and twirling a wooden crochet hook into the deep burgundy rug yarn of her project. Earlier in the day, when she and her sisters had strolled home from church service, her mind had begun to churn with thoughts about their husbands. Rebecca moved a sweat-soaked lock from her brow, smoothing it back in place so it would not moisten her clear gray eyes.

"We've all borne a heavy burden. For myself, the Lord has shown me a way to turn it over to Him."

"Turn it over, that's what He wants us to do," said Claudia, her eyes riveted on her embroidery. She would not lead the discussion but would second Rebecca's opinion.

Gracelyn did not speak at first, but she caught Rebecca's drift and nodded her head to show support of whatever Rebecca deemed appropriate when it came to turning troubles over to the Lord. As she waited for Rebecca to clarify the issue at hand and identify the "heavy burden" they had each borne, she sensed the discussion would flow less from spiritual insight than from expediency. That was fine with Gracelyn. A grasp of purely ethical considerations was never enough to sway her from consensus with her older sisters.

"Well, that is the Lord's way," was her amendment.

A low-register moan cut through Rebecca's thoughts. The sound came from the second story of the house where two of the front windows had been raised and the shutters flung open to receive the light spring air.

"That one doing poorly today," was Rebecca's succinct comment.

As if to accompany the moan, in the next few moments the women heard a series of thuds against the hardwood floors inside. Claudia Cates's head shot up from the tiny lavender stitches she was making on her linen square, her concentration broken.

"Damn!"

Gracelyn Cates dropped her fabric scraps and sucked the bubble of blood from her pricked finger.

"I'll go inside, make sure Lucy is all right."

"Lucy's fine. You just sit still so we can talk."

At Rebecca's instruction, Gracelyn lowered her half-raised body and sat back down in her chair.

And so the talk began. Rebecca characteristically led things off.

"You know the Lord's been good to Jake, keeping him alive after his head accident; and I just believe the Lord wants to take him over altogether. That Sacred Lamb Rest Home up in Springfield is a nice clean place, and they would have him in church service every afternoon. He's been a good husband to me, and I want the best for him right now. It stays on my mind that he could hurt himself when my back was turned, wandering around confused like he does."

Claudia and Gracelyn listened carefully. Here was the standard supplied by the indisputable leader of their now matriarchal clan.

But they needed Rebecca to say more. With the blueprint laid, they would both be able to follow suit. To their knowledge, Jake's offenses throughout his marriage to Rebecca were in no way comparable to their own husbands'. In fact, he was mild mannered and seemed to have a great fondness for his authoritative wife, even while tolerating her unmasked adoration of her father.

Rebecca's marriage to Jake had been perfunctory and unrelated to her ideas of womanly fulfillment. Her father was the man in her life, brilliant, dynamic, demanding. Rebecca was very much like him, strong and spirited, optimistic, sharing a physical resemblance and a passion for family. Mattie indulged the bond between her firstborn and her husband, actually relieved that her husband had another sounding board, since his bold energies had consumed her own fragile ones for years. Rebecca, however, more than matched his stamina, could keep up with his grandiose outlook and, by the time she reached puberty, had begun to echo it.

Reuben was interested in dynasty. When Jake, then a young man in his twenties, came calling on Rebecca, a year out of high school and home from college for spring break, Reuben assessed him quickly. He had finished Illinois Normal in accounting and begun working as a clerk for a white-owned banking establishment. He seemed bright and ambitious, albeit not too interesting. When her father mentioned to Rebecca that this young man would fit well into the family, Rebecca was happy. Jake's slight physique and pleasantly intense dark eyes excited her. She was not suited to a man who would dominate her, nor did she want someone she could intimidate. Jake seemed the right balance. They could talk for hours about people, politics, and the places they both wanted to travel. After their marriage, they made love often.

Jake was steady. He intended to make the most of his good fortune in landing Reuben Cates's eldest daughter. When he began working with the Cates family business following Reuben's stroke, he came to work early and left late. Growing up poor, Jake hungered for the acceptance that marrying into Peoria's elite would afford him, and even had illusions about ultimately owning the prosperous business.

When first wed, Rebecca and Jake took a road trip together every summer, venturing as far as Los Angeles one year. Entranced by the sparkle of sunlight sweeping wide clean streets, Rebecca spearheaded their visits to tourist sites, commandeering her husband early in the morning.

"We'll head over to the university today. I hear it's a big place, and I want plenty of time to find the greenhouse. Then, why don't we visit the Hollywood lots and see about going to one of Papa's game shows."

Jake acquiesced in his usual way with a brief nod of his head. He liked the welcome they received entering and exiting their hotel, where they had obtained a lush suite, including a kitchen, as Rebecca was not a restaurant enthusiast. He knew their car, a Mercedes sedan, meant something in this milieu when they drove up the first time and the valet came to park the car. Pleased as he was, it was not difficult for him to agree to Rebecca's wishes.

The evening before they left, Jake mentioned to Rebecca that his mother's distant cousin Betty lived in one of the suburbs and he would call her so they could visit the woman, a retired schoolteacher. Rebecca, already in her nightgown and curled up in the oversize bed, after yawning sleepily, told her husband, "Well, let's make sure we know exactly where we're going. Better get directions from the desk."

The next morning, Rebecca informed Jake that he needed to go see the relative alone, since she had developed a headache from swollen sinuses. Jake said sympathetically, "Must be the air pollution out here." He left shortly after.

During their drive home when it was Jake's time at the wheel, Rebecca hoisted the snapshots she had taken with her camera, examining each and ordering them for their scrapbook. "How was Betty? Did you have trouble finding that address?" she asked.

Jake replied offhandedly to his wife's query, "No, honey, everything was just fine. I'm sorry you didn't get to meet her. She was quite a gal."

In late August, Rebecca noticed a burning discharge coming from her vagina. She douched for a week with white oak bark, thinking that the heat and humidity had irritated her. After the second week, when the secretion continued unabated, she left the house with Jake early Saturday morning, dropping him at the store and telling him that she was going to look at antiques in Springfield.

She arrived at the Springfield clinic, an anonymous woman. The diagnosis of syphilis left her dazed. On her way back to Peoria, she stopped at a pharmacy for her penicillin prescription, and, standing at the counter, felt, for one of the few times in her adult life, truly embarrassed.

The rage hit during the rest of her drive home. The cold and intense feeling alarmed her. This was the first time she had felt such out-of-control fury. She pulled off the road to the shoulder and tried for several minutes to breathe deeply. Then her mind began constructing a balance sheet, first randomly, then methodically. A guttural sob escaped her.

Rebecca arrived in Peoria just as Jake was closing the office. She pulled up to the curb alongside the bank building and waited for him to come out. He had known she planned to be back with the car by the end of his workday, and was waiting inside the lobby. He waved excitedly upon seeing her, and came out immediately to open the passenger side of the car for her so that he could drive them home. Rebecca walked heavily around the elongated front of the elegant car and slid past Jake into the seat. Jake threw his attaché in the back and proceeded down the town's broad avenue.

"Do we need anything before we get to the house?" Jake asked his wife, thinking how he hated to settle in at home, only to remember they were out of toothpaste. "Did you find any antiques today, honey?"

Rebecca spoke quietly. "Is your syphilis taken care of?"

Jake gasped, the car swerved, and he abruptly put on the brakes. He steered the Mercedes to the side of the road and cut off the engine. He turned to look at Rebecca, his expression alternating between astonishment and belief. He continued to stare at her resolute profile but said nothing.

Rebecca continued to speak softly. "I have it, so you must have it. Get it taken care of, please."

The prostitute Jake encountered coming back from cousin Betty's a scant three blocks from their posh hotel had been a small woman, not any taller than five feet one. She was wearing a purple satin dress and had a purple netting shawl thrown over her delicate shoulders, and even with the three-inch purple satin–covered heels she wore, she was like a doll, a delicate princess needing protection. As soon as he saw her, he was drunk with desire, and after making love to her, he paid her double the price she quoted.

Jake, in the now-suffocating air of the Mercedes, remained tongue-tied for several minutes. There was no way he could deny to Rebecca that he had contracted the disease. He thought illogically that Rebecca was too noble to contract anything so vile. During their marriage his infidelities had been sparse, taking place two or three times a year, and always with someone from out of town. In his mind, it was no big deal. He sought variety and didn't feel that he was betraying his marriage vows, because the women were so unlike Rebecca.

"I'm so sorry, Rebecca; I am so sorry. I'm just a man."

Rebecca did not respond.

"You know, it's hard on a man to be faithful to one woman. But I don't know what I would do without you."

Rebecca had already made up her mind to stay with Jake. Though ill and weak, Reuben was still intent on his daughters' bearing offspring. Rebecca accepted this as a duty, and after Jake's presenting her with written clinical evidence of having been treated, she continued making love to her husband, separating the honest affection she had felt previously from her considerable carnal needs.

Rebecca's periods stopped coming four months after she was diagnosed. When she went to be examined again at the Springfield clinic, the physician told her she was sterile because she'd had the disease without symptoms for so long. Rebecca felt immense loss and disbelief that something so important to her could be snatched away. For several weeks she was unable to rally her energies. When she did, she threw herself into her prize-winning orchids, showing them at the country fairs around the Midwest, and even had an invitation to travel to France. She told no one about her infertility. She reasoned, it would just worry Reuben and Mattie and perhaps lead to questions she would not want to answer. Though she knew Jake wanted offspring, whenever he brought up the subject, Rebecca revealed nothing about her condition. As far as he was concerned, Rebecca felt he didn't deserve to know one way or the other.

Reuben Cates's daughters had maintained separate residences with their respective mates and adapted to the state of wifehood as best they could. But eventually, after decades of marriage, they all returned to live in the massive homestead built by their father, Reuben. It was as though they had been on loan temporarily for breeding, but actual bonding with their mates was not envisioned.

Rebecca and Jake moved back into the homestead when Reuben had his first stroke and Jake took over management of the store. Jake was efficient and turned a good profit, so that when a hundred-pound carton of Indian Mist perfume spray collapsed a neglected shelf and cracked his skull, causing brain damage, Rebecca was able to sell the store and amply support Jake, herself, and her elderly parents.

Some years later Claudia Cates returned home to help Rebecca care for their mother, Mattie, whose good health had not lasted much beyond her husband's final stroke. Claudia reasoned that Rebecca had done her share by tending to their father and her husband after he became a half-wit, so that she would come and assist now that their mother was ill. It was an easier decision for her to move home than it would have been to surmount the confusion she felt at her husband, Timothy's, drunkenness and repeated unfaithfulness. When Timothy became regularly dissolute and unreliable, she decided to abandon her lifestyle and move back home. Some part of her thought that a relatively stress-free life living in the Cates mansion would give her and Timothy a second chance at meaning. It would certainly provide her love within the bosom of her family. As she culled her thoughts, there was no doubt left in Claudia's mind that now her place was with Rebecca and her ailing mother. Rebecca's strength was the bulwark she required to subdue the chaos in her life.

Unlike Rebecca and Gracelyn, who were wed in church, Claudia had embarked on married life with an outdoor wedding and reception at a posh Bloomington country club. Reuben's money secured the all-white establishment with little protest from the membership. Mattie took her elegant daughter to Chicago to shop for a trousseau for the August wedding. Claudia was outfitted with a slim-fitting ivory dress with a beaded bodice and circular train. Mattie had decided a display of the family's wealth would be appropriate, since Timothy's mother was from a prominent Chicago family, and his father was a successful lawyer. Reuben indulged his wife's dreams of a grand occasion, knowing such a wedding would compensate for the humble ceremony the couple had themselves undergone years before.

On the day the date and locale were finalized, Mattie talked excitedly to her husband at bedtime about the preparations.

"Reuben, you know they're all pretty girls, but Claudia is our swan."

"Well, yes, that's fair to say," Reuben responded. "I never did see Rebecca in all that frilly nonsense, and Gracelyn is going to follow just what Rebecca did. It'll be good for Claudia's shyness, get her out in public."

For Claudia, the preparations were exhausting but exciting. With her mother's help, she attended to the most minute detail, anxious for Timothy's family to see her in the best light. They appeared to her extremely well bred, and she did not want them to think of the girl marrying their handsome son as a country bumpkin. Claudia's new in-laws were duly impressed by the ceremony. As she and Timothy pulled off in their decorated limousine, Claudia noted out the back window that her new mother-in-law pressed Mattie's hand while talking animatedly.

Claudia's dread of her husband's touching her began that day. She turned abruptly from looking at the tableau of family and guests they were leaving behind when Timothy shoved his hand down her dress and grabbed her breasts.

"Timothy! The driver!"

"He's getting paid to drive, not look at us. I'm sure he's seen worse."

Timothy went on for a few seconds, fondling her roughly until she could dislodge his hand from inside her fitted bodice. Then, leaning into her, he licked the arch of her neck and began sucking noisily. Claudia recovered from the shock and summoned enough strength to push him hard against the door on his side.

"Stop it! Timothy, please."

Timothy, surprised at her strength, leaned against the upholstered side panel and assessed his new bride.

"Her first time," he informed the driver and grinned rakishly at the mute, expressionless man. When Claudia began to gasp, hysterically clenching her throat, he watched her silently. As soon as she regained her composure, he spoke to her.

"You're my wife now, and I can have you whenever I get ready. Tonight, you'll see what a good man you married, and you'll be grateful."

Claudia, stunned and speechless, watched her husband warily as he pulled a flask from his inside pocket and swigged down a few gulps. He offered it to her, and when she looked blankly at him, tucked it away again. He wore a slight smirk on his face and seemed to forget her for the rest of their ride to the Cates mansion. Claudia went upstairs and changed into her traveling clothes. She later remembered feeling numb in the hours before their flight headed for Tijuana, where they honeymooned. Escape seemed unthinkable, her sense of duty clear, despite her muddled thoughts.

That evening, seated across from him in their hotel dining room, she watched the handsome man, whom she had thought of as shy during their courtship, down shot after shot of bourbon.

"You were damned pretty in that dress. You looked like an angel." Timothy's good humor had not yet waned. But the more drunk he became, the more his sweet talk disintegrated. He muttered the words "pussy whipped," "goddamn hobitches," and "tight-ass cunts." Claudia was insulted and embarrassed, even though there was no one around to witness the exchange.

Afterward, as they walked together toward the elevator, he staggered slightly, and she placed her arm around his waist to steady him. He jerked away from her and in the process almost lost his footing on the gleaming marble floor of the hotel lobby. Arriving at their room, Claudia felt anxious about not being able to subdue whatever coarseness the liquor was unleashing in him. Timothy managed to remove his jacket, becoming momentarily entangled in one of the sleeves. This done, he awkwardly grabbed his wife, steering her backward until she fell onto the queen-size bed. Not knowing what was to come, Claudia's instinct was to lie unmoving beneath him while he groped her, then fumbled at his zipper. Gradually, without success, he sighed once, then began to breathe heavily, lying still on top of her. She knew then that he had passed out and began to get free of his weight. Standing, she looked down at him and, shaking her head, began to right his still figure awry on the bed. This was the first of a ritual they would act out for the next three decades of their marriage.

Claudia did not resist Timothy's entreaties to her when he was sober. Rather, she steeled herself for the ten minutes or so that their lovemaking lasted. With only the vaguest notion of what constituted gratification, and no actual experience, she never made demands, nor did he ask if he was pleasing her. When other women talked about making love with their husbands, their experiences of rapture did not register with her. Beginning with their wedding night, Claudia did not enjoy sex with Timothy because of his drinking. Early on in their marriage, she made her disinterest clear. The couple settled into a pattern of cordial estrangement, talking minimally at the dinner table about household concerns and family news. Sex was something Claudia did not really miss, but she did miss the respectability she had had as a Cates daughter, and she had fully expected that to be enhanced by marrying and being a wife. So, when women began calling the house asking for him, they would bicker. When sober, Timothy smoothed things over ably, telling her she was the only woman he could ever love.

"These women, they just want some attention," he said. "They don't mean anything to me. We can't let it come between us. You're a lady, Claudia, and I can't always get you hot when I need to."

Claudia took Timothy at his word and wondered secretly that she might be deficient somehow in her womanliness. She buried her fear of being frigid and halfheartedly consented to his philandering. She was never able to talk to him about his drinking without his bringing up that her coldness was at the root of all their problems.

Ultimately, Timothy functioned as Claudia's escort to the lavish galas of Chicago's black uppercrust. In this milieu, Claudia kept very busy with parties, club meetings, and volunteer work. She had a pleasant circle of friends scattered throughout Hyde Park. These women were married, indifferently for the most part, but the shared discussions over their designer wardrobes, their Wisconsin and Michigan summer homes, the schools chosen for fractious children, and the rotating decoration of their lakeside apartments fueled a closeness dependent on each's respective place in their elegant, cloistered world, a world unknown to Peoria.

It was hard for Claudia to come back to the town full of people she grew up with, an excruciating dislocation, causing her to feel and behave oddly. She misinterpreted the requirements of local decorum because she had forgotten them. Her tastes and world-view were tainted by her Chicago years. She had to get used again to rising early, even though for the life of her, she couldn't imagine what was so urgent about the sun coming up. She was easily bored with church-related social activities, but had to attend. A repeated absence by any member of the Cates family would be too conspicuous. Claudia was strange, and despite her effort to do otherwise, she seemed to signal to her native community that she had no wish to conform. She desired apparently to remain as she was, in plain view of her neighbors, but out of reach.

Timothy came home with Claudia, thinking that Rebecca's money would make life easier and his access to it would attract more women. He was wrong; Rebecca fully expected him to work.

Gracelyn Cates experienced true passion. She married Bernard, a man she met at college. He was handsome, sensuous, and intended to teach English. They shared a love of literature and books, as well as each other. Their first five years together were bliss. But during this time, unknown to Bernard, Gracelyn had been writing a novel. He had no idea his wife, who had majored in home economics, was as skillful at crafting sentences as she had been at decorating their home and arranging their garden. She sent it off and received more than one offer for publication. Bernard was unable to reconcile himself to his wife's success as a published writer. His own writing had been curtailed by a rigorous teaching schedule. He withdrew from her emotionally in the face of her achievement. Her physical loveliness still held him bound, but he maintained a silence at home, and over a period of months Gracelyn lived with his torture of her, taking refuge in her garden. After her early success, she stopped her own writing regimen in an attempt to save their union. But she began to write again, secretly, during trips to the library, carefully hiding her work in their home when she returned. Again taking up her passion provided her with a glow she believed had been permanently lost. Still, she tread lightly around Bernard all those years, making certain he understood he was more important to her than her craft.

Gracelyn got used to walking on eggshells, taking pains to do or say nothing she thought might displease her husband. All the while, her longing for him was unabated. She prayed that their love would rekindle and they would resume the tenderness she had known for five years with him. After awhile, when this did not happen, Gracelyn, tense and unhappy, began to eat excessively. Bernard's response to her increased appetite and weight gain was to call her "Piglet."

Gracelyn fought her intuition that Bernard's professional envy had unleashed a desire to destroy her, but she continued to write in secret. One Sunday afternoon during a midterm break, Bernard discovered her manuscripts, hidden in the dining room beneath leather-bound scrapbooks in their breakfront. Leafing through each page to get the sense of it, it dawned on Bernard that this was Gracelyn's work. There were stories, poems, and worst of all, a new novel, unfinished.

"Gracelyn!" he commanded furiously, "Come in here!" Standing before her, he waved the thick mass of pages in front of her face. "Why have you done this? Why can't you just be my wife and be satisfied?"

Bernard continued, visiting insults upon her and irrationally attacking her womanhood. Gracelyn stood before him for long minutes in silence, then suddenly moaned and wrapped her arms around her belly. In a swift motion, she crumpled to the floor and began writhing. Bernard stopped his tirade, stunned and silent as the stream of blood flowed from beneath his prostrate wife.

After Gracelyn's miscarriage, Bernard was kinder to her. Noting this, and still hopeful of regaining his love permanently, Gracelyn began talking to him about moving to Peoria. Living in the Cates home would ease the pressure on Bernard to earn a living, she reasoned, and he could write full-time and catch up to her own success. At first he resisted, but with the possibility of artistic fulfillment and ego redemption dangled in front of him, he consented. Once they arrived in the town, Bernard threw himself into his own writing, isolating himself in an attic office in the Cates home for long periods. He did not welcome interruption. It was clear to Gracelyn that it was more important for him to outdo her than to resume his love for her.

Gracelyn lost her husband to his work. They made love occasionally; otherwise Bernard was distant. Gracelyn knew he used her body only for physical release, and that the spiritual union she once felt with him was no more. But she continued to hope. When Bernard contracted a terminal bone cancer, it was hard for her to think of him leaving her for the next life. In fact, she could not have missed him any more than she already had.

It was left to the sisters now to put their men away without scandal, and in the aftermath they looked forward to becoming each others' primary companions, as they had been when they were growing up. Without their husbands, their yearnings for a new lease on life could be realized. Each knew the mission had to be accomplished delicately. They had seen the way other women in the town absolved themselves of men who for years had not been able to make love to them, and who now could not dream or discuss doing anything with their lives, other than to survive the misery of their remaining days. The right places had to be found, not too remote and not too near, with good reputations, and expensive enough so that their community would know they had done right by their ailing partners.

The Cates women needed to be careful not to arouse suspicion of wanting to start their lives over, freed of partners who made them miserable, had not fulfilled them, or who could not have measured up to their father in the first place.

"We're losing the light," Rebecca noted after the women completed a second hour of piecework and conversation. "Let's go in; I need to pay Lucy before she takes off."

II

AT REBECCA'S BIDDING, the sisters placed their work into wicker baskets and went inside the house to reassemble around the dining table. Lucy had set out tea utensils for them, and, in the minutes before she knew the sisters would be coming inside, filled the teapot and placed it on the stove. For this part of their Sunday ritual, the Cates women put their handiwork aside to have tea and dessert baked earlier during the morning's elaborate food preparation. They sat in the stately room surrounded by hung photographs of Reuben and Mattie, Reuben's mother, Mattie's parents, themselves as children, and their wedding photos.

Claudia had baked dessert, her specialty, a sweet potato pie with a custardlike texture. When she heard the teapot whistling in the kitchen, the slender woman rose from her seat to prepare peppermint tea and slightly reheat the luscious pie. Rebecca and Gracelyn waited, excited as little girls, for their evening treat, though they knew their glamorous sister would take her time.

This Sunday, Rebecca told Lucy to lay out the gold-rimmed ivory Sheffield china with an orchid pattern, her favorite of all of Mattie's sets. Rebecca's earthy appearance belied her quite ethereal tastes. The orchids she cultivated in the estate's small green-house—*Laelia, Dendrobium,* and *Phalaenopsis* hybrids—were exquis-ite, and before bringing blooms into the house, she spent hours deciding on the right crystal or silver vase or porcelain urn. She would see the arrangement in her mind's eye first, then astonish Claudia and Gracelyn by how easily she executed it. To Rebecca, using the family's best china and silver service for tea added a visual feast to the gastronomic one.

Claudia carried over to the table a huge silver tray with slices of pie topped with fresh whipped cream on dessert plates, teacups and saucers, and napkins held snugly in engraved silver rings. The women ate leisurely, continuing their gossip and laughter until a long moan was dimly heard from the second story above their heads.

Claudia continued the discussion Rebecca had started on the front porch.

"I hear Briney Memorial's a decent place. Louella has Joseph up there and he's a drinking man like Timothy. Louella tells me they do very well with that sort."

"That near Chicago?" Rebecca queried. At Claudia's affirma-tive nod, Rebecca commented, "Be good for you visiting. You could see some of your friends in the city from time to time."

Claudia blushed, but she understood clearly Rebecca approved of her mixed motive for the selection of Briney Memorial for Timothy. Rebecca knew that Claudia had thrived in the social whirl of black Chicago society and reigned for years at formal balls given by the archaic clubs to which she and Timothy belonged. When Timothy's drinking caused him to miss out on important seasonal engagements, it had been uncomfortable for Claudia to make her entrances unescorted. Now in her mid-fifties and still stunning, Claudia looked forward to making public appearances sans scandal, amid the common knowledge that her husband's health had failed and she had had to institutionalize him. She loved being with her sisters in Peoria. It seemed they never had enough time to talk and laugh over vivid memories of their childhood. But she also longed to be a celebrated dowager in what was to her the exciting social network of Chicago she left behind when she returned home. Rebecca also realized that Claudia had never fully understood Timothy's drinking, but had at some point made her peace with the inevitability of it. She had accepted her responsibilities as his spouse as Rebecca outlined them, but was now well past the stage of wringing her hands over his lost potential and ruined health.

Rebecca added, "Be good for me to go up there and visit some of our congregations."

Gracelyn, understanding that this was her moment, chimed in.

"They always have important lectures at the University of Chicago. I keep saying I'm going to subscribe to their author series. It would be good for me to go up there with you from time to time." She added in afterthought, "When you're visiting Timothy."

Rebecca declared resolutely, "It'll be good all the way around."

Both Gracelyn and Rebecca were sensitive to Claudia's dilemma. Timothy, unlike poor confused Jake and terminally ill Bernard, was pretty much a quiet drunk, and his behavior was not considered serious enough to warrant permanent confinement. Also, though it was generally known that he chased women, his dalliances were somewhat overlooked because many people considered Claudia to be a cold fish. The general reasoning was she should be happy now that he had become too weak to betray her.

Claudia would have to unload Timothy at some distance from her neighbors' judging, so that even if their first reaction was disapproving, the memory of the once-handsome man peacefully imbibing too much liquor at local bars, would dim. Neighbors would have to be satisfied that Timothy was well taken care of at his remote location near Chicago, and the sisters' visits to see him at Briney Memorial would have to be grandly orchestrated.

Rebecca thought shrewdly that she would have Claudia stand up at church during the sick and shut-in announcements and inform the congregation each time they were planning to go see him. She knew that Claudia—who loved dressing up and making entrances, but who was actually shy about speaking in front of a group—would be nervous. Expressing concern for Timothy's well-being would call for some acting skills, but Rebecca thought Claudia would rise to the occasion. Timothy would continue to appear the focal point of her life, when in reality, she was, as were her sisters, women who could now pursue their own agendas. Rebecca, who could strategize like a general, knew these repeated announcements would eventually endear Claudia to their community and neutralize any antifemale sentiment Reverend Wilson might cull from the sisters' actions.

In between visits, they could all report on how their men were doing, Jake at Sacred Lamb in Springfield, Timothy at Briney Memorial, and Bernard at a nearby hospice. Bernard's prognosis was six months or less, yet Gracelyn had already stated her rationale for putting him away, rather than letting him die at home.

"I don't want him to suffer any more than he has to," she had informed Rebecca and Claudia on a Sunday afternoon a few weeks prior. "The doctors and nurses can do a lot more for him and I'll ask them to increase his morphine. I've been praying that maybe they can find out something more about this dreadful disease from examining him on a regular basis." She then told her sisters she had just a week or two before she would receive word from the hospice to call an ambulance to bring Bernard in.

Rebecca knew Gracelyn might never fully get over her love for Bernard, and that her furious writing activity was her way of distancing herself from his tragedy. Rebecca intuited that this was driven as much by Gracelyn's confusion and regret as it was by her younger sister's rekindled ambition. Rebecca knew that Gracelyn was also struggling with bitterness over the years lost to a futile love, and now, realizing that her hope of Bernard's loving her again was completely dashed, her bitterness might easily reach full flower and turn to rage. It would be best to remove the helpless man from the household sooner than later. In the meantime, Rebecca, while encouraging Gracelyn's distractions, would be a nonjudgmental confidant and do her best to soothe her sister's inner turbulence.

Rebecca, coming back to their primary issue, decided to raise the stakes.

"Reverend Wilson doesn't spend enough time talking about our sick and shut-in members to suit me. All these men falling by the wayside and all these new widows. I've decided to bring it up to him that we need to stay regular with telling who's in, who's out of the hospital, who's ailing, and so forth. Maybe we could work up a little ceremony for women who have had to nurse their husbands for a long time, a prayer ceremony to keep them filled with the spirit, and keep them going. I think I'll stop by the parish house this week and talk to him."

Claudia absorbed the import of Rebecca's statement in seconds. She was not the strategist her sister was, but she knew that Rebecca's plans for challenging Reverend Wilson had been thoroughly mapped out. Her head jerked up from her dessert plate, where she had just stabbed a last morsel of pie with her fork, and, midway to her mouth, Gracelyn's cup of tea paused for several seconds as they took in Rebecca's words. Both of them knew precisely what their elder sister meant. When Rebecca made a decision, they never questioned her motives or doubted the outcome would be in her favor. But this would be a bold strike indeed.

Claudia doubted whether the pompous Reverend Wilson had the faintest idea of what was in store for him. When she thought of the shock he would feel when he found himself deposed, Claudia's breath caught sharply in her throat.

Gracelyn, hearing the soft gasp, turned her attention from

Rebecca's steely expression and looked over at Claudia, who had raised her delicate hand to finger a choker of onyx and gold beads at her neck. Suddenly, Gracelyn's loud giggle broke through the ruminations of the other two.

"Haheeeee!" she squealed. "That calls for another piece of pie."

"You just better be careful how those hips are spreading," Claudia said.

Gracelyn, completely ignoring the admonition, raised her slightly plump frame and bounded into the kitchen, returning with the remaining pie.

"Rebecca, you could even become a deaconess and really run things!"

Rebecca looked at Gracelyn's flawless skin, her round black eyes, beautiful round face, and velvety black hair. Even as a child, Gracelyn had had a zany sense of humor and unquenchable spirit. She had also always been an acute observer of everything around her, and considered following in the footsteps of two older sisters with arresting personalities her life's great adventure. From watching Claudia, she learned the uncanny effect a strong sense of personal style had on other people. Shorter than Claudia and not as slender, Gracelyn refined a different look for herself, dressing conservatively but in a way that flattered her curvaceous build. She dressed daily in jersey or soft cotton fabrics in deep colors. On her arms she wore collections of bracelets, sleek European designs or ornate African or Asian pieces. Because her thick hair was hard to control, she kept it cropped. She made sure of always appearing well groomed and tasteful.

Throughout their growing up, Rebecca's bold brilliance had made Gracelyn unafraid of her own. Now, at fifty, she was extremely comfortable with her eccentricity, and, having survived years of Bernard's silent torture of her during their marriage, believed she was the intellectual equal of any man. Rebecca, her rock, was definitely up to the task of toppling the arrogant Wilson. He would never be able to outthink her or even fathom her motives.

Rebecca smiled patiently at Gracelyn.

"Now, why would I want to be a deaconess after all these years. I just want our congregation to have the pastor it deserves. I'm not talking against Wilson, just saying he needs a little straightening out."

Gracelyn was not ready to abandon her point.

"Rebecca, we need a woman deaconess or some kind of leader, something. You see how the women do all the grunt work at the church, all that cooking and setting up for programs, but then the pastor and the deacons make all the important decisions about money. Rebecca, that's our money they are spending. Yours, Claudia's, and mine. And we're women and we should have a say-so like all the other women should."

"Yes, dear, I know," Rebecca said calmly.

"Those morons nixed a day-care center. Can you believe that? A day-care center! That would have made things easier on most of the young mothers in the congregation."

"Now, Gracelyn, don't call our church elders morons." Rebecca tried gently to rein her in.

"Walks like a duck!"

Rebecca and Claudia chuckled. Gracelyn forged on.

"And something happened with that woman from the seminary. Nobody would just up and leave like that. We wait years to get a woman in the pulpit and she stays for all of four months. Somebody should at least have investigated what happened to her."

"Gracelyn, the first thing we have to do is get free ourselves. The way I see it, we'll start with Wilson because we have to. But we'll have our new lives, and if our sisters in the faith catch our drift, we'll keep our good name."

"Do you think they will?" Claudia asked, her eyes widening.

"That's the plan, honey child. Gracelyn's right about our deep pockets. But we want people's hearts to be in the right place, too. Ladies, we follow the plan and it's win-win for us."

Not one of the three women voiced concern over the ethics of what they were embarking on. They were united in one goal, to achieve power over their lives, and if Rebecca had not acknowledged any gray areas in their morality, the other two would not. Recapturing freedom and a new vision for themselves had been a powerful craving for the Cates women for some time. In these later years, past their youth but with many more years to live, given robust health, frustrations and yearnings could more easily translate into physical or mental ailments. Arthritis, headaches, metabolic disorders, chronic fatigue, depression—all awaited them if their spirits became mired in the hopelessness of nothing to look forward to.

Their uninspired marriages were like nooses around their necks. Either they would unload their husbands and renew themselves or suffer corrosive, deadening twilight years. The small community's standard for respectability would have to be met for the Cates women to retain their eminent profile, though. They would have to have the vocal approval of their church and community. Rebecca thought she knew how to sway their female neighbors. The men she would have to think long and hard about.

Rebecca's sisters understood that her intention to speak with the pastor about an issue involving the women of the church was like a declaration of war. Rebecca in fact knew Wilson would take her comments as mildly insulting, but he would not understand the full import of her action; that with this move, she would begin a campaign against him.

Reuben's power within the church had been considerable, though he had never abused it, complacent in the awe he inspired among his neighbors as a black man who could make money as competently as white men, and in the grudging respect of the pastors whose tenure he had lived through. The men of the cloth knew one word from Reuben Cates would more than likely result in their ouster. They both resented him and needed his support to undertake anything requiring money outside the congregation's meager budget. Without Reuben Cates, there would be no big projects, no photos of themselves and their parishioners in the local papers, and no worldly signposts measuring the extent of their dedication to holy purposes.

Gracelyn had zeroed in on and voiced Rebecca's own logic. It was still Cates money underwriting First Baptist's unquestioned prominence among Peoria's black congregations. And with no longer having to defer to Jake, Rebecca had inherited Reuben's clout as head of the most important dynasty. She knew she could never control the dogmatic Wilson. So, she reasoned, she would install a pastor that she could control. She was Reuben Cates's daughter, and with no direct male descendants and no functioning spouses, the matriarchal head of the Cates clan. Rebecca and her sisters, once freed from the constraints posed by their ailing husbands, could enjoy their community profile with renewed pride and enthusiasm. Wilson's exit would be their first milestone as healthy and purposeful women eagerly anticipating their new agenda.

Gracelyn's high-pitched giggle broke into Rebecca's thoughts. "Well, you go, girl!" was her animated response.

Rebecca's deep concentration broken, she looked at the mature woman she could never quite think of as anything except her baby sister. She never really knew what Gracelyn was thinking, but she knew her soft-featured, ultrafeminine youngest sister would be champing at the bit to do whatever she was bid, never flinching initially like prim Claudia.

Rebecca didn't realize that Gracelyn's bold streak was a mirror image of her own, and attributed her loyalty to seeking to uphold the Cates family name. Gracelyn was indeed loyal to her family, but whereas Rebecca worshiped Reuben, Gracelyn identified Rebecca specifically as her idol and found over the years that she could successfully imitate her straightforward actions. When Gracelyn, living on the Northwestern University campus with her professor husband, Bernard, first thought about writing a novel, a voice inside her head kept saying it would be an impossible goal. But she kept thinking about Rebecca's orchids, the perfection she reached with each species, and how people far away from Peoria, indeed, all over the world, had written to request photos and cuttings and were willing to pay enormous prices.

With this turn toward confronting Reverend Wilson, Gracelyn saw Rebecca entering a new era of womanhood in which she was finally conscious of her own power. The Cates sisters were on the verge of a new era of freedom from their earthly partners. To the younger Gracelyn, born into the generation of women who rediscovered feminism, Rebecca was the Chosen, the woman who would lead the women of their community into greater self-knowledge and maybe even the freedom she and her sisters felt was rightfully theirs. They would seize control of their church, the place they relied on for spiritual guidance, and because of this, their lives and potentially the lives of many other women would change.

Rebecca's agenda was more narrowly focused. She wanted freedom for herself and her sisters. She knew she had a knack for using what she considered to be each of her sister's strengths to best advantage. Having Claudia make repeated announcements at church would put her glamour to good use and give people a chance to get used to her and better, like her. Rebecca was sure that in the right situation, Claudia would warm to people unlike her, and they to her. Gracelyn, despite her conservative appearance, tended to have an overdeveloped sense of mission and could be extreme. Rebecca knew she would be best utilized in situations that required immediate action, enabling her to expend her manic store of energy.

Gracelyn's second peal of hysterical laughter finished off Rebecca's concentration completely.

"What's got you so tickled, girl?"

"Reverend Wilson's road kill," Gracelyn managed to blurt out, before giving way to loud, unladylike guffaws.

In spite of herself, Claudia's trim shoulders began shaking, she gave up on decorum, and she began laughing louder than Gracelyn. Rebecca broke easily into laughter that shook her frame.

Lucy made her last set of rounds and descended the back stairs of the house leading into the kitchen. Hearing the noise in the dining room, she cautiously pulled back one of the lace curtains. The Cates sisters were laughing uncontrollably. Opening the door just a crack, she managed to say above the din, "Sister Rebecca, I'll be leaving now. I'm all finished."

Rebecca, slouched down in her chair, pulled herself upright, and still chuckling, said, "Lucy, just a minute. I've got a check for you." She reached into her skirt pocket and pulled out a white envelope. "This is through the end of the month. I thought you could use it early, since Earl is laid up with that back injury."

"Oh, thank you, Sister Rebecca. You are certainly a Christian woman."

"As are you, Sister Lucy. I hope the men didn't work you too hard today."

"I was up to it. I left my notes on the counter. There shouldn't be too much to do except feed them tomorrow. You probably won't need to bathe Bernard until Tuesday. Only thing is, I would call Dr. Turner about that colostomy. The poor man doesn't look too comfortable. Even if Miss Gracelyn has to give him the bedpan for a day or two, it might be a good idea to have the doctor adjust it for him."

Lucy's suggestion destroyed Gracelyn's humor, but she was able to answer swiftly.

"It's not right to move that man about right now; it's so painful for him. I think we better leave that colostomy where it is."

Gracelyn's earnest protestation was enough to satisfy Lucy's tender concern for her charges.

"Oh, what am I thinking," she replied, remembering how tired she was from the day's work.

Rebecca, recovered and wiping her eyes, chimed in, "Sister Lucy, you know what each one of us is faced with. We're just trying to keep some joy in our hearts this evening before our work begins again tomorrow. I want you to keep us in your prayers this week."

"I always do, Sister Rebecca."

Claudia, on her feet and arranging the pleats on her shantung skirt, walked skittishly to the front door and held it open for Lucy's exit. "Thanks for all your hard work, dear," she proffered, echoing Rebecca's sentiment. "We sure needed this day of rest, and you never let us down."

Rebecca looked approvingly at Claudia's action. She was quite charming when she reached out to people, and Lucy Sims, known for her integrity and moral character, would need to remain an important ally for the Cates women. Rebecca would have Claudia reaching out to more and more people in the months to come.

Each of the Cates sisters relished the narrow sliver of evening left. The men would stay locked in their rooms until the morning. The sisters hoped each of the men would remain peaceful during the night.

"Damn!" Gracelyn, alone in the kitchen, inhaled a deep breath following her brief expletive. She was pained, thinking about Bernard's colostomy problem. There was little she could do about his body's disintegrating, yet she still did not know how to cope with his dying. She was angry also because Lucy's mention of the colostomy was one more worry cutting into her energy and time for creative work. She didn't suppose Bernard would be any worse off in the scheme of things, bedpan or no, though it would have been no use trying to explain all this to Lucy.

Her mind on these thoughts, she cleared the dining table of the dessert dishes and placed them in the dishwasher. She went into the living room and swiped chocolate truffles from the candy dish, thinking she would need extra sugar to keep her mind awake. She wanted to complete a long poem begun the night before and get started on a piece about her life with Rebecca and Claudia. Gracelyn, accustomed to her sisters' idiosyncracies, never grew tired of observing them. Sometimes, after they had talked until after midnight, she would climb eagerly upstairs to her attic garret and begin writing about the day's events in her journal, describing in detail Rebecca's anecdotes about neighbors and church members, and quoting Claudia's barbed evaluations of their friends' husbands and children, and the friends themselves.

After hours of recording everything she heard and saw during the day, she would run water into the ancient bathtub. The attic bathroom was lined with green ceramic tiles, and the uncurtained dormer window framed many lustrous moons and varying constellations. If, during the week, her caretaking duties wore on her nerves so that she could jot down only a few lines, then collapse in bed each evening, on Sunday Gracelyn was energized and productive enough to stay awake a few extra hours to soak in a scented bath while gazing at a hypnotic sky.

Gracelyn relaxed for a few minutes on her bed. Lying on her back and glimpsing the chunk of moon visible from the window, she thought about Lucy. Lucy worked with the children's group at church on special programs, and Gracelyn had been thinking about offering them a wonderful play she had discovered about Harriet Tubman in the Cates library. She had wanted to talk with her about doing the play, but thought this might make her look uninterested in Bernard's colostomy problem, the matter at hand. After Bernard was committed, she would definitely talk with Lucy, and might even offer to work with her on the project, thus having her ear more frequently. She would ask Rebecca when to proceed.

To recover her good mood, Gracelyn decided to put on some music. She roused herself and went downstairs to the third floor to see if Claudia's light was still on.

Claudia stood before her closet shuffling the orderly arrangement of dresses, blouses, and skirts. Stacked on her cedar chest were three pairs of pants that needed mending. Planning her fashion statement for the week and preparing her wardrobe was a Sunday night ritual. Though her daily chores as a caretaker were unglamorous, she had managed to find a smart set of casual clothes. An oxford shirt, khakis, a silk around her neck, quiet gold jewelry, a vintage Claire McCardell casual dress with pockets, impeccably ironed denim jeans, a light cashmere pink sweater set could all withstand dragging a staggering Timothy to the nearest chair to let him sleep off his drunkenness.

Toward the late afternoon, Claudia would excuse herself from the bustle in the kitchen and the trips up and down the back stairs to the men's floor. She would go up the front stairs to her suite, wash her face, and touch up her makeup for a trip to the pharmacy or grocery store. Sometimes she would even shower and change into something elegant and ladylike if she had multiple errands. Tomorrow, she thought, the green-and-white-striped cotton Geoffrey Beene dress cut on the bias would do.

Gracelyn peeked in at Claudia, who was folding a cashmere shawl.

"Claudia, will it bother you if I play some music?"

Hearing the footsteps, Claudia turned around and, seeing her sister, her humor of earlier in the evening returned.

"Did you give Bernard his bedpan yet?"

Immediately, Claudia regretted her gallows humor. Gracelyn smiled at her sister faintly; then the tears came.

"Oh, darling, please forgive me. That was so thoughtless."

Without answering the stricken and embarrassed Claudia, Gracelyn turned away and swiftly mounted the stairs to the attic.

Rebecca came in from the backyard greenhouse where she had gone to adjust the thermostat. The balmy spring weather they enjoyed earlier that day would turn into a night freeze, according to the weather report. All the orchid varieties were sensitive to sudden changes in temperature, and Rebecca, knowing which ones were particularly at risk, kept a watchful eye on them. Part of Rebecca's fascination with the flowers was their delicacy. Hale and hearty all of her life, she found frailty a mystery and the flowers brought out a deep-seated protectiveness in her character. She took pride in successfully nurturing things of such great beauty.

Coming in through the back door, she walked purposefully through the kitchen. She stopped abruptly when she spied Lucy's notes lying unobtrusively on the counter, slightly wet now so that the ink drizzled down the page. Snatching up the sodden document, she scanned it distractedly, then continued her trek through the spacious house, dimming the lights as she went.

In the small library adjacent to the living room, she plucked a copy of *Ran,* Akira Kurosawa's war epic, from a shelf reserved for videocassettes. Rebecca had seen the Japanese saga of war and warriors in the fourteenth century numerous times but had not grown tired of its massive scope and exhilarating battle scenes. She hardly noticed her long climb up the front stairs, excitedly anticipating the next few hours of her favorite film. Humming contentedly, she proceeded.

Before Rebecca reached the landing of the women's floor, she heard Claudia calling Gracelyn's name. Seeing the distressed look on the normally serene face, Rebecca walked over to her swiftly and put her arm around Claudia's delicate shoulders.

"What's wrong?" she asked.

"I said something cruel to Gracelyn about giving Bernard the bedpan. I didn't realize she still had a soft spot for him. I'm so sorry, and now I don't know what to say to her. Will you please help her?"

"Of course I'll help her, but you calm down first. Poor thing doesn't know whether to love him or hate his guts, so she's doing both. That man took something from her. He cut into her real deep. And now she knows she'll never have him back in a tender way. It's like he's already left her, and she can't hope anymore. She's lived on hope for a long time, and now she's lost that too. She'll get over everything in time, but right now there's a fresh wound. You stop worrying, because she loves you and she knows you didn't mean any harm to her. Let her rest, and I'll give her a talking to in the morning."

Claudia, comforted, lay her head on Rebecca's for a few moments, while Rebecca patted her hair. After a full embrace, the sisters departed each other's company, each anticipating a few hours' activity in her own quarters.

Rebecca settled comfortably in bed, clicked on her television, and fast-forwarded her video to her favorite battle scene, before, gradually, an uneasy feeling crept over her, distracting her from the movie. Sensing danger, her mind wandered to Gracelyn. She felt it best to go check on her.

> *I've got a cold, cold feeling, just like ice around my heart.*
> *I've got a cold, cold feeling, just like ice around my heart.*
> *I know I'm goin'ta quit somebody, every time that feeling*
>   *starts.*

Rebecca heard Ester Phillips's raspy singing clearly through the closed door of Gracelyn's attic quarters just as she mounted the last of the back stairs leading to the top floor of the mansion. When Gracelyn did not respond to her muffled knock, Rebecca opened the door slightly to let her know she had called to her.

Gracelyn sat with her back to the door in an overstuffed wing chair that had seen far better days. "Gracelyn, honey." When she didn't answer, Rebecca walked around the chair and perched on the ottoman in front of her. "Girl, you get that man off your mind for the time being. Go on and get in the bathtub. Give yourself a facial, or the like."

Gracelyn sat mute and stone-faced while Rebecca raised both her legs onto her lap and for several minutes massaged her feet.

"He was my whole life, Rebecca, my whole life. All that time, I tried to make him love me. Now he's leaving me. I can't stand this. I hate him so much, and I'm so sorry for him. One minute I can't stand to look at him like he is. The next minute, I want to make him hurt real bad, like he made me hurt. The bad thing is, most of the time, he doesn't know I'm there."

"Girl, the Lord has moved in your life, can't you see that? You're about to be free, free from all that pain. Bernard is about to be free. We're all about to be free. It doesn't matter what came before, because what's coming is so much better. You are lovelier and stronger than you've ever been, and when you know that, you'll find another man who will love you and all those poems and things you write. That man's gonna feel like the luckiest man alive."

"Oh, Rebecca, do you believe that?"

"You claim it now. All this time you held on and tended to him. Don't you think the Lord will reward the goodness in your heart? He didn't strike you, he struck the evil in your life. And so all you have to do is look beyond today."

Gracelyn mulled over Rebecca's words, knowing in her heart that her eldest sister was unfailingly honest and caring toward her. If this was the blueprint Rebecca saw for her life, she would embrace it.

"Are you really going to take on Reverend Wilson?"

"Yes, child, and I sure need you to work with me on that. I don't see suffering his foolishness any longer. Too many women in that congregation with the same burdens we have, and he just isn't going to say things and do things to make life harder for any of us. You follow my way, and you'll see what I'm talking about."

"Rebecca, you know I'll do anything. I'm a good soldier."

"Yes, child, you're about the bravest I know. But right now, you get some sleep. I can't have you up here moping around half the night and not ready to work tomorrow. I've got big plans and I need you to have a lot of energy."

Gracelyn grinned. "Rebecca, sometimes I think I have too much energy."

"Well, that's good and bad. Anyway, tuck in early enough to be ready for action tomorrow morning." Rebecca stood up and leaned over to plant a kiss on Gracelyn's forehead before going back to her movie.

III

THE CATES KITCHEN window faced east, looking out over the backyard. Rebecca loved to get downstairs early enough to see the sun come up. In warmer weather, she would already be out back checking her plants. This morning, her head full of the elaborately costumed Japanese warriors and their bloody battles, she stood over the sink filling the copper teakettle with water. Rebecca waited a few minutes before turning the lights on.

After meditating on the orange, fuchsia, and turquoise streaking the sky, she turned on the fluorescent ceiling light. Rummaging in the large pantry, she found Melita filters and a decorative canister of Kenyan coffee, a good strong blend. She turned her head, hearing Claudia in her low heels walk pertly into the kitchen.

"Kenyan all right with you this morning, dear?" she asked.

"That sounds good; how's Gracelyn?"

"She'll be fine. We'll keep an eye on her, but I think she'll be fine."

Claudia's eagle eyes spotted Lucy's note. "What's this?"

"Hmph," was Rebecca's comment.

Not waiting for a further response, Claudia took eggs and butter out of the refrigerator. She prepared to scramble the eggs with scallions and fix toast for their breakfast, accompanied by Rebecca's strong coffee. Gracelyn bounded hurriedly into the kitchen and set out glasses for orange juice she had squeezed the night before.

She grabbed the tattered note.

"Did you all see this?"

"Yes, dear, we did," Rebecca answered her. "Those are Lucy's suggestions on how we can make the men more comfortable. She means well."

The three met each other's glance. Claudia, understanding they were all in sync, gently took the soggy piece of paper out of Gracelyn's hand and threw it away.

"I'm not ashamed to say that we are doing enough, Lord knows," Rebecca said, "as much as any human beings could under the circumstances."

"So, we'll move on," Claudia added brightly, putting an end to the matter.

Monday's moderate breakfast was always the sisters' first meeting of the week, during which assigned tasks could be reviewed. This Monday morning, the mood was different. On top of their normal routine, the Cates women would begin to enact their plan for freedom. They were energized, even while realizing their responsibilities would now be double and triple until they achieved their goal.

"Ladies," commanded Rebecca, "we have to compartmentalize. Those eggs done?"

Claudia scurried to the stove and transferred the fluffy eggs onto a large white china platter, arranging them carefully in the center. Before bringing them to the table, she sprinkled them lightly with basil. She made a last trip to the oven, where she had been keeping the toast warm in a baking dish, shook the pieces of bread out into a wicker basket lined with a cloth napkin, and covered them over.

The three, seated at last, joined hands for a brief blessing of their food by Rebecca.

"Heavenly Father, we ask you to bless our meal as we do your will throughout this blessed day."

The Cates women ate for a few minutes in silence, spooning butter and apricot preserves on their warm bread, salting and peppering their eggs with abandon, and blending cream into their coffee. Well into their meal, Rebecca began to give instructions.

"Gracelyn, we need to get Bernard to that hospice. Then we need to see about getting Timothy up to Chicago. Claudia, all right with you if we head up that way around the third week of June?"

"Fine with me."

Rebecca continued. "Gracelyn, did you get a date from that place yet?"

"Yes," Gracelyn said slowly. "They're ready for him Saturday after next."

"All right." Rebecca smiled gently at Gracelyn. She continued soberly, "We could feed him just soup up till then, in case the oatmeal is running him off. That might ease him with that colostomy problem. But since the date is coming up that quick, you may just want to let the hospice people handle whatever it was Lucy was talking about."

"All right," said Gracelyn, thinking of the arduous collection and sorting of urine-smelling bedclothes that she carted off several times a week to Raphaela, a neighbor who took in laundry and foster children. "Rebecca, I can hardly believe this is real."

"Uhm hum," Rebecca responded. "It's real, all right." Rebecca was already onto her next thought.

"What you need to do next time you go by Raphaela's is tell her she can keep those sheets and things after she washes them, so she'll have some extra for all those children. Tell her Mr. Bernard took a turn and is going to a place where he'll be more comfortable."

Gracelyn, regaining her enthusiasm, shot in, "You want me to talk to Lucy about the Harriet Tubman play I found?"

"We'll get to Lucy a little later on; got other things for you to do right through here and—"

"Rebecca, please. I've got to do something!"

"Now, hold off, girl, I'm getting to this play of yours."

Gracelyn waited eagerly for Rebecca to continue, knowing whatever her sister had in store for her was completely well thought out. Her brown face shining, she poured more of the strong coffee into her mug, spilling droplets onto her hand.

"Ow!"

Efficient Claudia dipped a clean corner of her napkin into her ice water, took Gracelyn's hand, and began daubing the reddened skin. Crisis resolved, the two waited for their leader's next pronouncement.

"We've got to be careful about Timothy going around talking our business. Once he sees Bernard taken away, he'll be nervous. I have decided the thing to do is keep him sedated. That way, he'll stop shaking and won't remember he needs some alcohol. But we'll need a pair of male hands to help with him when we take the drive to Chicago to put him away. When you talk to Raphaela, see if she has any big boys with common sense over there. I'll go on and tell Lucy that Timothy's taken a bad cold and is sleeping extra, and she can just keep an eye on Jake. He'll be the last to go anywhere."

"Lord, I sure wish this could all be over," Gracelyn replied wistfully.

"Patience, girl. We're close now," was Rebecca's affectionate command.

A little nervously, Claudia asked her sisters, "Won't the people at Briney Memorial find out about the sedative?"

"Now, darling, don't you worry about that. I've already told Dr. Meyers about Timothy wandering around the streets at night, and he agrees he might hurt himself. He's ordered something so we can keep him subdued. I don't know why we didn't do this before. Now, Claudia, you're going to need to start testifying every Sunday about the men's sickness being a terrible burden, but that the Lord is giving us strength and showing us the way."

Rebecca paused while the other two absorbed her instructions, then continued.

"Wait two Sundays after Bernard goes in before you start talking about Timothy going up to Briney. Look specially pretty that Sunday, but don't smile too much. In the meantime, just keep it general. Let everybody know how we are suffering and ask for prayer. Make sure you thank the pastor for all his visits to our menfolk over the past months during our time of trial."

"Whew!" was Gracelyn's voiced approval at Rebecca's thorough strategizing. Rebecca had covered all the bases, creating infallible smoke screens for their actions. Further, Claudia's comment to Reverend Wilson would succeed in damning him with faint praise.

"What about Jake?" Gracelyn then wanted to know.

Rebecca met Gracelyn's eyes.

"He won't be a problem."

Gracelyn understood that Rebecca had already worked out what to do with Jake, but to reveal it now would be an information overload. She knew they needed full concentration on the tasks at hand. Gracelyn understood her sister's reasoning without having heard it directly stated. Noting Rebecca's momentary iciness when asked about Jake, Claudia coughed a little nervously, but she trusted her to make all the right moves throughout their undertaking.

Characteristically chatty in the morning, Claudia went on to review her schedule of pharmacy visits and shopping for the week. Like the other two, she would have little leisure time until the weekend, but since she had agreed to stand up in church, she might need to buy a new dress to make sure she looked her best and wasn't nervous.

"Y'all remember Susan Hayward in *I'll Cry Tomorrow*? Most drunks don't look that good, but that woman couldn't look bad if she tried. That dress she had on at the end was so pretty. I saw a dress like that the other week downtown. I think I'll try to go back by that shop and see if they have it in my size."

Rebecca listened without comment to Claudia's prattle. She knew that underneath her sister's seemingly frivolous interests was a mind capable of attending to the most minute detail. Claudia would leave nothing out in her church announcements and would be as meticulous in providing information as she was in her personal appearance.

Rebecca knew also that Gracelyn's energies would need to be distracted for a little while. She would keep her busy doing kind deeds for the town's leading gossips, starting with Raphaela, who gossiped continually as her twenty regular customers went back and forth.

"Ask Raphaela if any of her children want to be in a church play," Rebecca told Gracelyn. "Saturday morning when Lucy comes, sit her down for a few minutes and talk it over. I'll be going by to see the pastor come Wednesday. The Lord is shining the light in front of my eyes like I was Harriet Tubman following the North Star. We'll come through this just fine. We'll do what we have to do and keep our good name," was Rebecca's summation, ending their planning session.

The three women stood up from the table and began bustling around the kitchen. They gossiped hurriedly about what their neighbors had worn to church, who had sat with visitors, and the unpredictable May weather. Gracelyn put on water to boil for oatmeal and instant soup, and began a light cleanup of the kitchen. After checking the bed linens for soilage and gathering up the remainder of the laundry, she would do the men's first feeding.

Then, after emptying the dishwasher, she would begin the lunch preparations.

Claudia, still munching on the remains of a toast point, began to inventory their food and pharmaceutical supplies in order to compile a list. She was the first to exit, an all-weather coat slung over her arm as she went to run the household errands.

Rebecca's first mission of the day was to tend to her orchids. She had come downstairs to breakfast in her gardening clothes, a light blue denim work shirt and off-white painter's pants, which hid her massive curves. Monday was watering day, and she fell silent, thinking of one of her laelias that wasn't draining properly and might need some rocks added to its potting media.

Half-listening now to Gracelyn, who was going on about someone's outrageous hat and the Bartlesons' bad children, Rebecca opened the kitchen door that led to the enclosed porch where her gardening tools were stored.

"Uhm hum," she commented on Gracelyn's animated remarks as she grabbed a watering can. "Be back in an hour."

Rebecca was true to her word. Traipsing efficiently through the greenhouse, she first looked at the thermostat, which registered right at seventy-nine degrees, then went about checking the soil of each row of hundreds of plants as though she were inspecting troops, giving a dose of water to some and skipping others. When she arrived at the problem laelia, she took up a pinch of fir bark, charcoal, and perlite mixture the flower was planted in and rubbed it between her thumb and index finger. The last thing she did was to cut off about twenty blooms with her gardening scissors to bring them indoors.

After the allotted time, Rebecca reentered the kitchen door, her arms full of fresh flowers. Gracelyn had already gone upstairs with the men's oatmeal, leaving behind a spotless kitchen. Rebecca ran some water in the sink and plunged the tips of the flowers in while she went into the dining room to pick out three of the large vases lining the top of the large mahogany breakfront. Bringing them carefully into the kitchen, Rebecca laid them out on the tabletop and brought the fresh-cut blooms from the sink. She took her time arranging the flowers according to their color and length, reconsidering several times, until she discovered the most strikingly sculptural shapes.

By eleven-thirty, Rebecca had positioned the floral arrangements in the main entry hall on the first floor, in the library window that faced the street in the front of the house, and on the third-floor hallway adjacent to Claudia's bedroom, across from her own. Coming down to the men's floor, which she habitually skipped in her decorating, Rebecca went down the hallway to the bathroom. She gathered up a bar of Ivory soap, a washcloth, an old-fashioned ceramic basin, and a pitcher, which she filled with lukewarm water. It was time for her to give Bernard a sponge bath and perform sentry duties while Gracelyn took her lunch break.

Rebecca dunked the cloth into the hot water, soaped it lightly, and unceremoniously but with a light hand went over Bernard's limp body, including his genitals. Soaping the cloth again, she went over his face and neck. Once or twice he moaned weakly, most of his pain blunted by the morphine drip he was attached to.

Afterward, Rebecca picked up some newspapers Gracelyn had left on the seat of a ladder-back chair near the back-stairs landing and sat down. She began a thorough perusal of the news, pausing to look up when she heard a thud coming from Timothy's room. She waited to see if further noise would accompany what was either his falling down or knocking something over. Not hearing any wailing, she continued to read, finishing the local Peoria paper and going on to the *Chicago Sun-Times* to check on her stocks.

Rebecca started when Jake wandered from his room into the hallway. Even in his impaired mental state, Jake managed to dress himself nattily every day, sometimes wearing a tie and gold cuff links.

"You have to go to the bathroom?" she asked him.

"Such a nice day, I wanted to go outside. Can you take me out back, Rebecca?"

"Go on back inside there and rest," was his wife's no-nonsense command. "Lucy will take you out when she comes Saturday. Go sit in your chair. You'll get some sun that way."

Jake mumbled confusedly, "Who is Lucy?" before obediently turning around and slowly going back to his room.

Rebecca waited for him to be out of sight, then sprang up from the chair to look in on Bernard and Timothy. Timothy had indeed fallen from his bed and was sleeping soundly on the floor, saliva dribbling from the corner of his mouth. Rebecca hoisted the tall, angular man first onto his knees, then back onto his bed. She looked at him sprawled on top of the covers in an odd position. Shaking her head, she spent the next few minutes arranging his limbs so that they were less akimbo.

Looking in on Bernard, she noted that he lay still and was breathing evenly. By the time Gracelyn ambled back up to the second floor, a tray filled with medicines, glasses of apple juice, a plate of cheese sandwiches for Timothy and Jake, and soup for Bernard, Rebecca had finished her reading and torn off several pages from both papers.

"Everything's quiet. Jake was wandering around, but he's peaceful now. Timothy'll need a few more hours to sleep it off from last night. I heard him come in just before daybreak. Haven't heard a peep from yours since I checked him, but he's breathing. If they don't want to eat, don't force them. No point troubling yourself. Don't think anyone stinks too bad right now. Let's get going with that medicine before anyone else pees on himself."

Rebecca followed Gracelyn into Timothy's room, waiting just inside the door while the younger woman deposited a sandwich next to his bed table. It would be there when he awoke, and he might eat a few bites from it before performing his brief ablutions.

Later in the afternoon, he was sometimes awakened by delirium tremens. If not, he slept through most of the day. At night, he headed out to purchase liquor.

Jake still sat listlessly by his bedroom window when the women entered and did not turn his head when Gracelyn offered him his lunch plate. "Leave it," Rebecca supplied, and Gracelyn unceremoniously set the plate down on Jake's dresser.

Feeding Bernard was the last task for Rebecca and Gracelyn. Rebecca took charge of spooning the liquid into his mouth, oblivious to his faint moaning, as Gracelyn opened capsules of pain killers and vitamin supplements and stirred them into his juice.

The women tended directly to their men for the first portion of the day, checking their rooms and personal cleanliness, then provided them with a late supper. In between, things could get helter-skelter. As he became more and more immune to the effects of morphine, Bernard's intermittent wailing might fill the rafters of the big house. Startled and disturbed, Gracelyn put on Mattie Cates's classical music or Reuben's delta blues to drown out Bernard while she continued her light housecleaning chores and dinner preparation.

Rebecca told her repeatedly, "Nothing you can do about that; we've got to go on. Put it out of your mind."

Though shaken, Gracelyn always complied. For tonight's dinner, she decided on spring lamb, a watercress, endive, and radish salad, and wild rice. Before seasoning the lamb and dredging it with flour, she thought fleetingly that Bernard would miss all this and again have soup.

Jake wandered about the house with surprising deftness, rarely breaking things or hurting himself. However, Rebecca monitored his movements for the occasional odd activity his poor mind led him into. Once, she found him seated at the library desk convinced that all of the fountain pen cartridges needed to be refilled. Interrupting his earnest concentration, she led him perfunctorily back upstairs, thankful that the oriental carpeting had not been stained by a leak from one of the pens. Rebecca admonished him about coming downstairs again, but realized that he would quickly forget what she said to him and whatever had happened minutes before.

Returning from her errands, Claudia would make certain Timothy had not fallen to the floor, and if the sandwich was untouched, she would carry it downstairs and throw it in the garbage. Afterward, she disengaged herself as he came and went in his intermittent stupor, habitually making forays into town well after midnight. In his absence, she wiped streaks off hallway mirrors, misted Rebecca's floral arrangements, and filed receipts from her drugstore and grocery market purchases.

When Lucy returned, she would see an orderly house, ample medical supplies, and a store of clean linen. Based on the neatness of the house, including the men's bedrooms, she invariably reported to the Cates's neighbors that the sisters were circumspect in their caretaking. Once, when Lucy noticed that Jake was bruised slightly, Rebecca reacted with genuine surprise, thinking that he might have tripped on the stairs. When, in his conscious moments, Bernard muttered something about his wife not tending to him properly, Lucy uttered a "Tsk, tsk," as she shook her head and pitied the poor man's morphine-induced delusions.

In the few hours the sisters stole from their daily caretaking duties, they were busy keeping the massive house in order, determined to preserve the lifestyle Reuben and Mattie had worked hard to establish for their offspring. Each had ongoing projects. Rebecca never neglected her income-producing orchids and kept busy overseeing workmen doing the continuous small repairs inside and landscaping of the two-acre grounds. Her keen eye noticed any imperfection in ceramic tiles or molding, and a slightly sunken floorboard or tarnished mirror frame in the well-lit hallways would get her immediate attention. This month her concern was an army of bag worms that had invaded the pristine hedges lining the long walkway from the street to the front door. Alerted to the problem by Wayne, her landscaper, she researched the species in detail before calling an exterminator, so was able to thoroughly instruct him on the proper pesticide.

Wayne stood near Rebecca, an amused look on his face, as she gave her detailed overview to the befuddled man.

"Is all of that clear, sir?" she asked when she finished speaking.

"Yes, ma'am, I understood everything."

"Well, that's good. Wayne can show you which bushes are the worst. I declare, these creatures will be here long after we're gone."

"That's for sure, ma'am."

"Call me Rebecca."

"Oh, sure. Thanks, Rebecca."

As the two men headed off to attend to the row of bushes framing the front and side lawns, Wayne looked over his shoulder, his handsome face grinning at Rebecca. Rebecca grinned back. He had worked for her for fifteen years and understood her perfectionism. He was the same way about his landscaping, and Rebecca thought of him as a true artist. She felt close to Wayne in a sisterly way. She knew he had no family and his life hadn't been easy, although she did not have any details about his experiences. She remembered the day he rang the front doorbell and asked to show her some photographs of work he had done at other large estates. The man standing in front of her was well spoken, regal, and immaculate, and something about him had made her instantly trust him. He proved to be hardworking and a superbly talented designer, incorporating her suggestions when he thought they would enhance the undertaking, and letting her know sincerely and regretfully when he thought they would not.

Mattie's collections of sterling silver gleamed from inside the Jacobean cabinet in the dining room, owing to Claudia's diligent inspection and upkeep. Twice a month, she dutifully polished all of the flatware and spent as much time as she could arranging stemware, dessert dishes, jelly jars, and candleholders so that the light from one of the side windows would refract from the mirror directly opposite, illuminating the sparkling contents. On top of the breakfront under the mirror, she rotated displays of cups and saucers from Mattie's numerous china patterns. A year ago, Claudia had one of Rebecca's workmen install dimmer lights for the chandeliers in the living room, dining room, and hallway. Since then, every evening at dusk, she adjusted the dimmers to a soft, even glow.

Over the years, the Cateses had accumulated photographs of Reuben and Mattie before and after their children were born, family outings and community events, and each of the three girls at intervals during childhood, adolescence, and their adult years. Gracelyn was fascinated with these artifacts of the family's culture and spent hours cataloguing shots of school functions and picnics. She made certain to frame photos of her parents' parents, grandparents, and other relatives now deceased, and maintained a genealogy chart recording both sides of the family's migration from the South.

For the next few weeks, the sisters would be busy enacting the strategy Rebecca had presented to them at their morning meeting, their energies fueled by the freedom completion of their goal would provide them.

IV

By ten Wednesday morning, Rebecca had checked on her flowers and made the first round of attending to the men. In a few minutes, Claudia would relieve her from sentry duties on the men's floor and wait for Gracelyn to bring the lunch tray upstairs. Sitting pensively in the ladder-back chair in the second-floor hallway, Rebecca thought her beige linen suit and a navy cloche would serve her purposes well when she went to visit Reverend Wilson that afternoon. She decided to carry a pair of tan kidskin gloves, one of many that had belonged to Mattie. She knew she had sedate oxford pumps to match the gloves. The gold studs in her ears she wore daily would be the extent of her jewelry.

Never frilly, Rebecca knew that today especially a muted though impeccable outfit would both display her wealth and keep her femininity part of the equation. Catching Wilson slightly off guard, and for now having him think of her as a disgruntled matron with an unthreatening agenda, was critical to her overall strategy. By the time Wilson understood Rebecca meant to depose him, Bernard and Timothy would already be in facilities and, since Jake was still living in the Cates mansion, the reverend would not be able to point a finger accusingly at Rebecca. She would have plenty of time to discredit Wilson before carting Jake off to Sacred Lamb Rest Home in Springfield. She was not certain how she would bring this about, but she was certain she would.

Decided on her attire, Rebecca went back to reading the *Sun-Times,* expressly looking for the ad she had placed for laelia blooms. The Chicago market for her flowers was usually very strong this time of year with many of the leading downtown florists ordering from her throughout the spring months. When she and her sisters went farther upstate in July to deposit Timothy, she planned to check in with several vendors. A personal touch always increased her orders. Jake would be out of the house, she calculated, no later than mid-August. That meant a longer Chicago trip for the Cates women, with Claudia lunching with friends and Gracelyn able to do some extensive book browsing.

"Gracelyn, I'm gone," Rebecca shouted down the back stairs as soon as she heard her sister's footsteps coming up with the lunch tray.

"See you at dinner! Want a full report!" was Gracelyn's excited reply.

Rebecca hoisted herself up to the third floor to bathe and get dressed for her meeting. She had ample time to soak in a tub of pine-scented salts, then rub herself luxuriously with eucalyptus oil. Rebecca giggled at her reflection in the standing mirror adjacent to her bureau. With her softly corpulent build and abundant gray-streaked hair, she reminded herself of a grandmotherly sylph. Feeling fresh and lubricated, she pulled the linen suit still hanging in a plastic cleaning bag out of the closet. At 12:45 P.M. with military precision she drove her Mercedes down the long driveway and proceeded on to the parsonage.

Arriving at the Wilsons' home, Rebecca was guided through the entry hall by Julia Wilson. Stately and composed as they went through preliminary greetings, Rebecca accepted Julia's offer of tea. Once seated opposite Wilson in the living room, Rebecca noted the pastor's curious hand gesture as they made small talk. He persistently balled his left fist and, moving his forearm up toward his left shoulder, thrust his hand downward in a rhythmic swing, as though he were pounding on an invisible table. Rebecca thought Wilson might be unaware of this gesture and presumed he would not be aware of much else during their visit.

"Pastor Wilson, it was so good of you to make time for me today."

"Sister Cates, you are one of our outstanding churchwomen. I only wish you would visit with me more often."

"I intend to, Pastor. There are a few situations I believe we should work on together."

Reverend Wilson paused in mid-gesture and looked at Rebecca with the faintest surprise before asking, "What might those be, my dear?"

Rebecca had already decided to throw out a few things casually, but not to drive home any strong points. It was important that she be able to mention in conversations with other members that she had been having talks with the pastor, but that he not think it necessary to counteract any of her moves and lobby members to his own positions. At the moment, she intended that he have only a surface grasp of her motives.

"I am so grateful for your leadership. However, my sisters and I have felt somewhat neglected here lately. Our men keep us pretty much homebound throughout the week, and it would be so helpful to have you come by and bring us a spiritual message throughout the month to keep us going. Knowing how busy you are, it occurred to me that some of our committees could help you carry out your other duties. That way, you could have more of a personal touch with members going through hard times, such as my family."

Wilson cleared his throat, and resuming his hand gesture,

responded nonchalantly. "I see, I see. Well, perhaps I'll look into doing more visiting with you girls. Things do slow down a bit over the summer months."

Just as Wilson finished speaking, Julia appeared in the doorway carrying a service tray.

"Julia, see if Ms. Rebecca would like more tea."

"No, thank you, don't trouble yourself," Rebecca responded directly to the timid woman. "I'm doing just fine."

Julia nodded her head briefly. As she walked away, she glanced over her shoulder a few times at Rebecca.

"Oh, it would be so kind of you to come see us girls," Rebecca continued. "Of course, we wouldn't want to take away visiting time from other sick and shut-ins."

"I'm certain you won't, Ms. Rebecca."

"And if you discover the slightest shortfall in our church resources, you just let me know. My parents intended for me to continue providing for the church as much as they did when they were alive."

"Why thank you, Rebecca. I'll be in touch with you on that."

"Especially doing things for the children, Reverend. My sister Gracelyn just discovered a play about Harriet Tubman that would be a perfect activity for our summer youth program. I believe she intends to speak about it to Lucy Sims and see if they can't put on a big production with costumes and lighting and such. With your permission of course."

"Hmm," Wilson said with a degree of interest. "That sounds like a very good project."

"Then we will count on your support. It is so very important to keep our young people occupied. And I do believe my dear sister will need this sort of consolation soon."

"How's that?" the reverend asked, unable to follow Rebecca's flow of conversation.

"Well, you know that her poor husband, Bernard, is failing as we speak, and Gracelyn has decided that a hospice might make his last days less painful."

"I believe menfolk should die at home," was Wilson's succinct reply. "My mother tended to my father for seven long years before he passed on. She sat right at his bedside every night comforting him until he could sleep."

"How wonderful."

"Is Brother Bernard in his right mind?"

"He is lucid sometimes, Pastor. But the pain is very great now, and truly, I don't think my sister, being the delicate sort, can bear to watch him expire. In any case, please keep us in your prayers in these dark moments."

Silence built between the two as Wilson reflected on Rebecca's statements. Pulling a pipe from his shirt pocket, he waved it in front of his visitor.

"Mind if I smoke?"

"You go right ahead. I was just about to leave," Rebecca replied as she stood up. "And do thank Julia for her wonderful tea service. I will look forward to seeing you both this Sunday."

Wilson, slightly baffled, realized just then that their conversation had ended, and that Rebecca had not sought his approval of Gracelyn's actions. As he led Rebecca to the front door, he thought to himself that the Cates women were a peculiar lot; probably all that money made them too damned independent.

Rebecca's cheeks flushed with temper as she left the parsonage and climbed into her Mercedes. But she had been careful not to openly defy the authoritative man. Pulling away from the curb, she shifted her steely focus to how she would use the remainder of the day. After supper with her sisters, she would do some research on the church's finances during Wilson's tenure. She had a copy of the church budget from last fiscal year, and she would compare it with the budgets in Reuben's extensive files on church matters under Reverend Simmons.

Entering the hallway of the Cates home, Rebecca smelled the garlicky tomato sauce Gracelyn had prepared for their spaghetti dinner. She looked forward to the rolls with flecks of fresh basil that would accompany their main course.

"Gracelyn," she yelled out, "do we have any ice cream? Tell me before I settle in, and I'll run get some."

"Oh hi, Rebecca." Gracelyn smiled as she puttered in from the kitchen. "There's just enough of that mint chocolate chip for all three of us to have a smidgen. You can relax for a few minutes before we sit down to eat. Jake's dozing in his chair, Bernard is sleeping peacefully. Timothy was in the bed, too, when I checked him, but restless."

As if on cue, Timothy's wiry figure emerged, hurriedly descending the front stairs. He reached into the hallway closet, donned a fedora and a sport jacket, then walked past the two women, giving them the merest tip of his hat as a greeting, his eyes downward. Carefully shutting the front door, he headed out into the moist air of the descending dusk.

"That'll be all we see of that one this day," cited Rebecca, knowing Timothy would not return home until well after midnight. "Remind me to call Dr. Meyers about that sedative. If we can get him to sleep more, he won't be thinking too much about liquor. All this running in and out has got to stop. The other night, he must have forgotten his door keys. I don't know how long he pounded on that door. And do you know poor Claudia slept through the whole racket. Lord knows, I just had that door painted. Going Italian tonight, girl?"

Gracelyn giggled.

"You know how I get in my moods. And I really started thinking about spaghetti after I spotted those fresh bitter greens at the market. A green salad and some pasta is such a wonderful combination. And Lord, sister, we need our strength to go forward."

"Lord knows we do. I guess Claudia will be prancing in here shortly. What time did she tell you? My stomach's rumbling."

"She told me no later than six-fifteen."

"Well then, that's probably a go. I'll have time to change out of my clothes. You call me now when everything's ready."

"Sure thing." Gracelyn went back to her meal preparations as Rebecca mounted the front stairs. Entering her bedroom, she removed the cloche from her head and placed it inside a small hat box left out on an overstuffed chair. After kicking off her pumps, she lay her gloves and purse on the dresser.

"Whew!" Rebecca expended a grateful breath after freeing her feet from the confines of exquisite leather. She quickly removed her suit jacket and skirt, returned them to their wooden hangers, and filed them inside the closet. She slipped out of the sleeveless shell she had worn under the jacket, removed her enormous bra, and clad only in her satin slip, bounded onto her bed.

Almost immediately, Rebecca dozed off into a dream. She was walking, incredibly, through a field of orchids, completely nude, and the high afternoon sun was shining on her full figure. While still going forward, she felt a pair of long-fingered hands cupping her breasts from behind. Not turning her head to see who it was that had come upon her, she said, "I knew you would find me." Aroused and happy in the dream, Rebecca's catnap was interrupted by Gracelyn's calling out that dinner was ready.

Claudia indeed arrived as scheduled, so that by 7 P.M. the sisters were seated in the dining room spooning out healthy portions of pasta and Gracelyn's sublime *bolognese* sauce. They ate in virtual silence for a few moments, then began the chatter among themselves that they so relished at this time during their day.

"It's polka dots again. I don't care whether it's your blouse, or a shirtdress, or just a scarf helmut. That Anna Wintour is the bible for fashion, if you ask me."

"Do tell." Rebecca responded tongue in cheek to Claudia's frantic commentary.

"And I mean, you should see the way they have paired those polka-dot blouses with a straight python skirt." Claudia went on undaunted by Rebecca's mild sarcasm. "If I were a younger woman, I sure would be swishing around in one of those straight skirts. Not too short, though. The women in this country should learn to leave more to the imagination. The African women believe a man is most interested in what he can't see. Do you all believe that? I think there's something in it."

"They sure do cover themselves up. I wonder does that get hot." Rebecca reflected on this issue as she scooped more greens onto her salad plate. "Gracelyn, you have outdone yourself with these rolls."

"Why, thank you. I figured we should all have some hips to swish around in our straight skirts."

Rebecca chuckled at Gracelyn's remark. Claudia, unembarrassed, chewing on a roll, began to speak again.

"Yes, indeed, dear, these are excellent. Now, you could liven yourself up a bit with some polka dots. And Rebecca, you could buy some polka-dot accessories if you were of a mind to. I think they favor just about everybody."

"I'm lively enough to suit me. But you go right ahead. Um hmm. You all know I saw pastor today."

Once Rebecca spoke, the mood around the table shifted to sober concentration. Claudia stopped chewing momentarily.

Gracelyn asked, "What did the two of you talk about?"

"I told him about that Harriet Tubman play, for one thing. But mainly, I let him know we expected him to do more visiting to ailing parishioners. Nicely, of course."

Claudia coughed, choked slightly, but remained silent.

"He told me he would try to visit us 'girls' more often. And that was about it."

"What now?"

"Honey, you let me worry about that. Claudia, you have your speech ready for Sunday?"

"No, but I'm working on it."

"Well, I know you'll get it just right. And wear some of those polka dots so you look extra pretty."

Claudia blushed at Rebecca's comment. Gracelyn, frowning slightly, kept silent. Rebecca, noticing this, continued.

"I'm going to be in the library this evening going over the church budgets. Remember, Mama used to say, 'When you go a-looking for something, make sure you really want to find it.' Well, I'm a-looking and sometime this evening I'll be a-finding. Now, you fix your mind on talking to Raphaela and Lucy. Just keep talking up that play and after we drop off Bernard next week, you start getting them organized."

Gracelyn was ready to focus her mental energies on her children's production. While tending to the men, cooking, and doing housework, she had already begun to silently work out casting, lighting, and stage directions.

Claudia sighed deeply. "Well that's that."

With all three sisters prepped on their strategy through the weekend, the dinner conversation continued lightheartedly.

"Rebecca, I found a whole set of pewter vases in the basement. I want to do a flower arrangement on the breakfront. It'll be fresher than all that china for the hot weather. I need to cut some extra blooms to bring inside."

"That would be real nice, Claudia. There are some laelias in the back of the greenhouse. I brought some in earlier. You can carry more in this evening, if you've a mind to."

Snapping to from her reverie, Gracelyn teased, "The three of us can start thinking about pollinating before long, don't you think?"

Rebecca laughed, then said. "Girl, what's got into you?"

Claudia responded for Gracelyn, "Nothing! That's her problem."

"Our problem," Gracelyn parried.

"Lord, help us," Rebecca intoned in mock piety.

The Cates women enjoyed a session of raucous laughter before Rebecca stood up, daubed her mouth with her cloth napkin, and trudged straight to the library. Finding last year's church budget right where it belonged in the file drawer, she reached behind to find past budgets and financial statements that Reuben had maintained carefully until his death. Seated at the desk with the paperwork spread out in front of her, she easily compared Reverend Wilson's expenditures over a twelve-month period with those of Reverend Simmons. Wilson's church-related business trips, the parsonage upkeep, and the slight raise approved by the trustees six months after his tenure began showed he was not as frugal as Reverend Simmons had been during his long stretch as pastor. Nevertheless, everything appeared reasonable. Rebecca continued to probe.

Around 11 P.M., Rebecca's energies wound down, and she stood up from the desk for a long stretch and yawn. She sat back down, determined to keep going until midnight. After vigorously rubbing her eyes, she flipped through the pages of the Wilsons' itemized expenses. An insurance deductible of three thousand dollars was listed for Julia Wilson during the past year. The payment was made to the Horizons Medical Assurance Corporation out of Michigan. The procedure, listed as surgical, was performed at a clinic in Bloomington by a Dr. Randall Leighton.

Rebecca combed her memory, trying to remember if Julia had been absent any Sunday for the past year. Surely, if she had needed medical attention, the congregation would have been informed, if only to offer its support and well wishes. Rebecca could recall nothing said during announcements about Julia's being ill or needing an operation. Well, Rebecca thought, it could be something that embarrassed her, perhaps some women's procedure. But since Julia was in her mid-fifties, she was not likely to have had her tubes tied. But this was in fact minor surgery, so it was probably something other than gynecological, Rebecca concluded.

Intrigued, Rebecca pulled the page and placed it on top of the other papers. Fighting sleep, she stood up from the desk, found a paperweight to keep the stack of records intact, and proceeded upstairs.

V

"REBECCA? REBECCA?" Gracelyn called outside Rebecca's door. She had traipsed downstairs, in her excitement almost tripping over the antique petticoat she had pulled on underneath a coarse wool skirt. Her head swathed in yards of muslin, she held herself regally erect while she waited for Rebecca to respond.

"Hold on," Rebecca said.

Rebecca, already awake and in her bathrobe, was bent over, retrieving a stray house shoe from underneath her bed. She pulled the scuff quickly onto her bare foot and hustled to see what Gracelyn was so excited about.

"Everything all right?" she asked as she swung the door open. After a moment of silence, Rebecca let out a throaty chuckle. "Girl, what on earth?"

"Harriet Tubman! There's tons of this cloth upstairs in Mama's trunk. And I found about six petticoats for the little girls to wear. I was just trying everything on to see if you thought this was the right effect."

"I do indeed. My goodness, Gracelyn, you have a talent for costuming. Maybe the theater is your missed calling."

"You know what they say, 'The play's the thing!' I'm really excited now. Last night, I was almost too excited to sleep. I just had to show you what I came up with before I got breakfast started."

Gracelyn bounded back to her attic quarters to dump her creation.

"What on earth?" Claudia, peeking out from her half-open door, echoed Rebecca's sentiment.

Rebecca, seeing she was still groggy, instructed her, "Nothing. Just Gracelyn getting excited about her play. You go on back and get your beauty rest for another hour."

Claudia yawned sleepily in agreement.

Gracelyn's hyped enthusiasm persisted throughout their morning breakfast.

Rebecca was actually glad that once Gracelyn slowed down, Claudia began to talk excitedly about what she would wear on Sunday when she made her announcements in church for the first time. All the chatter allowed Rebecca to focus her thoughts on her plan to depose Wilson.

"I don't see how I can avoid driving to Bloomington Saturday. Marshall Field's is the best place for me to find something perky to wear. I'll probably leave right after Lucy comes in. I need to catch her to ask the best thing to use on all that pewter to get it sparkling."

When Claudia mentioned Bloomington, Rebecca's attention was recaptured.

"Bloomington? Well that will be a nice drive. I may go along with you. We can take the Mercedes. Gracelyn, do you mind being here alone for most of the day?"

"No. That'll give me the chance to meet with Lucy about the Tubman piece, if she can take some time away from the menfolks. She can lock up the two wanderers while we have our talk. Anyway, I'd just as soon not be in a car if it's nice. I'll probably walk over to the library and check out some slave narratives. I really believe this play can be something magnificent."

"Sure it can," Rebecca assured her animated baby sister.

"Rebecca, have I convinced you to look for some polka dots?" Claudia asked in mock seriousness.

"No, dearie. I'll leave the polka dots to you slender women. You know I'm not going to be poking around Marshall Field's for any length of time. But there are a couple of florists in Bloomington I can call on. It will be nice to be on the road for a few hours. It sure does help cleanse the mind."

Rebecca saw no need to reveal her agenda to the others right at that moment. While Claudia was shopping downtown, she would locate the very Dr. Leighton who had performed Julia Wilson's surgery. She planned to find out his specialty without probing for any confidential information on Julia, and she would in fact say Julia had referred her to him. If there was anything amiss in that three thousand dollars the church had paid for Julia's medical procedure, Rebecca knew the trip to Bloomington would be well worth her time.

As soon as Lucy arrived at the Cates home Saturday morning, Gracelyn greeted her in the front hallway, sat her down at the dining table, and proceeded with a rapid-fire description of her children's play.

"Now, you know Harriet Tubman is my favorite historical figure, male or female, I know for a fact that there are at least twelve children in the church who could work on this project—acting, lighting, doing stagecraft, and what have you. And we need to keep our young people occupied over the summer months. Lucy, your Melba would be wonderful in the lead. Is she in summer school now, or anything like that?"

The lightbulb went on in Lucy's head at Gracelyn's last remark.

"Matter of fact, no. She would love to do something like this.

Since school's out, she's always up late watching old movies and such. How soon do you need her?"

"I'm thinking we'll get started Saturday evening, a week from now. But it will have to be after supper, around seven. I've got something to take care of earlier in the day."

Right on cue, Bernard moaned from upstairs. Lucy stood to attention, ready to go up and tend to her charges.

Gracelyn continued, "I'm going to finish up in the kitchen; then I'll be going out. There are some pastries in the refrigerator. Rebecca and Claudia are driving to Bloomington this morning, so you'll have everything to yourself. Honey, don't let these menfolks wear you out."

Lucy smiled as she shifted mental gears from the excitement of Gracelyn's production to the task at hand. Entering the kitchen to start the breakfast oatmeal, she called to Rebecca, standing at the back window finishing a glass of juice.

"Mornin', Rebecca. Hear you and Claudia are heading down to Bloomington this morning. Ought to be nice weather from the looks of it."

"It does look nice and clear. I was out with my flowers for an hour or so just about when the sun was coming up. One of these days, I guess I'll be too old to get up so early."

"Not necessarily. You stay in the habit, you'll be just fine."

"You're a wise woman, Lucy."

"You all coming back for supper?"

"Hmm, don't think so. I have some business errands to run, and by the time Claudia finishes shopping, we most likely will have had enough to eat. And you know tomorrow when Gracelyn cooks our big meal, we'll make up for whatever we didn't eat today."

Both women laughed at Rebecca's reference to the sisters' full-course Sunday meal. Rebecca had made it clear that Lucy could join them whenever she desired, but she had never taken Rebecca up on the invitation.

Today, however, to Rebecca's surprise, Lucy told her, "I believe I'll sit with you all at dinner tomorrow and taste Gracelyn's cooking. We were having a wonderful conversation about that play she wants to do. Myself, I need to do some brush-up reading on that black history stuff. Melba sure will be excited. You should see the way that girl preens around, thinking she's Dorothy Dandridge."

"Now Dorothy Dandridge, that was some actress," Rebecca responded, encouraging Lucy's uncharacteristic divulgences. "I bet Melba has real talent. Wasn't she Mary Magdalene in the Sunday school Easter pageant last year?"

"Oh, yes, indeed. She went over that speech every day for three solid weeks. Lord help me, if I heard that piece one time I heard it a hundred times."

"Well, it's good for young people to be excited about something—"

Bernard's moan punctuated Rebecca's unfinished phrase.

"I better be heading upstairs now." Lucy, basking in motherly pride, quickly filled a tray with oatmeal, juice, and dry toast and headed for the back stairs just as Claudia reached the landing.

"I just looked in on Bernard. Can't really tell if he's awake or asleep. But he was pretty noisy there for a minute. How are you doing today, Lucy?"

"Very well, thank you." A smiling Lucy continued her energetic ascent.

Claudia, crisply chic in a pink-and-white-striped shirtdress with a matching kerchief, turned toward Rebecca.

"What's got into her?" Without waiting for a response, she filled a water glass and downed a multiple vitamin.

"Aren't you supposed to have food with that, dearie?" Rebecca asked.

"I figured we'd get something on the road. Anyway, it never bothers me to take these on an empty stomach. Let's get going."

Rebecca understood that Claudia's shopping addiction had

overcome her. Now, there would be no holding back. Rebecca was herself excited over their two-hour road trip. The highway from Peoria to Bloomington was lined with some nice woodsy patches and this time of year there would be spring flowers just past their peak, still glorious, and ready to succumb to the warmer weather.

Expertly backing the Mercedes out of the driveway, Rebecca indulged Claudia's persistent chatter while focusing on how she would cull the information she needed from Dr. Leighton. She had checked his office to find out if he took Saturday appointments, and been informed that she could come to the clinic as a walk-in patient up until 1 P.M.

Rebecca planned to feign self-consciousness and mention she had been referred to him by Julia Wilson. She would be as vague as possible about her symptoms, then vaguely ask if he would recommend that she have the same procedure. That would hopefully be all she needed to get him to reveal the specifics of Julia's case; then she would know definitively if this expenditure had been appropriate. If it had not been, there was meat for real controversy.

It didn't occur to Rebecca that Julia may have received treatment for some life-threatening emergency, or that her situation could be in any way pitiable and deservedly kept private. Rebecca would cross the ethical divide when it came to her, and, currently in war mode, she had not yet intuited that it would.

"Why, Rebecca, are you just going to let me talk to myself for the next hour? Girl, I don't know what, but there's something important on your mind. I guess I know you too well."

Called back to the present by her sister, Rebecca shook her head as if snapped to attention.

"I'm sorry, dear. You know I enjoy your conversation. It's the only way I ever find out about things like what to wear and such. I guess my mind wandered, looking out over these gorgeous colors. Which do you think dry out better, the forsythia or the hyacinths?"

Claudia's attention shifted to the pastoral, which up to now had escaped her view. "Honestly, I have no idea, but I imagine both will dry very prettily. You know, I just now noticed that milkweed. That makes a pretty arrangement all by itself in a tall vase. One of those pewter vases would be just the thing for a bunch of it."

"Well then, we'll stop on the way back," Rebecca swiftly responded. "Remember where we are right now, right at Exit 14 on the Interstate."

Rebecca had skillfully managed to divert Claudia's attention so that her own silence would seem less remarkable. Now Claudia was off clothes and onto decorating.

"Marshall Field's usually has some beautiful household accessories. I may give that third floor the once-over if you think we'll have time."

Rebecca, who had every intention of spending all of ten minutes inside the department store, said to her sister, "You take all the time you need. By the time I haggle with these florists, I'm going to need to go somewhere and have a cup of tea to calm myself. If you can occupy yourself until around two, all the better."

"Oh, yes. I can do that easily. If you pick me up then, we can go somewhere for lunch."

"Let's plan on it." Rebecca had succeeded in structuring the day to allow ample time for her visit to the clinic. She would get around to her florists later, if it turned out she had time to kill.

"Lord, talking about food makes me hungry. It's a good thing I brought this fruit." Claudia reached into her bag and opened a Tupperware bowl filled with apple slices. "Rebecca, you want some of these or you going to hold out?"

"I am on the hungry side, but after I drop you off, I'll grab some toast and coffee somewhere."

She knew Claudia's shopping urge would not permit her to stop and eat a full meal, so she didn't press her to have something substantial for the morning hours. Their size was the starkest difference between the two sisters, and Rebecca's need for fuel was never meager, while Claudia's was sometimes birdlike. Today, as always, Rebecca's agenda accommodated their differences as well as her need to conduct her investigation of Dr. Leighton without distraction.

Heads turned at the sight of the gray Mercedes pulling up to the entrance of the ornate department store, which took up a whole block of the small downtown. Claudia garnered further attention from the pedestrian traffic as she alighted. Claudia, used to receiving attention for her style and elegant bearing, still wore her kerchief. She had also retrieved her Dior sunglasses for the brief walk from the car to the store's main entrance.

Rebecca, noting the small sensation that her sister caused, was confident that her upcoming church announcements would produce the same effect. She was also confident that Claudia would select just the right ensemble to wear to morning service. With an impeccable eye for detail and the lines that suited her, she was devoted to her appearance even in casual mode, and with more time and planning for a special occasion, she would be totally arresting.

Before continuing on her way, Rebecca reached in the car's glove compartment to retrieve a street map for Bloomington. She was across town from Leighton's clinic, and the map indicated she would be best served by heading south for about three miles, then making a left onto the avenue where the clinic was situated.

The Aphrodite Clinic. Rebecca noted the bronze-plated sign alongside the automatic glass doors with curiosity. Inside she found a scrupulously clean, spacious, and well-lit waiting area. Four women were seated on comfortable plush green chairs with chrome frames. The Berber carpeting was a gray-flecked ivory. The women and the facility suggested affluence.

Rebecca walked over to the registration desk and gave her name to the casually dressed attendant. In return, she was given a form to fill out providing her medical history. Rather than inspecting the large, light-skinned black woman dressed somewhat androgynously in khakis and a neat oxford shirt, the other patients studiously avoided looking at Rebecca, as well as at each other. Rebecca was increasingly curious about this doctor and his clientele. The faintest tinge of embarrassment prevailed throughout the large room, and the attendant's ingratiatingly friendly manner only underscored it.

Rebecca took a seat and began filling in the form. She stopped momentarily and scanned the two-sided document to see if there were gynecological services offered. Never having been inside an abortion clinic, she imagined the tension in the room might be from something of that nature. She saw nothing on the form asking for anything other than routine medical history. There was a question about computer imaging, but in Rebecca's mind, this was an innocent enough procedure and these days could pertain to a range of ailments.

Several magazines were arranged on a long glass-topped table in between the rows of chairs where the women sat. Rebecca picked up a copy of *House and Garden* and began leafing through it. She was interrupted by a light tap on her shoulder. A woman seated directly across from Rebecca had moved to the vacant chair next to her. She was carrying the Bloomington newspaper folded back to a page showing a crossword puzzle.

"Do you happen to have a pen or pencil?" she asked Rebecca.

Rebecca reached in her bag and produced a pen.

"Thank you."

The woman smiled and, rather than return to her seat, remained seated next to Rebecca. She frowned over the puzzle for about two minutes, then spoke to her again.

"Excuse me. Here's your pen back. I guess I'm a bit nervous today." She seemed intent on starting up a conversation.

Rebecca thought nothing of telling the presumptuous woman

that she would rather read than talk, but right away thought better of it. She could certainly find out why she was seeing Dr. Leighton, and it could be helpful in discovering the type of surgery he had performed on Julia Wilson.

After the woman confessed to her nervousness, Rebecca interjected, "This is my first time seeing Dr. Leighton. Is he a good doctor?"

"Oh, I should say. I've been with him for years now, starting right after my youngest finished college. You know, the prices have almost tripled in the past ten years, but the way you feel about yourself afterward is worth every penny."

Rebecca waited for the woman to reveal more about her particular health complaint.

"I knew I had to do something to keep my husband happy. I wasn't getting any younger, and everywhere you look there are so many pretty girls. A woman needs to feel attractive and good about her assets."

"Indeed," was Rebecca's puzzled comment. "If you don't mind my asking, why are you here now?"

"Oh, just for a checkup. I had the last operation a few months ago."

Rebecca, knowing she was overstepping the bounds of politeness, asked pointedly, "What did Dr. Leighton do for you the last time?"

The woman, only too happy to reveal herself to Rebecca, glanced quickly around the room as if to make certain no one else heard her.

"The first time," she said, speaking in a stage whisper, "I had liposuction."

Rebecca's mouth flew open in astonishment. She checked herself immediately and responded dryly, "I see." After a decent interval, she asked further, "Did everything go well?"

"I had just the tiniest bit of discomfort after the procedure, but

Dr. Leighton really knows what he's doing. And the medication he gave me was superb, and I'm not one for taking a lot of pills."

Rebecca, still not fully recovered from the woman's revelation, prepared to ask her what her current visit to Leighton portended. Before she could think of a tactful way to raise the question, however, the attendant called out to her.

"Rebecca Cates Furness, the doctor will see you now."

Rebecca, for a moment disoriented at hearing her married name, thought fleetingly that she would drop Jake's surname and change her name legally back to Rebecca Florentina Cates once Jake was safely ensconced in Sacred Lamb. No one in Peoria remembered her married name, anyway. She, Claudia, and Gracelyn would forever be "the Cates girls" to all of their neighbors in their small universe. She quickly got over the shock of what her fellow patient told her, and in her steely mind, started planning how she would query the doctor.

Rebecca was led by the attendant to the doctor's office, a small, pleasant room with Impressionist paintings on the walls, prints of Cézanne's water lilies, and some of Matisse's portraits and still lifes. When Dr. Leighton—a man she surmised to be in his late forties—entered the room in his immaculate white surgeon's coat, Rebecca noted the same muted elegance as in the paintings. Tall, olive-skinned, and of medium build, he spoke to her in a well-modulated baritone.

"Mrs. Furness, I'm Dr. Leighton."

"Hello," Rebecca responded. Her eyes followed him as he sat behind a long teak desk positioned directly in front of a large picture window with old-fashioned blinds drawn nearly shut. Her eyes then swept the small room in totality and stopped at a credenza, above which were mounted several carved West African masks.

Noticing Rebecca's survey of his decor, Dr. Leighton began to talk with enthusiasm about his art collection.

"I'm very passionate about Yoruba sculpture, as you can see. There is such a spiritual quality to these pieces in addition to their beauty, and since I'm in the beauty business, it's good to have as much of it around as possible."

Rebecca thought initially that Dr. Leighton might be a black man. The tinge of cadence in his speech and the resonance of his speaking voice confirmed this for her.

"You've been to Africa?"

"I go as frequently as I can. I'm planning my next trip for sometime this winter. Are you a collector yourself?"

"No, not in the least. My business is orchids."

Without waiting for the doctor to give her a lead-in, Rebecca stated, "Julia Wilson, my pastor's wife, referred me to you. I'm interested in the same procedure and knowing what you think is best for me."

Dr. Leighton cleared his throat and paused before he began speaking.

"Mrs. Furness—"

"Do call me Rebecca."

"Oh, thank you. Rebecca, it's important to me that the women I see first appreciate their own special features before considering any surgery I might perform on them. Unless I misunderstand, you are interested in breast enlargement."

Rebecca, unflinching, replied, "Actually, breast reduction."

"Oh, I see, I see."

A trace of a smile came and went from Dr. Leighton's mouth.

"I was confused when you mentioned Mrs. Wilson."

"I can see how you would be," Rebecca probed, just to make certain she completely understood their exchange. "No, sir. I'm a bit overendowed."

"Well, I wouldn't say so, given your height and build. Your breasts are quite appropriate. Have you been having back pain or any other discomfort?"

"No, none. But I thought some surgery might enhance my appearance. I suppose that's vain."

"Well, possibly. But more likely you are saturated with American cultural images of the perfect woman. You should really travel to Africa and get another sense of beauty. Men there value larger women. To some extent, that's true of our people here as well."

Dr. Leighton continued talking to Rebecca, as though he didn't often have the chance to express his opinions about art, culture, and varying types of beauty. Listening with mild interest, she tried to conceal her excitement at having learned the truth about the three thousand dollars the church had paid toward Julia Wilson's breast implants. As far as Rebecca's strategy went, this development was beyond perfect. Noting that Dr. Leighton had stopped speaking and was looking at her thoughtfully while stroking his chin, she thought it best to tell him she was not going to do anything for now.

"But if you don't mind, I may want another consultation with you."

"Why certainly, I would advise just that." Leighton leaned forward earnestly. "Even if just to be assured that you're very attractive as you are."

Rebecca stood, and he immediately sprang to his feet and came around the desk to escort her out.

"I do not charge for up to three consultations, because I recognize these are serious issues, and I don't want my patients to hesitate to contact me. So, you keep that in mind."

"Oh, I will, Doctor. And thank you so much. I feel very much at ease after speaking with you."

It was just shy of one o'clock, and Rebecca decided to forgo seeing her florist clients and just drive around the town, since she would need to pick up Claudia at Marshall Field's in just over an hour. She was so happy with her discovery of Wilson's financial impropriety, she didn't feel she could talk to business clients coherently, and as far as she was concerned, her workday was over. She would just relax behind the wheel, get something to eat with Claudia, and enjoy the ride back. The next, more intense phase of her project was about to begin, and she would need to recoup her energies. Armed now with critical information, she would be able to launch a searing attack.

VI

REBECCA STOOD OUTSIDE the gothic building noticing the sky was cloudier than earlier that morning. The Cates sisters had abandoned their walk to church because of the grayness, and Rebecca had let the others out while she parked the Mercedes in the lot adjacent to the small backyard. If in fact it started to rain, the parishioners would not be in a rush for the service to be completed. That was a good thing for Claudia. She could take her time making announcements without hearing an impatient sigh or anyone's feet tapping. Rebecca realized that if her glamorous sister relaxed, she would completely charm the congregation.

Rebecca proceeded indoors, pausing briefly in the entryway to acknowledge two white-gloved ushers in starched white dresses and lace caps. One of the women handed her a program and the other led her down the center aisle to the sixth pew from the front, where she took the aisle seat next to Claudia, who sat primly in the middle of the pew reading her Bible. For most of the last century this had been the Cates family pew. Rarely did other members of the congregation invade the sisters' designated seating area. If they did, it was only when the church was completely packed, at Easter service or when a well-known guest speaker was present.

Claudia's dignity was enhanced by the ensemble she had chosen for this morning. Hatless today, she wore a sleeveless ivory linen dress that provided just a hint of an A-line over her slender frame. The bateau neckline was accented by a vivid melon-and-teal-printed silk scarf, ends clasped by a large onyx brooch resting on her sternum. The effect of the scarf was welcoming, and the subdued neutral dress created a regal effect. Sparse gray strands wound through the chignon at the nape of her neck, giving her an air of kindness and gentility.

A few moments after Rebecca was seated, Gracelyn appeared from a side door at the back of the church. Walking briskly up the aisle, she plopped cheerfully next to Claudia and began to fan herself excitedly. Rebecca knew she had spoken to Sunday school students about a meeting next Saturday evening to discuss the Tubman play. That morning, if everything went smoothly, they would have deposited Bernard at his hospice. Claudia would also mention the play in her presentation that morning, and ask parents to support the activity. Rebecca planned for Bernard's commitment to be kept quiet for a while, and she hoped any public interest in his plight would be muffled by the excitement over the children's play. In the weeks that followed, when rehearsals were under way, she would have Claudia refer soberly to his unfortunate decline. Rebecca herself would be able to drop the bomb regarding Julia Wilson's surgery before people had a chance to gossip about how buoyant Gracelyn seemed about her project, despite her husband's misfortune.

Strains of organ music halted Rebecca's rumination. She raised her head up to the choir loft, where tiny Shirley Breeden had seated herself at the pipe organ three or four times her size. Rebecca began humming softly to Shirley's signature prelude, "Is Your All On the Altar of Sacrifice Laid." Ever since Rebecca could remember, Shirley had begun playing this melody at the start of the church service as a signal for members to cease shuffling and whispering in their seats in preparation for the procession of the pastor and the choir.

The music segued seamlessly into "All Hail the Power of Jesus's Name." Reverend Wilson, with Deacons Smitherson and Johnson slightly behind him, walked down the red-carpeted aisle to the front of the church singing loudly. The choir followed, stepping rhythmically in their burgundy robes with gold satin collars. The congregation sang along with the choir, with many persons knowing the words by heart and holding their open hymnbooks out of habit.

At the end of the song, Wilson, standing at the pulpit, delivered the invocation in a sonorous voice. Smitherson and Johnson stood next to their chairs on opposite sides of the pastor's, looking out over the congregation like stern yet kindly grandfathers. The choir, assembled in the loft, the congregation, and the two deacons up front all waited for Wilson to finish speaking so they could be seated. At Wilson's instruction, everyone sat down in one motion. An usher scrambled forward, motioning to the just-entering Bartleson family to follow her. She was able to seat the clan, James and Amelia and their three children, in the seventh pew, directly in back of the Cates sisters. The children bustled and whispered uncomfortably after they were settled. Rebecca, turning her head and torso to face them frontally, narrowed her gray eyes to slits, intimidating the three into silence. This morning she would brook no disruptions to her agenda. Claudia would not be distracted by the unruly urchins.

The pastor gave instructions to read silently from the Bible, Timothy 3:1–6, as he read aloud:

> Thus, know also, that in the last days perilous times shall come.

For men shall be lovers of their own selves, covetous, boasters, proud, blasphemers, disobedient to parents, unthankful, unholy.

Without natural affection, trucebreakers, false accusers, incontinent, fierce, despisers of those that are good,

Traitors, heady, high-minded, lovers of pleasures more than lovers of God;

Having a form of godliness, but denying the power thereof: from such turn away.

For of this sort are they which creep into houses, and lead captive silly women laden with sins, led away with divers lusts.

Wilson's choice of scripture signaled to Rebecca that she should tune out the sermon. Claudia's announcement would come right after the offering. In the interim, Rebecca let her mind wander. She half-listened to the choir's selection of spirituals, catching the refrain of "We Are Climbing Jacob's Ladder," then drifting again into her reverie. A man appeared in her mind, tall and light-brown-skinned with large hands outstretched to her. She was brought back to alertness by the sopranos' high notes in "Lord I Want to Be a Christian, in-a My Heart" and by the shock of apprehending her fantasy: The face belonging to this man was Dr. Leighton's.

Her mind racing to make sense of this image from her subconscious, Rebecca indeed heard none of the sermon. How was it possible, she asked herself, that such a fantasy had taken root following a very brief meeting with a man she had not been particularly taken with, and who she suspected might be guilty of larceny? She brushed her thoughts aside for the moment.

Reverend Wilson had called the ushers to come forward for the offering, and as four women assembled in the front of the church, Deacons Smitherson and Johnson distributed a brass plate for the collection to each. Claudia, realizing the announcements were next, was certain Rebecca and Gracelyn, seated on either side of her, could hear her heart thumping inside her chest. She lasted through Wilson's highlighting of items already printed in that morning's church bulletin, his recognition of visitors, and carefully worded commendations on the work of the various church committees. At the end of his remarks, he called upon the congregation in general for additional information needed to be made known during that portion of the service. A slight murmur swept the congregation when Claudia rose from her seat.

"Brothers and Sisters," she began tentatively. "I have a word to share with you, should it please our pastor."

"Go ahead, Sister Cates."

"My sisters and I have decided that we wish to open our hearts more frequently to our church family, and ask for prayer in our time of great need."

Immediately, heads began nodding and Amens were shouted to punctuate Claudia's statements. Others listened silently, transfixed by the soft-spoken woman's queenly appearance and bearing.

"We know that many of you have loved ones who are ailing and, like us, wish to unburden yourselves periodically and witness to the Lord's great power to strengthen and save."

"Amen!"

"Do Jesus!"

"Testify!"

Encouraged by the vocal responses to her words, Claudia continued more boldly.

"I just want to say that, with all our tribulations, we don't feel no ways tired, and we want to thank the members of this congregation for their Christian example. We want to make certain that you let us know how you are faring so we can mention your loved ones' names whenever we bow our heads and come before the presence of the Lord. Lastly, I want to thank the pastor for all his visits to our menfolk over the past months during our time of trial."

As Claudia's final statement registered, there was a momentary pause in the twitters and murmuring of approval for her plea for spiritual connectedness through their common plight. Rebecca attributed the brief silence to puzzlement, since Wilson seldom made visits to members. She felt confident that, according to her plan, a small controversy had been sparked.

Outside the church building following the service, several members embraced Claudia, offering words of encouragement and thanking her for stating what was in so many of their hearts. She had completely surprised the congregation, accustomed as they were to her reticence and seeming indifference. Now, any resentment toward her was utterly dissolved, and her attire and attractiveness would be remarked upon with utmost approval for the remainder of the week. Rebecca knew that this initial response would heighten, and Claudia's role as the Cates family mouthpiece would bring both credibility and admiration to the sisters' apparent sacrifice as they continued boldly in their strategy.

That evening, Rebecca, Claudia, and Gracelyn sat along with Lucy at their massive dinner of London broil, mashed potatoes, and stir-fried zucchini and red pepper. Lucy had been totally mesmerized that morning by Claudia's speech and was also reeling from excitement over Gracelyn's upcoming play. The Cates women's vibrancy had always inspired her, and this evening, sitting alongside them at their dinner table, she displayed a newfound confidence and enthusiasm.

"Oh, Sister Claudia, you made my heart glad this morning. You are just a beautiful soul, inside and out. And you just keep the faith. I'm going to help as much as I can with these menfolk. You can rest assured."

"Thank you, Lucy. I really do take that to heart."

Claudia took quiet pride in accomplishing her duty that morning, and so was less chatty than usual. She knew Rebecca was proud of her and she intended to do even better next Sunday.

"Sister Gracelyn, I would be pleased to have a bit more of your potatoes. How on earth did you decide on such a wonderful mixture?" Lucy went on, referring to the puréed celery Gracelyn had blended with the whipped concoction.

"Oh, Lucy, they are really just mashed potatoes with a little milk, butter, and salt, and the celery adds a nice flavor. I've been known to throw in some scallions or some grated cheddar when I'm out of celery."

"Well, my tongue is telling me I'm in heaven."

"Lucy," Rebecca broke in, "we're so glad you could be with us today. We couldn't make it around here without your helping us out. How's our young Dorothy Dandridge getting along?"

"Miss Rebecca, she can't wait to get started. But I told Melba that when you do something like this, you have to audition. There's other talented young girls out there. You can't always expect to be the best."

"Well now, that's wise counsel. But keep in mind that Gracelyn is already very impressed with Melba from that Easter show last year. She stands out in a special way."

"Thank you, Miss Rebecca. I—"

"Lucy, finish up eating so we can go upstairs," said Gracelyn, in her excitement cutting off Lucy's comment. "You can never start too early on a project, and I need you to help me sort some petticoats and a trunkload of fabric. I want the children to look like real slaves, with headwraps and stuff. I'm not too handy with a needle, but Claudia is, and maybe Raphaela can give her a hand with costumes."

"Now, hold on, Gracelyn." Rebecca spoke mildly. "Let Lucy have some strawberry shortcake and fresh cream before you put her to work. I'm surprised you're ready to miss out on dessert."

"Oh, of course. There's time. It's still early in the evening. I'll make us some coffee, unless Lucy would rather have tea."

"Miss Gracelyn, coffee sounds wonderful."

The four women resumed their leisurely chat, with the three sisters filling Lucy in on as much history from the slave period as they could remember. Each of the Cates sisters, bookish in their younger years, had excellent memories.

Gracelyn began the animated discussion. "I know one thing about Harriet Tubman. She pulled a gun on people who wanted to turn back before they reached the North. She told them, 'Dead Niggers don't talk.' We can't have the children using that language, though. Maybe our lead character could say 'Dead Negroes don't talk.' "

Lucy was delighted to be included in what seemed to her a learned discussion.

"Oh, I think 'Negroes' wouldn't offend anybody."

"Uhm hum." Gracelyn continued, "I think there should be a scene or two where she falls asleep. You know, she had that somnambulism from being beat over the head by her master. Imagine going through life being beat like that whenever you turned around, or whenever the people in charge of you got ready. And to go out with no map, just following the North Star, and being responsible for hundreds of people who put their lives in your hands."

"Sounds like you know quite a bit about her," Rebecca said, smiling at Gracelyn's flushed face. She knew her excitement about the play was building to a fever pitch.

"And risking death over and over. There was a price on her head, and you know those white posses would have been happy to shoot that little black woman on sight. She kept making such a fool of them."

"She did well," Rebecca said feelingly. "Didn't end up like poor Nat Turner tied up to the hanging rope. I remember Papa used to talk about how he thought Turner was like a hero from another age. He always said there wasn't anyone braver, except maybe that Henri Cinque who took over the *Amistad* slave ship."

Claudia ventured, "Now, I know you all don't think much about her in the heroic way, but I kind of admire Sally Hemmings. I have a picture in my mind of President Jefferson entranced by a beautiful young girl who reminded him of his dead wife."

"She should have strangled him!" Gracelyn exclaimed, while Lucy's eyes widened in mild shock.

"Well, maybe, maybe not. You just don't know when or how love is going to blossom."

"Claudia, he owned her! That is not love."

"But Gracelyn, honey, she went along willingly."

"As far as we know, but we don't really know, since there's no evidence. It's not like she was a person with rights, and if she did go along, it was because she was young and stupid."

"Fourteen, I think," Rebecca said calmly. "Lucy, you're the mother of a fourteen-year-old daughter. What do you have to say on this topic?"

"I just think that's terrible. If any man, black or white, tried to even so much as look at my Melba in that demon way, I would shoot him."

The Cates sisters, all astonished by Lucy's frankness, erupted into laughter.

"Well, I just don't know," Claudia went on unfazed, "love comes in many guises."

"Claudia," Gracelyn earnestly remonstrated, "what planet are you from? Sally Hemmings was property. Her children were property. On his deathbed, Jefferson didn't free them. They became his white children's property. Sally Hemmings should have stabbed that white man."

Rebecca, amused by the heated exchange, asked mischievously,

"Let's see now: We've got stabbing, shooting, and strangulation. Are you all sure you're Christian women?"

The laughter resumed.

"I see I just can't win with my romantic notions," Claudia said as she pushed back from the table to follow Gracelyn, already in the kitchen preparing their dessert tray.

"Lucy, I'm so happy you joined us tonight," Rebecca said to the beaming woman. "We appreciate your taking time away from your own family to be our Sunday guest."

"Thanks, Miss Rebecca. I did want to ask you something."

"Go right ahead."

"When does Pastor Wilson come by to visit? Is it normally on Sunday or during the workweek?"

"Well, now, Lucy. He really doesn't."

"But Miss Claudia thanked him for visiting you all."

"Why, yes, I remember she did. But I think Claudia was just being diplomatic. We're hoping he starts to come by more frequently."

"Well, I wondered about that, because you know when my Earl had that back injury a few weeks back, I did expect Pastor to come by and check on him. But he never made it. Miss Claudia is right; we need pastoral prayer especially during troubled times."

"You are so right, Lucy," Rebecca agreed. "And you know, I am so glad you were listening. I wouldn't feel right bringing up any strong criticism of our pastor over something that just concerned me. But if there are other members who have had the same experience, it is probably something we need to bring out in the open. I for one don't believe in keeping my light under a bushel, and if I can help out somebody else, I feel it's my duty."

"Oh, yes, Miss Rebecca. That is a true statement. And I just want to say—"

Before Lucy could complete her thought, the doorbell rang. Rebecca stood up to go answer it.

"Lord, who on earth would that be? Honey, we'll talk more about this later."

Rebecca practically skipped to the front door, so happy was she that Lucy had caught Claudia's drift from her morning speech-making.

It crossed Rebecca's mind what a huge irony it would be should this in fact be Pastor Wilson come to call at the Cates residence. Through the glass rim on the side panels of the oak door, Rebecca could vaguely see the shadowy outline of a tallish, broad-shouldered man in casual clothes. Certainly not Wilson, but she thought perhaps one of her workmen needing reimbursement for yard supplies. When she opened the door, Rebecca's mouth fell open. Standing before her smiling slightly was Dr. Leighton from the Aphrodite Clinic.

"I can see you are surprised to see me." Leighton spoke in the slight cadence Rebecca had first noted seated across from him in his office.

Rebecca, recovered, said evenly, "Why, yes. This is totally unexpected. May I ask if there is something amiss?"

"Oh, not at all, Rebecca. But I did feel the need to explain something to you in person. This is not my regular procedure."

"Do come in."

Leighton followed Rebecca's gesture to come forward. Sensing that their conversation needed to be private, she motioned him again, this time toward the library.

"This is a beautiful house. Is it quite a hundred years yet?"

"Just over; one hundred two. It requires a fair amount of upkeep. Please do have a seat."

Leighton sat dutifully in one of Reuben's softly burnished leather club chairs. Rebecca sat directly across from him on the leather sofa, facing him, as she had done in his medical office.

"Dr. Leighton, what did you come here to tell me? I don't intend to be rude, but I have a dinner guest waiting."

"Of course, I understand totally. You see, Mrs. Furness—"

"Rebecca."

"Rebecca. When we spoke at my clinic, I offered up to three free consultations on your decision about having surgery. I came here tonight to tell you not to plan on coming back to see me."

Rebecca looked slightly baffled but said nothing, waiting for him to explain why he had driven just under two hours on a Sunday evening threatening a thunderstorm to confront her.

"I think most people would agree I am both an ethical man and an ethical doctor. Certainly, in my professional life, this has never happened to me before."

Hearing this, Rebecca thought he must suspect her motives for coming to his clinic. She waited for him to accuse her of prying into Julia Wilson's medical affairs for her own less-than-ethical purposes.

"You see, Rebecca, since you visited me, I have felt it was not appropriate to perform surgery on you or to advise you in any medical capacity."

Rebecca waited for him to state clearly that she had been prying. However, Leighton looked at her without saying anything.

After what seemed several long moments, he blurted out, "I can't stop thinking about you."

Rebecca's thoughts converged as she considered this curious statement. Had this handsome man, several years her junior, really driven all the way from Bloomington to initiate a courtship with her? Could her first thought have been wrong, that he was not Wilson's collaborator in larceny, just a moonstruck romantic? Knowing she needed more time to sort this out, she decided to stall this discussion for the time being.

"Do you care for strawberry shortcake?"

VII

REBECCA, EXPERIENCING mild shock, noted that Leighton was smiling at her. It took her several moments to remember her offer of food and, doing so, she felt this would be the best follow-up to their awkward exchange.

"Will you have some dessert?" she repeated.

"That's very kind of you, Rebecca."

Rebecca opened the doors to the library and motioned for him to follow her down the hallway into the dining room. Gracelyn and Claudia had resumed their seats and were chatting casually with Lucy, a delectable portion of shortcake piled in front of each diner. Rebecca's entry into the grand room with the handsome Leighton stalled the conversation.

"Ladies, we have a guest. This is Dr. Leighton, who's en route back to Bloomington. He has graciously agreed to share our dessert while waiting out the storm. Doctor, these are my sisters, Claudia and Gracelyn, and our dear friend Lucy Sims. We are blessed to have Lucy tend to our menfolk on weekends. You'll be interested to know she is a very skilled nurse."

"It's wonderful to meet all of you."

Gracelyn spoke eagerly. "You can't chance this weather, Doctor. You did the right thing by stopping here."

"Oh, yes!" Claudia echoed. "It would be too treacherous to try to go anywhere on a night like this. I'm sure Rebecca told you, we've got plenty of room, so you're no trouble at all."

"Would you ladies mind calling me Randall?"

"Oh, not at all, Randall," Claudia chimed in. "With all that moisture out there, we had better offer you something hot as well. Tea or coffee?"

"Tea would be wonderful."

"I'll reheat the kettle, just you make yourself comfortable. And you will help us polish off our dessert?"

"I'd be delighted." Leighton smiled as Claudia scurried into the kitchen. By the time she reappeared with a tray, Rebecca had reclaimed her seat at the head of the table while Leighton sat to her right, next to Lucy. The conversation resumed at a clip, covering tornadoes and hailstorms predicted throughout the region. A loud thunderclap made everyone pause. Without discussion, Rebecca realized that settled it. Randall Leighton would be their guest for the night. The confusion in her mind was louder than the din of several voices chattering and the intermittent rumbling of thunder. However, she joined in the polite conversation, wanting everything to appear normal.

Rebecca turned to Lucy, who stared entranced at the handsome doctor. "Perhaps you should settle in here tonight also. These storms can go on for several hours without much letup."

Shaking her head slightly, Lucy responded, "Well, now, Rebecca, what I will do is call Earl and have him meet me here during the next lull. He can drive over in the truck, and I can leave my car here until morning, if you wouldn't mind."

"Oh, not at all, dearie. I believe that's the most sensible thing to do. Claudia and Gracelyn, would you mind clearing everything away? I need to show Dr. Leighton—Randall—to his room."

"Don't worry, I'll take care of everything. Claudia's been tidying up behind me all night as usual anyway. There's really not much to do."

"By all means, Rebecca. We'll handle it. I'm sure Randall needs to get some rest after all that driving. Sleep well, Doctor."

"Thank you all."

"I'm a bit tired myself," Rebecca said, in an effort to keep the conversation casual. "Lucy, let me know if Earl has any problems getting here, because we could really put you up as well. There's a pull-out sofa in Claudia's bedroom."

"I think I'll be all right, ladies. It shouldn't take him long to get here. And you know men, he'll fret all night if I'm not in the house."

"Lucy, that's so romantic." Claudia sighed.

"Perhaps so. More likely, he'll be worried about missing out on his breakfast."

At that, everyone stood up from the table, the women giggling and Leighton surprised, but chuckling.

"Good night, ladies. I can't imagine spending a more pleasant evening, bad weather notwithstanding."

Leighton raised his hand to wave and, trailing Rebecca, reentered the hallway.

Rebecca was determined to avoid saying anything in response to his earlier declaration.

"Our guest room is small, but I hope it will be comfortable for you. You'll have your own bathroom; I apologize; there's only a shower stall."

"Don't apologize, Rebecca. It sounds fine" was Leighton's answer.

Rebecca, uncomfortable with the silence between them and the gentle way he pronounced her name, intended to keep him talking or listening to her talk.

"There's an alarm clock on the night table, in case you need it.

We tend to be early risers, but feel free to sleep in. We'll leave some breakfast for you."

"I'm sure I'll be awake, Rebecca. Thank you."

Hearing her name again, Rebecca flushed. For the first time, climbing to the third floor seemed interminable, as though there were a thousand stairs. Opening the door to the guest room, Rebecca was aware of Leighton brushing against her as he entered.

"You won't get much sun from this back window, but there's a nice view of the backyard. Sleep well."

"Good night, Rebecca."

Dawn sunlight streaking across Rebecca's face awakened her. Rather than bound out of bed as usual, she lay there, astonished by the eroticism of her dreams. Throughout the night, there had been no letup in the *Kama Sutra* of images of her with Leighton. And even now, recovering her alertness, she was sick with longing for the man.

"I'll be damned!" Rebecca sat upright, realizing her body could easily betray her resolve to keep Leighton at a distance. She began to think there must be a way her urges would not be at cross-purposes with her other priorities. She had made a commitment to her sisters and herself to achieve freedom from their husbands, and Leighton had already unwittingly helped her in getting compromising information on the pastor's embezzlement of church funds.

Rebecca's feelings toward the doctor were powerful and pure, and she was unhappy thinking of further duplicity involving him. She wanted him as a lover, but how to square that with her initial dishonesty in going to see him was troubling. It could not be squared, she knew, without letting him know what she had done, and risking his turning away from her. Moving quickly now, Rebecca dressed and made her way out the back door to the green-house. After watering the middle row of her plants, she spent several minutes trying to identify a soil problem with her laelias. Unbeknownst to her, Leighton, awake and fully dressed, stood at the guest room window watching her.

Rebecca and Leighton arrived at the breakfast table at the same time.

"Good morning, Doctor. I'm glad you made it down for something to eat."

Puzzled that he had not asked about her marital status, Rebecca stated matter-of-factly, "Our husbands are all ill and not able to join us."

"I'm sorry to hear that. Your own husband is bedridden?"

"Well, no. He suffers from a brain injury. I am looking into a facility where he could receive twenty-four-hour care."

"I assumed you were a widow."

As Leighton's words trailed off, Claudia entered from the kitchen, carrying a tray of breakfast food.

"Good morning, Randall. Please take your seat. Gracelyn has everything ready; I'm just helping out a bit. Did you sleep well?"

"Very well, and thank you for calling me Randall. Perhaps Rebecca will begin to follow suit. This is a very grand house."

"I'll remember to do that now," Rebecca said casually.

Gracelyn entered next with the coffeepot.

"Lucy get home all right, Gracelyn?"

"Earl got here pretty quick, so I imagine they did just fine. We didn't hear anything more from them."

Rebecca, quiet during the breakfast conversation, took the opportunity to further size up the younger man while he chatted easily with her sisters. She managed calm as he unexpectedly turned the conversation to her orchids and politely answered his questions about her business.

"This is a brisk time of year for orders, so I'm busy with those. Also, I have a problem right now with my laelias. The soil mixture isn't quite right for several of these plants, and they're not growing properly. So, when I should be marketing, I'm spending most of my time remixing and repotting so I can keep them blooming."

"Rebecca is just amazing with those flowers. Why, I don't know too many people who can grow anything so delicate," Claudia chimed in. "Rebecca, you should take Randall out to the greenhouse before he leaves."

"I'm sure Randall needs to get back to Bloomington today, but perhaps he will accept a rain check on that."

"Oh, Rebecca, that's good!" Gracelyn broke in. "The poor man gets trapped overnight in a storm and now you'll give him a 'rain' check." She laughed infectiously.

"Well, I didn't mean it quite like that. Excuse us, Randall, we can be silly sometimes. Humor relieves many of our burdens."

"As it should. Rebecca, I'm down this way often. I'd like to call you about touring your greenhouse."

"I'll look forward to it."

Claudia and Gracelyn did not suspect from the dialogue that anything out of the ordinary had occurred between the two, and after their meal, Rebecca casually saw Leighton to the door.

"Well, now, we can get back to normal," Rebecca sighed, entering the kitchen where her sisters were tidying up from their breakfast and preparing the men's meal. "Since we didn't do our planning, we need to make sure we're together on everything. Gracelyn, did you ask Raphaela about lending us a big boy to help us get Timothy to Briney Memorial?"

"No, I haven't asked her yet."

"Ask her today when you go by there, because we need to pin that down. We'll need help with our luggage and keeping him still."

Gracelyn nodded in understanding of her mission at the laundress's, and proceeded in her kitchen chores.

"Should I tell her about the play?"

"I'm counting on it. Claudia, you set for this morning?"

"All set; I see Dr. Meyers at eleven-thirty to get Timothy's sedative. Gracelyn gave me the grocery list already, so I can meet you at the produce market around noon."

Leighton was quickly forgotten by Claudia and Gracelyn as the household's culture of women again took shape. Gracelyn began loading her vintage Saab with soiled bed linens and other laundry and headed to Raphaela's.

"Bye," she called, carrying the final load as she sailed passed Claudia. Then, noting that Claudia was busy setting out an arrangement of cups and saucers, asked, "Are you looking for something?"

"No, honey. When that handsome doctor was here I was embarrassed about using those ugly dishes. Lucy's family, but what does real company think? If we're going to start having more people come by here, we should be using Mother's best dishes, the Sheffields and the like. Anyway, you get going. I'll have this all done in half an hour. You tell Raphaela about that play, it will be all over town."

"I suspect. That woman runs her mouth. It'll be like having a one-woman public relations vehicle. As long as she doesn't bad-mouth me about putting Bernard away."

"She won't; not if we give her enough other stuff to talk about. That's what Rebecca thinks, anyway. Bye, girl."

Immediately after breakfast and their brief conference, Rebecca went back to her orchids, determined to make progress curing her ailing plants. Coming back inside, she walked through the house and out the front door to collect newspapers. Posted on the second floor during Gracelyn's absence, Rebecca alternately read and fantasized about Leighton's tall physique and handsome face.

Shaking her head abruptly, Rebecca retrieved a small pad from her pants pocket and plucked a pencil from the bun wound at the base of her neck. She began compiling a schedule of the men's planned confinement dates, Claudia's Sunday speeches, Gracelyn's play rehearsals, and for revealing the Wilsons' indiscretion to the church's Board of Trustees. She bracketed this last entry and reflected on her earlier thoughts about Leighton. She was certain he would view her deception as betrayal, and there would be no hope for further intimacy with him. Her enthusiasm was curtailed momentarily by regret.

Rebecca soon regained her resolve. She needed this man. Her dreaming about him and her conscious yearnings consumed a good deal of her thinking. And he made it clear that he wanted her. For what, other than lust, she wasn't entirely certain. But she was willing to risk finding out. Rebecca knew she had to do everything in her power to depose Wilson, since it was the only way she could free herself and her sisters. But for the time being, she would not use Leighton's information. In the meantime, she would balance her head and her heart, and make sure her head was leading.

Rebecca continued with her strategizing. She decided on a tea at the Cates mansion for the churchwomen, inviting them to pray and commiserate over their ailing spouses. Her thinking was that such an activity would keep the caretaking issue alive in their minds and conversations, and bolster support for the Cates sisters' actions toward their husbands. By the time of the tea, Bernard would have been out of the house for over two weeks. During the following week, the Cates sisters would drive to Briney Memorial to deposit Timothy.

Gracelyn arrived at Raphaela's fully concentrating on her mission. She pulled up the driveway alongside Raphaela's house and sat silently in her car for a few moments, breathing deeply. She was let in the side door by a large bowlegged boy who seemed to be expecting her. He immediately relieved her of her bundle.

"You have any more, ma'am?" he asked eagerly.

"Yes, in the car. Two, I think."

"My name's Herbert. Glad to help you."

Gracelyn smiled warmly at the boy and handed him her keys. Just then, she noticed his left eye was unmoving.

"I don't remember if I locked the door or not."

The side door of the house opened and Raphaela appeared. A tall, thin woman, her long face, large black eyes, and black hair made her look mystical.

"Good morning, Gracelyn. How's Rebecca doing?"

"Rebecca's well. Thank you for asking. That nice young man . . . Herbert, is getting my other two bags out of the car. Is something wrong with his eye?"

"He's blind in the one eye. In the other eye, he sees pretty good. He loses his glasses left and right. It's too expensive for me to keep replacing them. I have to wait on the state to send the money. I can get these things finished by this evening. But you can pick them up anytime tomorrow if you're not in a hurry."

"Tomorrow will be fine. Raphaela, Rebecca said to ask if you could spare one of your big boys to go with us to Chicago next month. Timothy, Claudia's husband, is going into Briney Memorial, a home up there."

"Is that so? Has he taken a turn?"

"Yes he has. He's wandering around at night more than he used to, and we're afraid he'll hurt himself. Claudia wants to see if the people at Briney can help with his drinking problem. They do well with that sort."

Gracelyn watched carefully for Raphaela's reaction before continuing.

"Dr. Meyers says it's best," she lied smoothly. "My husband, Bernard, has to go into a hospice this Saturday. He's in the last stages of his cancer. I want him to be as comfortable as possible."

Raphaela's dark eyes filled with pity looking at Gracelyn.

"Oh, now, bless your heart, I know you've done everything you can do. It's in the Lord's hands now. You just stay strong and keep praying for His peace." She paused, shook her head, and continued. "Herbert, matter of fact, is the biggest child here, so he would suit when you take Timothy in."

"I think Herbert would be perfect. He's so cheerful. We need help with the suitcases. He can ride along with us in Rebecca's car. We'll be gone a few days, and the extra pair of hands will make things go easier for us."

"You're staying awhile to get him settled?"

Gracelyn lied again. "Well, yes. Claudia said she'll feel better if she gets to spend at least a day or two seeing how they're handling him."

"Just relax for a minute, dear. Herbert won't be long."

Seated at Raphaela's kitchen table, Gracelyn listened as the energetic woman gossiped about their neighbors and church folk.

"You know those Bartleson children, they have wonderful musical talents. But I hear they can be hard to control. Probably since James left Amelia, they've gotten worse."

"Oh, my. I didn't know."

"Oh, my, yes. He took off in the middle of the night for a good two weeks. He's back now."

"That's good."

"It's good in a way. But if menfolk want to have their cake and eat it too, they may as well stay gone, I always think. He's been running around with Viola's niece for the better part of the year. They've been seen all over."

Deciding she wouldn't get a word in easily, Gracelyn blurted out, "Raphaela! I found the most wonderful play about Harriet Tubman, and Rebecca asked Pastor if I could put it on with the Sunday school. We're going to have a meeting with the children Saturday evening. I was hoping you would send some of yours over."

Raphaela looked confused by Gracelyn's interruption, but it didn't take her long to realize she was offering a children's activity.

"That will be mighty fine, thank you. How many children can I send? I have five here right now."

"I'm sure I can use all five. There are three main characters—Harriet Tubman, her husband, and the slave master—and there are a lot of other slaves, townfolk, and people that helped with the Underground Railroad."

"Then this is really going to be a history play?"

"That would be fair to say."

"Why, I think that's wonderful!" Raphaela's excitement combined with her eagerness for an evening free of children.

"Does Herbert read well?" Gracelyn asked.

"He does fine with his glasses," Raphaela replied, then sighed. "But I told you, he always loses them."

Herbert ambled in with laundry dropped off by other neighbors and descended the basement stairs.

"You get that sorted, then come back up here. Ms. Gracelyn has something she wants you to do this weekend."

"Yes, ma'am," Herbert responded swiftly and seriously.

Gracelyn returned home in time to prepare lunch and relieve Rebecca from her second-floor sentry. She bolted around the kitchen preparing the lunch tray, anxious to complete the men's feeding so she could work on sketches for her set design and drag more of Mattie's trunk contents for costumes.

By Tuesday morning breakfast, Rebecca had completed a schedule for the sisters' visits to their men at their new residencies. She explained to Claudia and Gracelyn that these visits should occur at regular intervals and must be grandly orchestrated, in order for their community profile to be maintained.

"Claudia, you keep standing up in church service, and every time we go visit the men, make sure you make an announcement afterward to report on their progress. We'll always travel in the Mercedes, because people notice that car. After awhile, when they see us driving off together, they'll know we're going to visit our sick. Gracelyn, you make sure Raphaela and Lucy always know when we're about to take a trip to see the men, 'cause they'll talk it up."

Rebecca's sisters both understood that the desired image of the Cates women's devotion to duty would be upheld.

The remainder of the week leading to the women's Saturday departure was hectic. Gracelyn hustled through her usual cooking and light housekeeping chores, all the while maniacally pausing to jot down ideas for costuming and casting. Claudia was assigned the job of packing Bernard's suitcase and sorting through the items of his clothing to be given away.

"No point cluttering up the closet longer than necessary," Rebecca had said. "But don't let Gracelyn know what you're doing, sweetheart. She'll be upset enough without dwelling on all of that. Hard for her to let go, even after everything he did to her. Love's a wonder."

"It is that," Claudia agreed emphatically. "Gracelyn's so excited about her play, I hope it will keep her mind off things."

"I truly believe it will. But we'll keep an eye on her just in case. You can cart some of those things over to Raphaela's. I know she has the big boy over there who can probably fit some of that stuff. See you at the market."

"Bye, Rebecca."

The sisters' activity was fueled by an understanding that they were about to take the first big step toward starting their lives over, and their energies remained high. They went through their motions as caretakers, but their hearts were in their burgeoning passions. As they anticipated more and more reemergence into lives as independent women, the Cates mansion took on new significance for them as their place of origin, a symbol of their status and the things they cherished most about their identity as Cates women.

Rebecca, when not with her orchids, directed the laborers who

manned the grounds and did the indoor maintenance. She homed
in on a problem with the dimmer lights for the hallway chandeliers and had one of the workmen totally remove the ornate fixtures to investigate the wiring. Claudia saw the three chandeliers
lying dormant on the dining table and decided to clean the massive crystal lights with a solution of vinegar and water. This done,
Rebecca oversaw the rehanging of the lights, and Claudia took on
Mattie Cates's pewter collection, polishing dozens of vases, bowls,
and serving pieces brought up from the cellar. Gracelyn, engrossed
in her children's play, took evening hours to meticulously archive
family photographs; she kept a notepad by her side to record
spurts of creative thought. Periodically, she accosted her sisters
with an idea about her Tubman play.

By Wednesday evening, tensions in the Cates household were
high. The week of impending freedom had presented unexpected
travails. Timothy's newly introduced sedative caused him to be
incontinent, which generated an immense amount of laundry. The
odor emanating from his bedroom at one point threatened to over-
take the entire second floor of the house. Gracelyn made two additional trips to Raphaela's, enlisting Claudia to make the third.
Rebecca repeatedly changed his bed linen. While Rebecca fought
thoughts about Leighton, Jake's memory confusion segued to a
time during their marriage when he and Rebecca were compan-
ionable and happy. He rambled about the large house more than
usual searching for her, looking at her dreamy-eyed, and calling
her name out loudly and frantically when his sedative wore off.

The commotion continued the next day, and the sisters focused
on Saturday as their day of salvation. When the various emergen-
cies disrupted the women's cleaning, polishing, and archiving of
estate items, the emptied rooms each had the appearance of an
elaborate still life. Rebecca kept a watchful eye on Gracelyn, and
with both her sisters busy and close at hand, she was able to rein-
force each's role in her overall strategy, frequently mentioning

their time frame and specific tasks. Rebecca could not curtail her fantasies about Leighton, but managed to talk offhandedly about men, arousal, and courtship. At dinner, after she outlined Saturday's trip to Springfield one last time, she intentionally turned the conversation to what her sisters would perceive as a lighter theme.

"Now, Gracelyn, you know when Bernard leaves this world, don't you sit around being lonely."

"Oh, Rebecca, I can't think about that now."

"Didn't ask you to. I'm thinking about it. You're beautiful and intelligent. Any sane man would fall all over himself to be with you."

"Do you think so, Rebecca?"

"Stranger things have happened." Gracelyn smiled at Rebecca's sarcasm. "And don't you or Claudia worry about what our neighbors have to say. I'll make sure everything appears in the right light. You take your time, but don't be too long turning away suitors. When the right man comes along, I expect both of you to do exactly as your heart tells you. And if your heart's not talking too loud, there's nothing wrong with a tune-up from time to time."

Gracelyn managed to laugh, while Claudia was faintly shocked.

"But Rebecca, I'll still be married when Timothy goes in," Claudia said delicately.

"Honey child, a woman has needs. We'll get these menfolk situated, get rid of that pastor, and by the end of the year, Gracelyn will be a widow and you and I will be free agents."

"You're right." Claudia, her usual way, totally acquiesced to Rebecca.

"And both of you, this time around, study your mule. You can't dream some of these people up. We've all had awfully bad luck and we don't want to go down the same road twice."

"But Jake—" Gracelyn started to point out that Rebecca's marital life was altered because of Jake's accident.

"There's things you don't know and don't need to know. The same goes for me. I don't know everything about what went on with you and Bernard. I only know how Claudia suffered because she told me everything. And it was fine with me if she wanted to unburden herself. Not one of us has been a happy woman, I do know that. That's all I'm looking at now for myself and I want the both of you to follow suit. And Claudia, you in particular need to get used to a man touching you in a tender way. Because any man who does a woman like Timothy did you from the start, that man needs to be horsewhipped. Lord, sometimes I wish we could hand all the rotten apples over to the white women. Lord help me for thinking that evil thought."

VIII

REBECCA, UP EARLIER than dawn, met Claudia frantically scurrying down the third-floor hallway.

"Rebecca, did you hear?"

"I heard. I'm going up there and see if I can calm her down."

"Shall I go with you?"

"Yes, please. But calm yourself down first."

At Rebecca's instruction, Claudia took several measured breaths, then followed her sister, already advancing swiftly up the stairs to the attic.

Rebecca pushed open Gracelyn's door and walked over to her bed, where she sat upright, crying hysterically. Sitting on the edge of the bed, Rebecca put both arms around her.

"Oh, Rebecca, he's leaving me! What do I have now? I wanted us to be lovers again, even if he couldn't touch me anymore. We don't have a chance now. Why is God taking my life away?"

"Gracelyn. Gracelyn. I'm here. Claudia's here. You'll have a good life. This is a wall you can't push against, but it will go away soon. It will go away on its own. Have I ever lied to you? You'll be strong very soon. Just let go. Let go. Turn your mind to the things you can have, the things you can't see now."

"Rebecca, I'm trying." Gracelyn's cries subsided as she leaned against Rebecca.

"He'll be taken care of where he's going. And when the cancer takes him, he'll be in a better place. It's out of your hands now, and you need to let it go. You've done what you could do. Now the Lord has another work for you."

"Do you mean my play?"

"Yes, that's one thing."

"Just think how wonderful it's going to be for all those children who never heard of Harriet Tubman," Claudia said gently. "You never know what kind of seeds you'll be planting."

"That's true, dear. Claudia's right."

Gracelyn sniffed back tears and nodded her head. "I want that so much. I've been so excited over doing it. It just seems like it shouldn't make me so happy right now. I feel like I should be thinking more about Bernard."

Rebecca, pulling a handkerchief from her pocket, wiped Gracelyn's wet face.

"Of course you're thinking about him. He's been your husband for a long time. But you can still have your joy. It's the Lord's will for you to turn Bernard over to Him. That's the power he needs now. Your power is for other things."

"Joy always comes in the morning, Gracelyn," Claudia said brightly.

"I love that song," Gracelyn replied thickly. "Can you put that record on for me, Rebecca?"

"I sure can. I know right where it is." Rebecca paused for a moment, still holding Gracelyn, then turned to Claudia. "We better get our day started."

"It won't take me long to get dressed, and I'll go ahead and put breakfast on so Gracleyn can take her time."

"Thanks, dear. Gracelyn, I'll put that record on soon as I go downstairs, and I'll see about Bernard. Don't you worry about anything except getting yourself together."

"All right. I'll be downstairs soon. I don't want to be by myself too long."

The Cates women ate breakfast in relative silence. Claudia, noting Rebecca's expression, did not find extraneous things to chat about. She announced, "I picked up these apricots yesterday. They're early, but they should be sweet enough. If not, I can squeeze some more juice." When the other two did not respond, she let the matter drop. Though nervous, she understood the best thing was to let Rebecca manage the day's ordeal. Gracelyn had been distraught, and only Rebecca could bring the situation back to normal.

Rebecca herself spoke then. "They look fine to me," she said calmly, slicing one and arranging the pieces on top of Gracelyn's bowl of oatmeal. "Gracelyn, you get down as much of that as you can."

"Yes, I will."

"You finish that up, then go and sit out back until the paramedics come. I want you to see how well that side garden is doing. All the sedum came back strong this year. The azalea blooms are about to go, but with the sun getting stronger, the caladium will make up for the color; their leaves are looking pinkish already. And you should see those begonias. Such pretty girls. You head on outside and think about all those flowers coming and going every spring, about how everything comes and everything goes. It's all beautiful, honey child. Even when we're losing something, we're gaining something."

"Yes, Rebecca," Gracelyn said weakly. "Can you play that joy song again?"

"Certainly." Rebecca moved quickly from the dining table to the library and restarted the cassette tape. Coming back in to finish her coffee, she watched over Gracelyn's progress with her oatmeal, and after she had eaten, led her by hand to the backyard. Pulling a handkerchief from her skirt pocket, she wiped the dew from a wrought-iron garden chair and motioned for Gracelyn to sit in it. "We'll be leaving in an hour or so. You just sit still till then and keep your mind peaceful. It's out of your hands what happens to Bernard, but only good things will happen to him now."

Rebecca and Claudia awaited the medics in the front hallway, taking turns pulling aside the front door curtain panels to look for the ambulance. The car arrived noiselessly, without lights flashing, and backed up the long driveway, stopping just abreast of the porch.

"Claudia, open up for them. Maybe move that urn out of the way. I'll bring Gracelyn inside."

Claudia, instantly obeying, dragged a large urn holding several umbrellas out of the front hall and into the library. She opened the heavy door and placed the doorstop in position. Stepping out into the sunlight, she called to the two men, wearing white uniforms and caps, unloading equipment from the back of the vehicle.

"Door's open. We're waiting inside."

The taller of the two looked Claudia's way and, with both his hands occupied, nodded his head vigorously to acknowledge her instruction.

"Won't take us long to finish this up," he called back.

Rebecca led Gracelyn, an arm around her waist, through the kitchen and into the dining room. "We can wait here for the men to bring Bernard downstairs, honey," Rebecca told her.

"I want to go upstairs and say good-bye," Gracelyn said brokenly.

"Well then, let's go on up."

Maintaining their embrace, Rebecca and Gracelyn climbed the broad front stairs to the second floor and entered Bernard's room. Gracelyn walked over to the bed where Bernard lay sleeping.

Bending over, she kissed him lightly on the forehead. His eyelids fluttered briefly, but closed again.

"Maybe this is one of those times he'll sleep through the day," Gracelyn said, glancing back at Rebecca.

"Probably will, dear. That would be best. You know the Lord has a blessing for us every moment."

"Yes, Rebecca, I know." Gracelyn remained silent for a few moments, then, hearing footsteps on the stairs said softly, "Goodbye, love."

The medics, working efficiently, placed Bernard, still attached to his IV, on a stretcher and expertly descended the two flights of broad, high stairs. The Cates women watched as they loaded Bernard's lifeless form into the back of the ambulance.

"We'd better load up ourselves," Rebecca said, and the sisters began gathering their purses and travel paraphernalia. Seated in the Mercedes, they followed the ambulance down the driveway and progressed up the street. They drove through Peoria's main thoroughfare to the notice of several passersby. It entered Rebecca's thoughts that before long, they would follow the same route in a funeral procession. She looked over frequently at Gracelyn, who was pensive but seemed all right. Once on the highway, she reached over to hold her hand. Claudia kept up intermittent chatter from the backseat. One hour after leaving home, the Cates women pulled up to the stately redbrick building.

The hospice staff was courtly and professional. Gracelyn signed off on forms already completed; then she and her sisters were invited by a nurse to go look at Bernard's room. The nurse waited with them until the paramedics brought in their new patient, transferring him from the stretcher to the bed. The hospice staff left and the family of women looked down at the anguished body. Rebecca, placing an arm around Gracelyn, said quietly, "We should go and let Bernard rest."

Riding back to Peoria, Rebecca and Claudia alternately kept an eye on their younger sister, watching for signs of distress. But her beautiful face was serene, and halfway through their return trip, she began to talk about the Tubman play.

"Raphaela is sending over all five of her children," she began tentatively. "I guess I need to decide what to do with that blind boy."

"What blind boy?" Claudia wanted to know.

"Her big boy, Herbert, is blind in one eye. Raphaela told me he reads well with the other eye, but he loses his glasses all the time. She can't afford to keep buying them. He's awfully good-natured."

"Oh, I've seen that fellow. He's sweet as pie. We could get him some glasses, couldn't we?"

"Sure could," Rebecca replied. "What about that, Gracelyn?"

"That would solve the problem. Especially if we got him a spare pair."

The three women were in mutual agreement.

The play rehearsal brought out thirty children to the church's basement auditorium, some of whose families did not normally attend Peoria First Baptist. Raphaela and Lucy had done their work successfully as unofficial information disseminators. Herbert was there, and at fifteen, was one of the oldest children. Surprised at the turnout and forced to think quickly, Gracelyn told everyone to take a seat.

"I'm so glad you could all be here. The name of our play is *Harriet Tubman's Triumph.* I need to learn all your names, but first, does anyone here know anything about Harriet Tubman?"

A skinny red-haired girl raised her hand.

"You, over there, give us your name, please."

"I'm Renee Bartleson." In an assured voice she recited, "Harriet Tubman was a freedom fighter who escaped slavery, then led other slaves to freedom."

"Very good. Does anyone know when this activity took place?"
Renee immediately raised her hand.

"Yes, Renee."

"In the 1800s."

"Thank you again. Why don't I describe the action of the play; then all of you can be thinking about parts you might play. Remember, every part, no matter how large or small, is very important."

Gracelyn gave a brief description of the play, act by act, then began a discussion of the characters.

"Herbert is going to lead our chorus," she told the entranced gathering, "and the chorus narrates the action of the play. Everything I just told you the members of the chorus will announce to our audience. We're doing our play the way the Greeks did their theater thousands of years ago. We need eleven more people to be part of our chorus."

Several excited children raised their hands. Gracelyn selected eleven. Then, taking Herbert by the arm, led them to one side of the auditorium. She arranged the group in three rows in order of height and instructed Lucy to hand out bound scripts to each child.

"You all will have to memorize your lines in the script. So take them home with you, but be careful to keep them neat."

Crossing back quickly to the center of the room, Gracelyn addressed the remaining seated children.

"We need a stage manager and five people to help with costumes, lighting, and cue cards. You'll be very busy."

As hands were raised, Gracelyn selected the team and began outlining their duties while Lucy handed them scripts. Gracelyn instructed the remaining twelve children that they would audition for parts in the cast, and to get their bodies limbered by bending and stretching. When the children's faces looked blank, Gracelyn began leading the stretching. Her arms raised over her head, she tilted her torso from one side to the other, then slowly lowered her head and curled her back until she could grasp her ankles. A series of facial contortions followed as she had them pronounce vowel sounds to get their voices ready.

By the end of rehearsal, the chorus looked disciplined and engrossed, and the stage managers had neatly recopied the list of props they would be responsible for. Lucy's daughter Melba was cast as Harriet Tubman, and the other children as her followers, paddyrollers, and abolitionists. Lucy passed around a sign-up sheet for each child's name and phone number as they filed out. When the auditorium was emptied, except for her and Gracelyn, she jumped up and down excitedly, clapping her hands.

"Oh, Miss Gracelyn, you just something! You are wonderful to be doing this for our children. All you Cates women are so smart." She embraced Gracelyn.

"It helps me, too, Lucy," Gracelyn said, moved and happy.

The following morning at church, a general buzz was afloat regarding the children's play. Entering the sanctuary before the service began, the Cates sisters were the target of warm smiles from members of the congregation already in their seats. Two women rose to accost Gracelyn with a hug. Lucy, on duty as an usher, beamed with pride as she seated the sisters ceremoniously in their accustomed pew.

As the service proceeded, Reverend Wilson made the announcements, acknowledging the Tubman play without fanfare. He mentioned he had given Rebecca Cates the green light on the project some weeks back.

"Sister Cates, it's good to see that you followed through on our discussion." Rebecca sat stonefaced and immobile, as though she had not heard anything he said. When Wilson finished speaking, she nudged Claudia, who rose gracefully.

"Good morning, church family. Rebecca, Gracelyn, and I would like to thank you for your warm reception this morning."

The congregation responded with murmurs of "Good Morning."

Claudia went on. "We ask you to keep us in your prayers today, particularly. Our sister Gracelyn's husband, Bernard, has taken a turn for the worse, and she has entrusted him to a hospice. We're waiting for God's hand to move. I hope that others of you who are in a similar situation with loved ones will make this known to us so we can remember you in our prayers."

Several of her listeners, enchanted by Claudia's elegance and touched by her humility, called out "Amen" and "Keep the faith, Sister Cates." Hearing this, Rebecca calculated that Wilson likely looked boorish to his parishioners, having missed the opportunity to both express empathy with Gracelyn and align himself with her success.

The Cates sisters' excitement carried over to the remainder of their day. Sitting together on the front porch with their needlework, they talked about how well things were going, and how swiftly. The few weeks remaining with Jake and Timothy seemed bearable and, even for no-nonsense Rebecca, bittersweet.

"We have to keep reminding ourselves this is all for the best. I'm thinking Jake will get a lot more attention from the people at Sacred Lamb than I'm able to give him here at home. They have hobbies too. I've never known him to be good with his hands, but he can probably still take photographs. I'm praying he'll find somebody's company to enjoy. Anyway, we'll be visiting all three of the men often enough. We can have our tears, but I know in my heart we're doing the right thing."

"Rebecca, you're right. I know you're right."

Claudia furiously twisted a cable needle full of bright blue mohair yarn.

"You of all people know my life with Timothy hasn't been a picnic. I know there's good in him somewhere, but that man is full of demons. At Briney Memorial, they can probably control him a lot better and maybe keep him calm. There's nothing like peace of mind, especially for someone that far gone."

"And you, ladybug. How are you feeling today? Everyone sure appreciates your doing that play."

"I'm fine, Rebecca. I think about Bernard, but it seems like once we left the hospice, I felt more at peace than I have felt in years. Everything had become so twisted between us. For so long, I've been so hungry for him to love me. Maybe one day, like you said, I'll find somebody who will."

"You will, and take all the time you need. You'll know when you're ready."

Hungry for him to love me.

Gracelyn's words reverberated in Rebecca's mind. She recognized that her sister had just voiced her own longing. Immediately she thought of Leighton. His desire for her was clear, but she didn't imagine that he wanted her in a union that transcended lust. And should he, there were so many things she had to consider before her own happiness. She would not betray her sisters' interests by abandoning her opposition to Wilson. She would do everything in her power to ensure they remained the esteemed Cates women in the eyes of their small community. That meant neutralizing the libel Wilson was certain to inflict regarding their actions. And, she was convinced, even Leighton's lust would be dampened by knowledge of how she had deceived him. Rebecca would lead with her head. The family's good name was now and forever her priority. She would never betray the sense of duty to family that Reuben, her father, had instilled in her.

During the Cates sisters' Sunday dinner of lamb roast, turnip greens, sliced fresh tomatoes, and cornbread, the conversation was optimistic. They talked of future outings and experiences they could have once they were free.

"Gracelyn," Rebecca ventured, "I read something about a rare-books fair in Chicago in a few weeks, right on Michigan Avenue. We might have to take Timothy up to Briney Memorial a little earlier than we planned so you can go by there."

Gracelyn's squeal confirmed for Rebecca that she had hit a target.

"I read about that! I've been dying to get my hands on some first-edition Russian novels and a few other classics. But I didn't want to make the trip alone. I want lots of company right through here."

"Well then, that's what you'll have, baby. Claudia, it's all right with you if we make our Chicago trip a few weeks early?"

"Lord knows, as far as I'm concerned, we can make that trip tomorrow."

Rebecca silently footnoted that Peoria First Baptist's trustee meeting was scheduled for Wednesday following the Tubman play. If she attended, she would have an opportunity to bring up Julia Wilson's surgery at that time. However, she wanted to confess to Leighton before doing anything that proved she had breached his confidence. And, if there was any other way to discredit Wilson, she would choose that way instead. The longing Gracelyn had voiced filled her thoughts again. If she lost whatever chance she had with Leighton, she was afraid the passion he engendered would be absent from her life forever.

Rebecca realized she was fortunate. She had her beautiful home, her orchid business, her sisters, and enough wealth and influence to pursue a variety of interests. Still, Leighton's face and physique created a restlessness in her that surfaced in her thoughts throughout the day. In her mind's eye she saw clearly his tall figure standing in her hallway and heard his Southern-inflected voice saying her name.

She decided to put off saying anything to the trustees for a while. However, the Cates women would take Timothy to Chicago the week following Gracelyn's play.

Jake continued to be restless during the week, wandering around the house calling for Rebecca. Though he interrupted her repeatedly throughout the day, she managed to steer him back to his room patiently each time. Rebecca's focus did not shift from her other activities, but she resigned herself to the fact that his remaining time with her would not be smooth sailing. On top of this, Leighton continued to press his suit, seemingly well able to match Rebecca's own patience. He had begun sending her expensive gifts, chiefly small art objects and beautiful note cards, several times a week. The first few times, she wrote polite but stilted thank-you notes, then decided it was too much trouble to keep up the acknowledgments. But the gifts and cards kept coming. When Leighton wrote to ask if he could visit, she promptly wrote back that it wasn't possible, thinking of Jake's confusion and the resulting chaos in the house. Though he continued to be the object of her fantasies, Rebecca couldn't imagine how to blend any time with Leighton into her overextended schedule. His seeming passion forced her to keep in mind her own, assaulting her clarity. Rebecca knew she required complete focus to move forward with her strategy. Before her plans were consummated and she nailed Wilson, nothing must stand in her way.

Rebecca spent most of a balmy Wednesday morning in her greenhouse, fretting and shaking her head over yet another drooping laelia. She had already changed potting media three times this month, shifted the plants to different tables in order to intensify their exposure to sunlight, then decrease it. She had tried altering the watering schedule and checking and rechecking drainage.

"Maybe I should try talking to these ladies," she muttered to herself in a half-laugh. "Lord, have mercy, my mind is going."

Rebecca continued to concentrate on the problem plants, poring over her checklist of symptoms and remedies. Hearing a loud honking from around the front of the house, she abruptly raised her head. Rebecca carefully secured her checklist beneath one of the flowerpots and rushed across the yard to the back door, through the small entry, and into the kitchen.

"Gracelyn, Gracelyn, you in here?" she called out, thinking

her sister would be getting lunch preparations started. Not hearing any response, she walked through to the front hallway. Wiping her hands on slightly dusty khakis, she pulled open the front door.

"Good morning, ma'am. I'll need you to sign for these here plants."

The deliveryman had lined up six crates marked FRAGILE along the porch railing.

"Plants from where? I didn't order anything."

"Ma'am, it says right here: Rebecca Cates Furness. Thirty laelia plants. Looks like they're from all over: Brazil, Florida, Hawaii. Even some from . . . I'm sorry, I can't read this too good."

Rebecca looked at the list the man held in front of her. She was impressed with what must be a grower's promotional campaign.

"Côte d'Ivoire. That would be Ivory Coast. In Africa. What company did you say these were from?"

"Ma'am, there's a card in that first box."

"I'd better check in case there's some mistake."

Rebecca sidled past the man and plucked a small linen envelope wedged between plants in the box nearest the door. Opening it, she pulled out a stiff card written in large, orderly handwriting.

Rebecca,

I hope this small shipment helps your laelia problem. I did some research, and these plants are among the hardiest of the species. I am told they can be repotted in clay pots a week after delivery, and their breeding prospects are excellent.

Best,

Randall Leighton

Rebecca's mouth fell open. Stunned, she reached for the pen the deliveryman offered her.

"Thank you," she muttered as she signed the transmittal

receipt. "I'll need you to take these out to the greenhouse. Just set them on the floor."

"Certainly, ma'am."

It took the deliveryman three trips to cart all the crates around to the back. Before he finished, Rebecca started prying open each crate. She was so busy inspecting the flowers that she didn't see him leave. In each crate, plastic pots were wrapped around the bottom with jute and tied to each other, keeping the lush plants secure. Rebecca immediately decided to isolate her new plants from her ailing ones, and dragged in a long table from the garage to hold Leighton's gift. She spent the afternoon cataloguing each according to its place of origin, and began to code each group with strips of colored tape. She plucked her master diagram from where it hung on the wall and amended it to include the new arrivals.

Rebecca's hours of work partially distracted her, but with the plants placed in order and her records updated, her thoughts returned to Leighton. Previously, his gifts were tasteful and expensive, but this time he had gone for the jugular. The plants connected him with her interior life. Their color, their smell, their essence consumed her senses. Leighton's painstaking gesture truly touched her. Her thoughts of him were now on a deeper level than her physical yearnings. He had, in one afternoon, erased what was absent from her life by making it visible. Because of this, for her, now the physical was entirely possible.

Rebecca remained trancelike until evening. She functioned normally enough during dinner, asking Claudia, "What are your plans for the weekend?"

"Saturday morning, I'm going to meet with some women at the Masonic Temple. We're the welcoming committee for Hillary Clinton. I can hardly believe she's really coming here to Peoria. Would you like to come to the meeting?"

"No thanks, dear. I've got some things to take care of in the greenhouse. I have to make sure some new plants are situated."

Rebecca added matter-of-factly, "Do you remember Randall Leighton? He may be coming by to look at some orchids. I believe he's got some kind of gardening project under way."

"That's lovely, Rebecca." Claudia resumed her Hillary mania. "I'm so thrilled she's making a visit here. It's a bit warm, but I just might wear my pashmina. I bought it as sort of a tribute to her. She's always got one draped around her shoulders. You think that's silly?" Without waiting for a response, she continued, "Gracelyn, would you like to join me?"

"I can't, Claudia. I have the play rehearsal that afternoon, and I'll actually be running some errands before going over to the church."

"Oh, that's right. I should have remembered. You're working so hard on that. Anyway, soon as Lucy hits the door, I'm out of here!"

Rebecca smiled lovingly at both her unsuspecting sisters. It was too soon to present them with anything outside their main agenda. The play, Claudia's announcements, transporting the men to their new residences—her whole plan for them had to unfold seamlessly. Rebecca knew Claudia and Gracelyn's temperaments and how to keep them focused. They couldn't have extra things to think about, especially something as distracting as Rebecca's link with Leighton. This knowledge would captivate them, and neither would be able to suppress her curiosity.

Later, alone in her bedroom, Rebecca found the card Leighton had given her when she visited his clinic. She called the first number and got a recording. Without leaving a message, she called the second number.

"Randall Leighton," a voice said crisply.

Rebecca paused momentarily. "Were you sleeping?" she asked, without identifying herself. "I'm calling to thank you for the laelias. It was totally unexpected."

"Rebecca. I'm glad you called. I'm used to waking up suddenly. I suppose most doctors are. Did you like the flowers?"

"Yes, very much. I'd like you to see what I've done with them. Are you available at ten Saturday morning?"

"Yes, Rebecca. I'm available then. But must it wait that long?"

Rebecca smiled to herself before answering firmly, "I'm afraid it must."

"I'm anxious to see what was delivered. You already know how much I want to see you."

"Then it should be a pleasant visit," Rebecca replied. "I'll be in the greenhouse. Come straight around to the back. Don't ring the front bell. Lucy will be upstairs, but I'll let her know you're coming, and she won't need to answer the door. You can pull your car to the end of the driveway. I'll be waiting."

Rebecca hung up the receiver, happy, and too excited to sleep. She spent the next half hour sitting naked on her bed, thoroughly brushing her hair, something she rarely did. When finished, she walked to her standing mirror and looked long at her face and body. She had always been aware of her Amazonian beauty, but even as a younger woman was not terribly vain. Tonight, her beauty counted to her, and she inspected herself carefully. Her neck was just faintly lined. Her ample breasts were smooth and rounded. Her torso was longish, with a well-defined waist above the curve of her stomach. Her thighs were large but firm. Her hands were hands that worked, but her nails were clipped and clean. Her feet were thick and deeply arched. Rebecca's features taken together were not imposing. From Mattie she had inherited prominent cheekbones, a pert nose, and from Reuben a strong jawbone. Her earthy appearance would have been unremarkable, except that her cool gray eyes were startling, and her tan skin had a pinkish glow. The gray streaks throughout her hair contrasted with thick black eyebrows. Her physical appearance was as dual as her nature. She could appear kind and intelligent, or fierce. It was never possible to know what Rebecca was thinking.

After smiling slightly at her image, Rebecca turned from the mirror and climbed into bed.

IX

LEIGHTON ENTERED THE greenhouse without knocking, while Rebecca stood over the new plants, misting them, her back to the visitor. Hearing the door, she turned to look at her suitor and smiled. Leighton smiled back at her, looking intently at her face and dress, a white muslin smock belted with a red velvet cord. She laid down her implements and motioned to him.

"Come see the new family. So far, they all look happy. I can't thank you enough—"

"Seeing you is thanks."

Leighton walked the ten-foot distance between them and stood beside Rebecca, his eyes sweeping the repotted orchids. They were arranged by color, the blooms cascading from deep fuchsia to ivory-tinged white. He leaned over to smell the rows of plants, his pants leg brushing slightly against Rebecca.

"They're lovely. You're lovely. How long did it take to arrange everything?"

"A few hours. How was your drive?"

"Pleasant. No. I could barely stand it."

"There was traffic?"

"No. You have to understand."

For several seconds neither spoke. Then Leighton spoke again, his voice rasping.

"Rebecca. You have to understand. I have wanted to see you so badly. When I first saw you, I knew I belonged with you. I couldn't explain it to myself, let alone to you. When you called, it was like my life started over. I know I can't force you to do anything, to want me back—"

"I do want you, Randall."

Rebecca took Leighton's hand and led him to a windowless wall at the back of the greenhouse. Leaning against it, she pulled him against her. He immediately began kissing her while holding her face. His hands began roaming over her broad shoulders and down her back while he kissed her neck. When his lips glided down her throat to her neck, she found both his hands and placed them over her full breasts. Drawing back from her, he looked into her eyes. Her gray irises had darkened to midnight blue, and her tan skin reddened to bronze. She smiled at him, her lips parting to release even, heavy breaths. As he continued to gaze at her, he held her with one arm around her waist. With his free hand, he untied the cord around her dress and, reaching under the gauzy white cloth, raised the hem of her skirt above her hips. Leighton gasped as his hands felt the naked roundness of her hips, then again, as Rebecca forthrightly undid the clasp of his belt.

By the end of their lovemaking, Leighton fell exhausted against Rebecca, his head leaning against her shoulder. Rebecca's eyes darted in disbelief at how transformed the large, familiar space seemed to her. The white half-walls were barely visible in the dim light, and she could barely see the view out of the long windows into the backyard. Suddenly, thunder railed across the sky, followed by heavy rain.

"This is the second time you've brought us bad weather," Rebecca teased him. Leighton remained silent.

"Randall."

"Yes, Rebecca."

"We really can't do this on a regular basis. I want to, but I'm still married to Jake. We're going to be divorced before long. I plan to divorce him, but for now, I need to make sure he's comfortable where he's going. I suppose you think I'm terribly dishonest."

"I don't think anything, Rebecca. I've had three wives. I know how things can be in a marriage. I would never judge you. I have no right. I know how I feel about you, and I'm willing to wait awhile. Will you be able to come to see me soon?"

"Yes, I'll come. I wish I could fix you something to eat, but Lucy is in the house all day. Will you be all right?"

"I'll be all right. But I have to see you soon."

"Then we'll make it soon."

Rebecca walked Leighton to his car and waved as he drove off.

That evening, Rebecca soaked for a long time in a pine-oil bath. She scrubbed herself with olive soap, recalling Leighton's scent and the release she felt after being with him. The clean smells filled her nostrils, adding to her feeling of calm. For over an hour Rebecca luxuriated in the warmth, then sat on the edge of the tub watching the water swirl slowly down the drain. She scooped up a handful and lifted it to her nose, reluctant to relinquish the smell that was so pleasurable for her.

Rebecca lay in her bed, not yet sleepy, when she heard Claudia outside her door faintly calling to her.

"Claudia? Come in, honey. I'm awake."

Claudia walked in, her outstretched hand holding a page of linen paper.

"Rebecca, I wanted you to see this."

Rebecca took the page out of Claudia's hand and began to read.

My Darling Reuben,

I cannot bear this anymore; I will not. As long as I have breath, you will not leave this house. It is hard enough for me to think of your leaving on that final day. Do you think I can bear to have this come any sooner than necessary? Nursing you is a burden I will gladly bear as long as I can see you smile at me and hear your voice. Your big girl Rebecca won't hear of it, either. She works tirelessly, and besides herself, trusts only me to look after you. Do you honestly think there is any way I could convince her otherwise? You are my fate, and I am glad of it.

Your loving wife,
Mattie

Rebecca glanced up and saw that Claudia's eyes were wet. She placed the letter on her night table and pulled her sister beside her in bed.

"Aren't you happy they had that much?"

"I am, Rebecca. But I am so selfish. I envy them. Maybe I don't deserve to have a love like they had."

"That's not for you to say, Claudia. Believe me, we get what the universe sends us when we open our hands."

"What do you mean?"

Rebecca wasn't ready to tell Claudia about her afternoon with Leighton. It was too fresh and private still. But she wanted to convey her awe of what had happened to her through no concerted effort of her own. After she had told her sisters it was possible for all of them to have what they desired, Leighton had come to her. In trying to keep their spirits up, she had achieved the far reaches of her own faith.

"I always feel that if I plan carefully what I want to happen, I can make it happen. But some things we need we can't plan or control. That doesn't mean we can't have them. It just means it's out of our hands, in more powerful hands. It has nothing to do with being capable. You have to let go. Your faith is your power."

"How do you know this, Rebecca?"

"I haven't always. But I wouldn't be telling you something I didn't believe, now would I?"

"No, you never have."

"Just don't rule anything out. You'll see. Go to sleep."

Rebecca kissed the already sleeping Claudia's forehead.

Reverend Wilson's sermon the next morning confirmed for Rebecca that he did not yet understand she had prompted a sequence of events intended to lead to his ouster. Without connecting the dots between Rebecca's visit to his home, Claudia's announcements, and Gracelyn's play, he preached about women upholding their wedding vows "in sickness and in health," and encouraged the women of the church to stand by their husbands in later years. Once she got the drift of his message, Rebecca tuned him out and began making plans. She knew intuitively she needed to coalesce a strong group of women at the church.

The next morning at breakfast Rebecca instructed Claudia to announce an afternoon tea for the churchwomen at the Cates mansion.

"We'll have a whole gala that weekend, with the play on Saturday and the tea the next day. Lord knows, we need some light-hearted moments to share with our sisters in the faith."

"Yes, that is the Lord's truth," Claudia agreed. "Rebecca, I will use your very words when I make the announcement. And since Gracelyn will probably need to rest after her theatrical debut, I'll take care of all the preparations."

"That's so sweet of you Claudia. I'm sure Gracelyn appreciates that."

"Well, I appreciate what she's doing with the children, using her talents that way. Anyway, you know I'm good at those little tea sandwiches with the crusts off the bread and the pink-and-green cheese spread and the thin cucumber slices. Rebecca, can we afford caviar? I imagine champagne would be a little worldly."

"We'll save the champagne for when Wilson's gone," Rebecca said flatly.

Gracelyn's large eyes lifted to meet Rebecca's, shifted briefly to Claudia's, then went back to her oldest sister.

"You think he's really going to go?"

"I think he's really going to go. Now, don't fret about it. Get that play finished and then get yourself some rest. Those creative juices need pampering."

Gracelyn smiled at both her sisters. "I couldn't have done it without you both believing in me."

Rebecca smiled back, then continued her instruction to Claudia.

"The weekend Gracelyn does her play and we have the tea, it will be three weeks since we took Bernard in. The week before, at morning service, you announce we're taking Timothy up to Briney Memorial. That way, any fallout we can put to rest because the women will be guests in our home that afternoon. In case some of them want to start gossiping about us, it will be better to have them on our home turf. We'll leave two days following, on Tuesday, get Timothy settled, and just make a week of it in Chicago. Gracelyn can relax at that book sale and you can do some shopping. I'll be happy just to know when we come back our home will be peaceful."

"What about Jake?" Gracelyn asked earnestly.

"Jake's time is coming. No need rushing. The weeks go by fast."

"They sure do. It seems like Bernard just left here. But it's been a lot longer, more than a few weeks. Isn't that strange?"

"Probably because you've been so busy. We've all been busy."

Rebecca's brow furrowed momentarily before she spoke again.

"Claudia, you make the point in your speech about Gracelyn wanting to witness to being a hospice widow when the women are gathered. And be sure to say that Pastor cannot be expected to take up all of the congregation's time with our concerns."

Claudia's concise nod let Rebecca know she had rapidly processed these instructions.

As the week went by, Rebecca indulged her fantasies, her mind fully registering her feral desire for Leighton. She caught herself smiling at frequent daydreams, and by Thursday decided to call him. Pleased that he sounded so happy to hear from her, she invited him to come see her again Saturday morning. Both her sisters would leave the house early, Gracelyn off to her play rehearsal and Claudia to the dry cleaners and hours of shopping.

Leighton's car arrived at the Cates mansion at 10 A.M. Saturday. Following Rebecca's instruction, he drove far down the driveway and stopped adjacent to the house, leaving room behind him for additional cars. Rebecca expected Wayne to arrive at noon and spend a few hours inspecting the hedges for parasites. Leighton's car would not be noticeable even after Wayne left, as it was parked in the shadow cast by the house.

Rebecca pulled swiftly back from Leighton, who enfolded her the moment he stepped through the front door.

"Follow me," she said softly but firmly, and turned to mount the front stairs.

Rebecca climbed briskly, pleasantly aware of Leighton close behind her, his body warmth and smell increasing her excitement.

"Here," she directed, once they achieved the third-floor landing. Taking his hand, she led him the short distance down the hall.

At first, Leighton's eyes took in the tall, wide windows and sparse furnishings of Rebecca's bedroom, then quickly returned to her face.

"Everything looks like you. Beautiful and strong."

Rebecca, her gray eyes darkening, reached for his face, laying her open hand alongside his jaw. Taking her wrist, Leighton noted her thumping pulse.

"Do we have time?"

"I think we do. Lucy has Jake and Timothy out back. I told her I needed to rest today. She won't disturb us. My sisters are out. They'll be gone all day. No one will know. Are you comfortable here?"

"I have nothing to hide."

Rebecca smiled at his frankness.

"Randall, I do. It's different for women. I have to be careful."

"I respect that, Rebecca. I'll leave whenever you say. This time. You called me Randall. I love hearing you say my name."

Leighton kissed Rebecca slowly, letting his tongue spread over her lips, then loll inside her mouth. She sucked it in as far as it would go while he began unbuttoning her shirt. His large hands traveled inside the starched cotton caressing her shoulders; then the tips of his fingers ran lightly over the edge of her brassiere. Pulling back from her, he undid her buttons and allowed the garment to slip to the floor.

"Do you ever wear lace?" he asked pointedly.

"Never," Rebecca responded flatly.

"What about silk?"

"No."

"If I brought you some things, would you wear them?"

"I might."

"I would like you to."

Leighton slid both hands around Rebecca's back and undid the clasp of her brassiere. Looking at her large round breasts for the first time, he drew an audible breath.

"Only goddesses look like you, Rebecca. Did you know that?"

"I want to lie down."

"I do too."

Their lovemaking lasted through the morning. Rebecca guided

him, saying, "Here. Move your hand here. Put your mouth here." Leighton touched her body as though he were creating it, molding her breasts, stomach, and thighs with his hands. They were able to climax together by the second time he entered her, and she stroked his back after he fell onto her, soon to be asleep.

Rebecca knew that at noon Lucy would lock Jake and Timothy in their rooms and head downstairs to make sandwiches for them. She would rouse Leighton when Lucy was still in the kitchen. They could shower quickly, and when she heard Lucy mount the stairs with the lunch tray, Leighton could leave unnoticed. Rebecca thought how strange it was for her to be so calm, given their risk of discovery. But she was grateful for the peace she felt, and that everything between them could be tender and unhurried following their fierce coupling.

Sunday morning, Claudia pulled a crisp, short-sleeved linen dress from her closet and pulled it skillfully over her head without mussing her makeup. Turning back and forth in front of her full-length mirror, she decided a little extra blush on her cheeks would complement the lavender color of the dress and look nice with her just-begun tan. Primping usually helped with her nervousness, but she noted with mild surprise that this morning she had none. She mulled over her announcement, completely comfortable with Rebecca's instructions and confident that she would remember everything.

The church people were eager for her to stand up now, just as Rebecca had predicted. She was amazed how warmly they received her, and wondered why it took her so long to realize that her chic wardrobe and quiet glamour could work for her or against her. It seemed that now, with her reaching out to the congregation almost weekly, people saw past the things they had once envied and distrusted and fully embraced her. Claudia felt powerful for the first time in a long time. She was grateful to Rebecca for opening this path to her.

Claudia was excited about this morning, as well as the remainder of the week. Next Saturday morning she would go hear Hillary Clinton speak, and that evening, Gracelyn would put on her play in the church's basement auditorium. The following afternoon, on Sunday, she and her sisters would host their tea for the church women at the Cates mansion. She didn't remember being this excited since she left Chicago. Claudia realized that along with her excitement she had begun to feel a new affection for the people of her home community. She was always polite, but her shyness had sometimes kept her from extending herself to people. Since making the church announcements, she had grown more confident, noting how the somewhat plain people of her hometown responded to her movie-star bearing. Her style created a small sensation for her audience, and for them her presentations were a fashion event. Claudia noticed the two or three women who began to copy her simple hairdo, hatless style, and the subtle neutrals of her dresses and strong colors of her accessories. During her years in Chicago, she had relished being noticed and setting trends. Having the same thing happen for the first time in Peoria delighted her.

"Brothers and Sisters," a fully composed Claudia began her statement, "my sisters and I have another heartache and we need you to pray with us and for us. We are blessed that my brother-in-law Bernard is resting comfortably in his last days, but now, under the advisement of his doctor, we're faced with placing my own husband, Timothy, in a rest home. Next week, we'll be traveling to Chicago and would appreciate having your prayers for our safety and for the courage to face this transition in this phase of our lives. We appreciate every kindness you have shown us, and in return would be so honored to have the women of our church attend an afternoon tea in our home next Sunday. This will be the day following my sister Gracelyn's play, and I hope it will not be too much activity for all of you. Gracelyn is happy to give of herself to our young people, but in her heart she also desires to witness to the women of our church about being a hospice widow. Perhaps, when we are gathered, there are others of you who have hearts that need unfolding in the company of caring fellowship. We feel this is one way we can minister to each other, since we know that Pastor cannot be expected to take up all of the congregation's time with our concerns."

Upon hearing her sister's speech, Rebecca leaned her head forward to cover a slight smile. This was perfection beyond even her high expectations of Claudia. Timothy's impending committal to Briney Memorial would be submerged in the excitement of the play and a luxurious tea the next day at the mansion.

Rebecca was sure the women grasped the point that they were left to comfort themselves, their pastor engrossed in other priorities. "Like his wife's breast size," she muttered inaudibly.

Sunday evening, the Cates women ate a meal of chicken, which Gracelyn had marinated in garlic and wine vinegar and covered with a rich tomato sauce flavored with Dijon mustard and white wine. She spooned the savory mixture over wide, flat egg noodles on a serving tray and prepared another tray with asparagus covered with fluffy wine-enhanced egg whites.

"Gracelyn, this is wonderful," Claudia said, trying the main course and the asparagus eagerly.

"I thought you would like it. I know we're in Provence with the chicken, and I think we're still in the south of France with the asparagus, but don't ask me to swear it. Anyway, we deserve pampering today. I have a feeling everything is going to be spectacular for us very soon. What do you think, Rebecca?"

"If this meal is any indication, we're on a serious roll. I'm praying for all of us, even the men. Gracelyn, honey, you go put your feet up after we finish. I'll do the cleanup this evening."

"Thanks, Rebecca. I hope Lucy comes down soon, so she can

share a plate with us. But there's a lot, so she can take something home if she wishes. I heard her say Jake has been restless since yesterday. Oh, Lord, I guess we don't need to hear that right now."

"Whatever it is, I'm sure she can handle it," Rebecca said, refocusing the discussion. "If not, she would let us know. Now, let's see. To be on the safe side, I'll take the car for a road check tomorrow. Claudia, you make an appointment for Dr. Meyers to come by right before we leave and make sure Timothy's had enough sedation, maybe a little more than usual. This is one time we don't want him getting belligerent. Gracelyn, did you speak with Raphaela about Herbert?"

"He'll be here at seven in the morning."

"Good."

Rebecca, pleased that her past instructions had been carried out, and confident that her current ones would be also, anticipated a journey to Chicago without tension. She understood that Claudia, unlike Gracelyn with Bernard, had little or no emotional investment in the dissolute Timothy. Claudia had constructed a life with Timothy on the periphery. In her eyes, he had done the same. Early in their marriage, she shut down emotionally, confused and alienated by his behavior. She sensed that even when sober, he had very little regard for her, and that the demons chasing him had taken him over long before they became husband and wife. Though not bold like Rebecca or Gracelyn, she possessed, like the rest of the Cates clan, an orderly psychology that allowed her to relentlessly weigh the pros and cons of her marriage in much the same way she made her clothing choices. Over the years, she catalogued Timothy's infidelities for Rebecca, but decided against confronting him with her unhappiness. Her remoteness signaled that she would respect his distance if he respected hers. Since he never quite knew what Claudia was thinking, it made him unwilling to risk being violent toward her. His impending confinement would keep him from alcohol. Whether there might be the slightest piece of his soul to salvage she would leave to God.

The week flew by. Gracelyn was relieved of her cooking duties so she could attend to last-minute details for her play. Rebecca had Wayne set up the barbecue pit in the side yard early Monday morning, so Claudia could get started roasting a small turkey and a cut of beef. For the next few days, the Cates women's customary formal meals would be given over to sandwiches, fresh fruit, and crudités, which they could grab as they ran in and out. Claudia carefully planned everything out so they would have ample food and no cooking time, and could concentrate on the upcoming weekend's events.

Claudia watched with interest as Wayne replaced a screw in the rotisserie cover and blushed, realizing she was taken with the muscles rippling his arms.

"This should do it, ma'am. I'll get your fire started, and if you have any trouble keeping it going, wave at me out front and I'll see what I can do."

Claudia blushed even more, realizing he was appraising her as well. They had never really been alone, since Wayne reported to Rebecca, but she noticed him and the easy rapport he had with her sister whenever he was in the house. Rebecca spoke highly of the caliber of his work and his honesty, and Claudia was always happy to get a glimpse of him because he smiled warmly at her.

"Oh, thanks, Wayne, I appreciate that. I expect I will have a struggle if a breeze kicks up. You'll be out front for a while?"

"Really most of the day, working on the border hedges. Rebecca likes them thick and low, but I talked her into letting me trim the outer ones a bit higher and keep more of the blooms so they'll kind of slope. I think it will be a nice effect."

"Sounds like it."

Claudia paused for a few seconds, thinking silently.

"Wayne, I'll be making some iced tea with fresh mint after I get this meat started. Please stop in for a glass later on. It's supposed to get pretty hot."

"Thanks. I'll do that."

"Good. If you like, pick up a sandwich too. We're eating off trays this week."

"Too busy for regular meals?"

"Yes. You know, Gracelyn has her play, and we've got to make arrangements for Timothy. He goes in next week."

"In where?"

"We're taking him to a home. Briney Memorial. It's outside Chicago."

"I'm sorry to hear that. Is he ill?"

"Well, yes. You know, he drinks, and with his shaking and wandering around, it's too much for me."

Wayne looked at Claudia's lowered eyes, thinking primarily how thick her eyelashes were, but he replied with what he knew was appropriate.

"You're doing the right thing. I hope everything goes well."

Now it was Wayne's turn to think silently. He finally spoke.

"Rebecca asked me to take you shopping Friday night. That still on?"

"Oh, good. Yes. I need your help. There'll be a lot of groceries. We're having all the churchwomen over for Sunday tea."

"You all eat that much?"

Claudia smiled at Wayne's sarcasm.

"Not really. We're going to have little tea sandwiches that take a lot of different ingredients, some home-baked cookies, and some punch. You've never been to an afternoon church social?"

"I must have with my mother when I was small. But you said this was for ladies."

"Well, really it is, but I'll save you a plate."

Wayne laughed. Claudia started to go back in the house, turned, and waved.

"Remember to come in for tea."

"I'll do that. Thanks."

By late morning, Claudia had removed the beef roast from the pit onto a marble cutting board and brought it inside. Standing at the kitchen counter, she began to carve succulent rare meat. Concentrating on making thin, even slices with the noisy electrical knife, she didn't notice Wayne entering through the back door. Feeling a light touch on her arm, she turned to see him standing beside her. Without words, he gently took the knife from her. A trace of a smile stretched Claudia's lips as she stepped aside and watched him take over the job she knew full well she could have done alone. Outdoors, she had noticed his muscled arms. Now, she found herself appraising his entire physique. The years had been kind. Only the lines in his face and more salt than pepper hair hinted at his age. He was medium tall, his body proportioned and lean. Claudia's nose twitched as she noticed his smell, comforting and masculine. She didn't remember ever before noticing a man's smell. She also noted his hands, large and strong. A workman's hands, she thought to herself, but she also knew these were hands that could fashion incredibly shaped topiaries, as well as till the earth.

Several minutes later, Claudia still felt his touch on her arm. Catching herself staring, she crossed the room to remove Dijon mustard, mayonnaise, and horseradish sauce from the refrigerator. When Wayne had completely carved the roast, she took several slices of meat, which she arranged on a serving platter with her usual efficiency. Next, she scooped dollops of each condiment into jelly jars, and placed them in the center of the platter. Reaching into the bread box she brought out an assortment of whole wheat, sesame, and rye slices and placed them in baskets on the table next to the meat tray.

"Oh, I forgot, Wayne, we have pickles also."

"Is this what the ladies are going to eat?"

Not realizing he was teasing her, Claudia began earnestly to quote her menu of colored cream cheese and cucumber sandwiches with the crusts cut off the bread, pâté and caviar on toast points, homemade mayonnaise, salmon prosciutto, and an assortment of olives, capers, and prepared artichokes.

"I keep thinking we're going to need a round or two of brie to go along with the fruit. But I really think a tapenade would be too much since we're serving olives anyway. Do you think our guests would miss it?"

"I don't think your church ladies are going to feel like anything's missing. Remember to save my plate."

"Oh, I will." Claudia, pleased by his compliment, and feeling very comfortable with him, began making sandwiches. "You go on and dress these however you want."

"Yes, ma'am."

Watching her move with birdlike quickness around the kitchen, Wayne came to the conclusion that Claudia was the most beautiful woman he had ever seen.

X

THE CATES SISTERS' excitement over their multiple activities reached a fever pitch by the weekend. They resumed having meals together at Friday breakfast. Rebecca expected Leighton to be coming by later in the evening while Claudia was out grocery shopping with Wayne and Gracelyn was at the final rehearsal for the church play. Not ready to share with her sisters her liaison with the doctor, Rebecca took pains that their conversation proceed normally. Always a week ahead in her planning, she briefed them on the next week's trip to Chicago.

"I know we're all excited, but let's try to focus. I'm taking the Mercedes in Monday for a road check, so, Claudia, I'll need you to run me by the post office. I have some boxed seedlings to pick up before one o'clock. Lucy is coming back over Monday afternoon. That way, we can all rest up from the weekend. We can't go up to Chicago dragging our feet. Lucy's going to stay here with Jake, which is a real blessing. I told her I would be back by Wednesday noon. If you two want to spend extra time and take the train back, it's fine with me. I don't mind coming back alone, since there'll only be Jake here."

"Lord, I can't believe it. We're almost all unburdened." Gracelyn shook her head, amazed at the rapidity of the changes in her life.

"Well, yes. But it's about time we drove up to see Bernard. That will be our next free weekend."

"Yes, Rebecca. I don't mind that. After the play, I'll have so much time. I'll have so much time to write. I almost feel guilty."

"Well, don't. You take as much time as you need. You've worked hard on that play, and I can't wait to see it. When it's over, you hole yourself up and I'll tell whoever calls or comes by that you're unavailable. I know how you writers are."

"Rebecca, you are so right," Claudia put in. "I read where Toni Morrison's concentration is so deep, she doesn't leave her home for days at a time. And you know how Emily Dickinson was a real stay-at-home. I believe Lillian Hellman had to move way out somewhere on the beach. You hear these stories all the time. We won't have anybody disturbing our Gracelyn."

"Uhm hum. Genius has to be nurtured. So, Gracelyn, you can crank out poems and things for twenty-four hours a day, if you decide to."

Gracelyn, moved by her sisters' understanding of her passion, took the hand of each, tears salting her eyes.

"That's all I want to do right now. I'm so hungry." She lifted her head. "What about you, Rebecca? When's your time coming?"

"My time's already come," Rebecca said, not intending to sound mysterious. "I'll do right by Jake and have my life too. You don't know how God has blessed me. Just to have my sisters with me and for us to have peace."

"Do you think a man can bring you peace?" Claudia asked.

"No, dear. But what we all know, I guess, is that a man can disrupt it. But not every man. Not the one the Lord sends you."

"How do you know it's the Lord that's sending the man, Rebecca?" Claudia continued in her questions.

"I'm not sure, dear. I guess we just have to give it time enough until we know."

Rebecca smiled at Claudia, understanding that perhaps even more than she and Gracelyn, her delicate, pristine sister had been bruised severely in her marriage. She had missed out on a man's giving of himself, and didn't really understand her own body. Rebecca felt for Claudia; to be so exquisite and so deprived of warmth seemed criminal. Gracelyn, she knew, enjoyed her sensuality and was unafraid of where it would lead her. Her confinement with Bernard over, it would not take long for her to reopen her heart, and her art would always sustain her, be a place for her to pour out her love and be loved. She hoped that Claudia was not afraid of what she had never known, and that her inkling of it had not faded from her consciousness. If Rebecca could herself be blessed with meeting Leighton, she reasoned, Claudia could be similarly blessed.

Leighton. She was certain they were soul mates, that theirs was a spiritual union. Rebecca knew she could make short shrift of Reverend Wilson by telling the trustees about Julia's breasts. But she would have to talk to Leighton first, letting him know she had deceived him to get the information, even if it punctured his trust and aborted the growing intimacy with him she found herself craving. In her heart, Rebecca knew she would have to trust the universe to right things for her.

Her bond with Leighton was strong. He came to Peoria three times without calling her first or coming to the house. Somehow, he managed to find her. The first time this happened, she was in a furniture store looking for nesting tables. She and Claudia had started collecting bonsai. Rebecca had imagined the small trees terraced on the tiered tables in the library. When she found the store clerk, he directed her upstairs to the sales floor, knowing he had seen several nesting tables in various woods. Rebecca strolled slowly through the large room past a row of ergonomic lounge chairs from the Caribbean, a half-circle of elegant slipper chairs covered in pastel suede, brocade sofas, and pine wardrobes.

Thinking she had missed the nesting tables, she peeked behind a partition. There they were, at least a dozen, reminding her of papa bears, mama bears, and baby bears from an alien planet. Rebecca smiled at her thought and thoroughly browsed the trios. Many of the tables were crafted with the Shaker simplicity she liked, but they were made of lighter woods—teak, cedar, and pine. Then she saw a larger set, lacquered a dark green, and knew this one would be perfect. She leaned over to the low surface, stroking the grain.

"Hello, Rebecca."

Rebecca turned to see Leighton standing a few feet from her.

"Randall." Rebecca spoke her lover's name, confused by their meeting in such an unlikely place.

Reading her surprise, he stated simply, "I knew you would be here."

The second time Rebecca encountered Leighton, she was driving east along the Interstate just leaving the Missouri border. Her appointment that afternoon was with a consortium of florists who bought top-of-the-line species in larger quantities at lower cost. They grunted appreciatively over Rebecca's album of photographs of her orchids. Pleased with the meeting and wanting to relax, Rebecca decided to take a longer route home, and pulled off onto a road where she knew she would spy antiques vendors. Stopping at the first sign, she pulled into the rocky driveway of the shop.

Inside, a prim but pleasant-looking saleswoman called out to her, "We have several new items. Let me know if anything catches your eye. Take your time, dear."

Rebecca smiled and began ambling carefully down rows of small knickknacks interspersed with larger furnishings. While browsing the shop, she enjoyed a pleasant reverie about her sisters, Harriet Tubman, the food she anticipated having for dinner, and Leighton.

"Rebecca."

Hearing his voice, Rebecca turned, a glass angel in her hand. Leighton stood before her, touching her arm.

"I knew you would be here."

"How do you always find me? How do you know where I am?"

"I don't know how I know."

The third time Leighton found her in an unlikely place, the periodical section of the county library, Rebecca accepted their mystical connection as natural.

Leighton arrived Friday evening, a few minutes after Gracelyn had left for the church and Claudia had sauntered off to do grocery shopping with Wayne. An hour before, Rebecca had fed Jake, then gave him an oversize book on the Negro baseball leagues, and closed him in his room where he sat engrossed in photos of lean, muscular players. She made sure Timothy ate something and was clean, and knowing he was heavily sedated, expected him to sleep through the night. She prayed that Jake would do the same.

Rebecca led Leighton upstairs to her room, then closed and locked the door behind them. He began immediately to undress her, unbuttoning her blouse.

"When do I have to leave?"

"It's best to leave around eight, before my sisters get back."

"Couldn't I stay the night and leave while they're still asleep?"

"No, Randall, you can't. It's too much of a risk."

"Why can't you just tell them I'm your lover? We're both adults."

"In a few days, after Timothy's gone. I have to keep them focused."

Leighton stroked Rebecca's breasts, his long fingers caressing the roundness above the edge of her bra. Then, pulling the fabric down, he leaned over to cover her nipples with his mouth. He let his tongue dart quickly over her aureole, sucking and wetting as much of her breast as he could hold in his mouth. Rebecca watched him, happy and aroused, through half-open eyes. Leighton pulled back from her, and watching her face for a moment, smiled broadly.

"You're wearing lace."

"You said to wear lace."

"I said I wanted to buy you some lace to wear."

"You still can."

Leighton was happy, understanding that in her desire she wanted to please him. He pulled her close, locking her in a long, slow kiss on the mouth. They sat on the bed, undressed, and talking about when they could be alone and travel together. Leighton told Rebecca he would be leaving the country again sometime in August, traveling to Senegal by way of Paris, and wanted her with him.

"Is that a good time for your business?"

"I can work that out. I'll have Jake settled by then."

"Good. Then it's a promise?"

"Randall, I promise. I'd love to be in Paris and Africa with you."

Leighton, in one strong and sudden motion, moved Rebecca underneath him, and locked her eyes in his gaze.

"You'll come as my wife?"

"I won't be divorced."

"Then I'll make you my wife. Now."

Leighton kissed Rebecca fervently; then brushing her face and neck with his lips, murmured her name over and over. Rebecca, overcome by his ardor, let her hands travel down his back to his buttocks. She held them firmly while he moved on top of her, the length of his torso grazing her breasts and stomach until he hardened. She gasped when he entered her, and not wanting him to pause, she wrapped her legs around his waist. She held on to him with both arms, freeing one hand to stroke the stiff waves of his hair. Rebecca heard herself moan as Leighton altered his rhythm, coming in and out of her slowly, then plunging into her hard, then slowing his thrusts again. After several minutes of their love dance, they climaxed together. Rebecca knew in that instant that while Leighton claimed her body, he had given his soul.

They made love again after sleeping. Rebecca heard Claudia come up from the kitchen around ten-thirty, and Gracelyn climbing the stairs to the attic sometime after one. Discovery seemed unimportant to her as she lay beside Leighton, watching him sleep. She loved that each time he awoke he kissed her. The last time, an hour before sunrise, she whispered to him that this would be the last time she asked him to leave, but that he should go. Leighton, sleepy but cheerful, obliged.

Saturday morning, after sleeping a few hours, Rebecca sat on her bed, languorously brushing her unwound hair. She noticed she wasn't at all tired in spite of the missed sleep. Sensing Leighton would call, she answered the phone when it rang.

"Hello, darling. I met Wayne. I hope that's not a problem."

"Wayne? Was he here at that hour?" Rebecca asked, thinking that he may have come by to retrieve some tools he needed for early Saturday work at another job.

"Yes, he was in the hall when I came out of the bathroom."

"He was upstairs?"

"Yes. Nice guy. But he was wearing a pink bathrobe. What's his story?"

"Wayne is my landscaper."

Rebecca knew immediately what had transpired. Wayne had been with Claudia that evening, and had spent the night. Rebecca smiled to herself, mildly shocked. Thankful that Leighton didn't press her to explain, Rebecca listened as he told her he would start making plans for their trip in the next few days.

"If we go to Paris first, we can fly to Senegal for about a hundred dollars. And, I'll book a hotel on the beach."

"How long will we be in Paris?"

"As long as you like."

"I can't believe you. You are so wonderful to me."

"That won't change."

Rebecca believed her lover. Etched in her mind were the words she could not say. *I lied to you. I came to Bloomington to get information on Julia Wilson. I plan to use what you told me against her husband, our pastor. He has to leave our congregation and leave this town. My sisters and I deserve the lives we are starting over. We are everything he despises. We are women, and he has no control over what we do. And we frighten him. We frighten all men like him. We frightened our husbands because we were who we are. We are Cates women. We have a legacy. Our legacy is each other, not our wombs.*

Rebecca felt that without her clarity of purpose, she would not survive. She also understood that today, being with Leighton, was the happiest day of her life. If the war she waged against Wilson cost her this happiness, she would go on with her life, filling her loss in the way she always had. She would run her orchid business, see to the family estate, have her sisters as companions. But the whole point of the war was to have something more. Perhaps, she thought, something more for her would be the memory of Leighton's loving her with such intensity.

"I have to tell him. He has to know," she said out loud. "If he can still love me, I'll make it up to him."

Rebecca rewound her hair and went to pull out her clothes. Excited about the Tubman play, today she would wear something colorful.

Claudia, already bustling about the kitchen, encountered her sister.

"I've never seen you in that shirt, Rebecca. You look wonderful in lilac."

"Thank you, dear. How was your evening?"

"Good," Claudia replied, poker-faced. "I'm making headway

on the tea sandwiches and Wayne made the shopping a piece of cake. He even stayed to help me roll out the cookie dough. I think he's a natural in the kitchen. He looks so strong, but he's got such a gentle touch—with women's work."

"I can imagine. He's a very nice man. You should ask him out sometime."

"Oh, Rebecca, I'm glad you said that. I already have. He's going to meet me at the Hillary speech. Turns out, he likes her as much as I do."

"That's wonderful, Claudia. It's good for you to have a companion."

Gracelyn, dressed in a turquoise jumpsuit of Indian cotton, bounded frantically into the kitchen, grabbed a Granny Smith apple from the enormous fruit bowl, and bounded out.

"See you all this evening," she said, blowing kisses. "I'm too nervous to sit still."

"Try to calm down," Rebecca advised, advice she knew was futile. "Everything will go well."

Claudia protested, "Gracelyn, you better take more than that to eat. You'll faint by lunchtime."

Gracelyn reentered, walking rapidly to the refrigerator. The shelves were full of Claudia's tea sandwiches.

"Take a few sandwiches," Claudia advised. "Wait, you sit down, and I'll pack your lunch. Hand me your backpack."

Claudia worked efficiently making Gracelyn's lunch, chattering at her about going too long without food and getting all worked up over things. Rebecca, amused by the exchange, stifled a smile.

"Lucy meeting you at the church?"

"Yes, Rebecca. Claudia, thanks."

"Break a leg."

Gracelyn exited, racing toward the front door, leaving as hastily as she had come in, her energy at an all-time high.

"And be calm!" Claudia yelled after her as she watched Gracelyn jogging toward her car, her backpack bouncing up and down like an ill-attached papoose.

"That girl," Claudia exclaimed, bustling into the kitchen. Seating herself at the table, she returned to her croissant. She paused, looking sidelong at Rebecca.

Rebecca, noticing, said to her, "What are you thinking, dear?"

Claudia finished chewing the pastry. "Do you think Wayne's a good catch? I mean, for someone, a mature woman."

"I think what's important is what you think."

"What I think? Well, I don't really know him that well. But he's pleasant company, that's certain enough. And he's a very tender man. I imagine a man like that knows right where to touch a woman, not going too fast and making her feel like she's a sack of potatoes."

"Uhm hum. Probably so. He looks the sort to make a woman feel precious, like a jewel or a flower. Definitely not like . . . what was that you said, potatoes?"

"Yes, that's the best way I could think of to describe it."

"Honey, it's good you're thinking that way, because I believe that might be a common problem. It's hard to unlearn menfolk in that vein. Well now," Rebecca sighed, "I myself think Wayne would be a very good catch, that is, if he wants to be caught."

Claudia blushed, now sipping her tea. She was silent, having heard from Rebecca what she wanted to hear.

Rebecca finished her coffee and made oatmeal for Jake and Timothy. When Claudia rose from the table, she turned back to her sister.

"Leave all that. You get a move on so you have time to do your makeup. I want you and Wayne sitting right in front of Hillary."

"Thanks, Rebecca."

"And be sure to ask him if he wants to come to the play. We can all go together. That way, there won't be any heads turning around to inspect."

After a clear morning and afternoon, the evening of the play performance was balmy and pleasant. The parishioners arrived early and gathered outside the church, enjoying a breeze and stars that began to emerge as dusk fell. They filed slowly into the church basement, their heads turning to admire the newly draped stage with very professional-looking lighting fixtures. On one wall, they noted blown-up black-and-white photographs of Harriet Tubman, Sojourner Truth, Frederick Douglass, and Nat Turner. Smaller photos showed anonymous slaves working in fields, young black girls holding white babies, and several men whose heads, arms, and feet were confined by torture instruments. Underneath the photos on a large mahogany table was a book exhibit of slave narratives and bound abolitionist speeches.

The playgoers milled around for several minutes, enthralled by the display, until all but one row of the overhead lights was turned off, signaling the play was about to begin. They lifted red fold-over programs from their seats and began to inspect them carefully, murmuring the names of their children as they spotted them listed underneath the parts they were playing. The parishioners assumed a curious silence as the Greek chorus, Herbert leading, filed in and took its position in three rows to the left of the raised platform.

The first voice they heard was Herbert's, ringing out, *"Harriet Tubman. A play by Constance Enright."*

Herbert adjusted his glasses, took a deep breath, and signaled the other chorus members with a nod. They began their narration in perfect unison.

Gracelyn, watching backstage from behind a thick curtain, relaxed after the strong beginning. She knew then that her scrupulous rehearsing of the children would reflect in the evening's performance. As the first narrative ended, the curtain rose to reveal Melba Sims as Harriet Tubman, standing alone center stage, a single beam of light highlighting her frame. As Gracelyn had instructed her, her eyes were focused slightly above her audience's heads, and she began speaking after drawing a deep diaphragmatic breath.

"Massa beat me for the last time," she said in a defiant tone of voice. "In a week, I'm gone from this place. Whether my man goes with me or not, I'm leaving here."

Her head raised and her arm pointing overhead, she continued.

"That should be the North Star. My, it's pretty. That star is going to show me the way north. I'm not meant to be a slave, and I'm not going to live like one. If they want to stop me, they'll have to kill me. But I know sure enough they bleed too."

At that, Melba pulled a gun from inside a cloth pouch tied around her waist just as Carl, one of Raphaela's boys, playing her husband, entered from stage right. Quickly, Melba replaced the gun in her pouch.

"Harriet, what are you doing out here so late? Massa see you, he'll beat you again."

"Massa will beat me again anyway. That's why I'm heading north."

"We talked about that. You can't go north without me. I'm your husband."

"Slaves don't have husbands or wives. You want to be married to me, you'll go to freedom alongside me."

"You're my wife and I love you, Harriet. But I can't do it. I want us both to stay here so at least we can stay alive."

"I choose death over being a slave. I'm going without you."

"Lord, woman. I know I can't stop you. But be careful. I'll be your lookout as far as the next county."

"God bless you. You're the only one I can trust not to say anything."

The couple embraced and exited hand in hand.

The performance continued seamlessly. The one exception to Gracelyn's agenda was Renee Bartleson, who appeared onstage as part of a procession of runaways behind Melba. Renee had endowed herself with an enormous bosom by stuffing two rolled-up dish-cloths inside her blouse. There were scattered snickers when she first appeared onstage, though much of the audience failed to notice, and afterward everyone remained engrossed in the drama. Backstage, Gracelyn quickly pulled out Renee's padding and tossed it aside.

At the end of the play, the audience stood to applaud the young performers. At the reception following, Gracelyn was hugged and kissed over and over by the children's mothers, and her hand grasped and shaken to soreness by their fathers. Graciously forgiv-ing of Renee Bartleson's improvised costume, she delivered the girl to her sheepish parents.

"I was happy to work with Renee," she told them. "She's extremely bright, and I was often overimaginative as a child myself. Don't worry about anything, it all went fine. The next play we put on, we'll give her more to do so she won't be bored."

The Bartlesons left the church hurriedly with their brood, grateful that none of their neighbors commented on their daugh-ter's misstep.

Reverend Wilson, however, was one of the audience members who noticed Renee's indiscretion, and the next morning at service he did indeed comment, citing "the ways of wanton young folk" as cannon fodder for his sermon. Rebecca was certain he would return to this topic over and over in the weeks to come, in concert with the subject of keeping women shackled to their men. By meeting with the trustees and revealing his misappropriation of church monies, she could easily silence his offensive message and send him packing. But understanding what she stood to lose, this power was of small comfort. Rebecca, her teeth clenched, resolved in her heart to bear Reverend Wilson's hostility for the time being, and wait for a door to open.

But the pastor's rant escalated.

"The Devil has entered our parish in the guise of womanly flesh. What was presented to me as an innocent idea, a children's entertainment, has turned out to be an opportunity for debasement and self-exhibition by a young girl. It pains me to say that youth has been led astray by a trusted role model. We must face this evil directly. Wily Satan has sown tares in the precious field of our young people's minds. He has caused the unseemly display of our precious young womanhood, and should we stand still, God's enemy will certainly reap a rich harvest within our midst. I charge the director of this work to make full apology to our congregation at large, and especially to this young girl and her parents. I charge her parents to commit to more attentive guidance of this child on the brink of throwing away her virtue. If you doubt what I am saying, just look at what we are able to see every day on television, our young people's morals continually deteriorating."

A stunned silence, then noisy twitter engulfed the congregation. Amelia Bartleson, seated with Renee and her other children, began sobbing, her hands covering her face.

Rebecca could not believe what she was hearing. Glancing over at Gracelyn, she was alarmed at the pained look on her sister's face. Claudia, her head erect and delicate jaw set, instinctively placed her arm around Gracelyn's shoulders. She understood, as did Rebecca, that Gracelyn's victory of the previous evening was a hard-won feat, a way that she was able to mend what had broken inside her over the years. It attested to her creativity and ability to do something difficult and worthy, offsetting the enormous wound of her marriage that cast such a broad shadow over her spirit. Rebecca feared it was too delicate a triumph to withstand the malice and brutality of this assault.

Wilson ended his diatribe by announcing an unscheduled meeting of the trustees for Wednesday evening.

Stunned, but quickly composing herself, Rebecca rose from her seat.

"Thank you, Pastor, for your announcements. My brothers and sisters, as you know, I seldom contribute to the length of our service, but today is a very special day. My sister Claudia has made grand preparations for our afternoon tea, and we are excited to welcome our churchwomen into our home."

The parishioners had seen Rebecca stand up in church on just two occasions, following the deaths of Reuben, then Mattie, and each time to thank them for their expressions of sympathy.

"I want also to inform the pastor and trustees that I will be attending their meeting. The matter I will be presenting is of grave concern to our congregation, and it will need to be first on the agenda. Due to the seriousness of the matter, I must hold it in strictest confidence until I am able to disclose it to our respected leaders. I am glad Pastor has voiced his concern with the spiritual destiny of our youth, because there is a great threat among us to this very destiny and the moral fiber we have preserved over the years as a congregation."

Rebecca sat down again, checkmate accomplished. She heard the volume of the twitters increase and saw the slight scowl on Wilson's face. She knew he had no inkling of the information she was to present, and was merely irked that she had not asked permission to attend the impromptu meeting. Rebecca had stated deliberately that she would be attending, and that she would be first on the agenda. Rebecca's announcement accomplished two things. First, she trumped his sensationalism, refocusing the entire crowd's attention on the mysterious problem she alluded to. Second, she declared war on Wilson, openly and unmistakably, apparent to all except him.

Rebecca was gracious later that afternoon, as dozens of ebullient women filed into the Cates mansion, lingering first in the front hallway, transfixed by the polished brass mirror, gleaming tile floor, and flower arrangements. Next, they filtered into the dining room, where a lavish table of miniature sandwiches, hors d'oeuvres, and crudités awaited them. Claudia had placed two of Mattie's crystal punch bowls at either end of the table, one filled with cranberry juice and ginger ale, the other with soft peaks of lemon sherbet afloat on pineapple juice mixed with sparkling water. Still reeling from the previous night's performance, several of the women spoke about how polished the children had been in their roles. None of the women questioned Rebecca about what she would tell the trustees, all respecting the confidentiality she had mentioned earlier that day, some more because of her authoritative bearing than of a lessening of their curiosity. Claudia, however, was complimented over and over for her food preparation. Some of the women, not accustomed to eating caviar and pâté, understood that they were being very specially treated, in addition to being transported by the elegant surroundings.

Nearly all the women embraced Gracelyn at one point or other during the afternoon, entreating her to do more projects and offering to assist. She quickly recovered the euphoria she had felt before being upbraided from the pulpit. Rebecca, noticing, sighed deeply and offered a silent prayer of thanks.

After the women had been at the mansion for an hour, Claudia, in a navy-and-white-checked circular skirt and sleeveless white cotton shirt with generous pointed collars, and looking as though she never sweated, walked to the center of the living room and raised her voice above the din.

"We are delighted that all of you were able to come to our home today and continue our Christian fellowship. We wanted everything to be festive, and hope you have been enjoying yourselves. But we also wanted the opportunity for ourselves and for all of you to witness to some of the hardships we face as women. My sisters and I have made known the burdens we have carried with our menfolk, and we invite you to share your own with us. We believe that in the mutuality of prayer, we can truly gain strength and understand the way the Lord wants us to walk."

The room quieted immediately when Claudia began speaking. She continued, encouraging the women to give testimony of their travails and offer them up for prayer. Claudia paused, thinking that the women needed to overcome an initial shyness. She had not heard the front door open and did not turn her head as a number of women trickled in, positioning themselves some distance from her in the large front hallway. But when the faces of her audience registered shock, she turned her head to see who had entered her home. There, behind her, unassuming and interested, stood Hillary Clinton with her entourage. Without giving it any thought, Claudia immediately rushed over and hugged her icon.

"You came! I am so happy and honored you came!"

Turning again to the church ladies, Claudia acted swiftly and with flawless composure.

"Well, we are truly blessed today, are we not, ladies? Mrs. Clinton needs no introduction. After hearing her speak yesterday, I told her I wished my dear friends and neighbors could share the experience. She told me she would try her best to stop by today, and I see that she is a woman who keeps her word."

Claudia, taking Hillary's arm, steered her to the center of the room. Beaming and relaxed, the First Lady spoke to the hushed group of women. After noting the beauty of the Cates mansion, she congratulated the churchwomen on the Harriet Tubman play, saying Claudia had told her about it and mentioned how it was important to provide women with role models at an early age. She recounted other things Claudia had told her the previous day about Peoria as a community and the history of the First Baptist Church. She encouraged the women to stay in touch with her by writing letters and making her aware of concerns they had about their children's health, education, and welfare. After speaking, Hillary accepted a small plate of hors d'oeuvres handed to her by a delighted Lucy Sims. She spoke easily with the women who approached her, asking them questions about their lives. After an hour, Hillary departed with her attendants, cameras flashing from the edge of the front lawn as she climbed into her limousine. The women, elated following Hillary's appearance, talked excitedly about her intelligence and friendliness. They were amazed at Claudia, at how she was so comfortable having Hillary as a guest in her home, reacting to her like an old friend. Rebecca, reading the thoughts of the mesmerized women, smiled to herself, thinking how inexhaustible were her glamorous sister's resources.

Claudia again positioned herself in the center of the room and invited the women to begin their testimony. Many women spoke, asking for specific prayers for a husband or child, or for themselves to have bodily strength and clear minds to support their loved ones. Many also asked for blessings for the Cates sisters as leaders of their church and community. Amelia Bartleson alluded to Wilson's tirade of earlier that day.

"I don't intend to keep apologizing for my daughter. She's a good child and doesn't deserve to be slandered, especially not from the pulpit."

"Amen," several of the women commented.

To everyone's surprise, Julia Wilson spoke next.

"We need you to stand up for us, Sister Rebecca. You make your own living and you're powerful. None of us knows how to do what you've done, but we can learn from you how to be strong women. I don't know how somebody can see, always facing the ground."

Though not elaborating on her personal experience, she had said enough to alert the churchwomen. Many of them had already detected her air of unhappiness. They also noticed how her husband dominated her. They looked at her admiringly for the first time, understanding at what price she mustered such candor. Rebecca, who had no concept of being dominated, knew Julia Wilson singled her out because that morning she had stood up publicly to the pastor.

"We'll get together again soon and talk over these things," she responded sympathetically but with characteristic caution. "I promise we will."

Soon after, the women departed. The Cates sisters happily did the cleaning up from their event, then headed up to their rooms.

Rebecca climbed into bed, her thoughts of Julia Wilson. The normally timid woman had opened herself during their female camaraderie, in the process confessing how much she admired Rebecca. Rebecca felt even more dismal about her plans to tell the trustees about Julia's implants, and her worry increased. Not only would she be injuring Leighton's professionalism, she would also hurt and embarrass Julia. The unassuming woman had stirred Rebecca's protective nature like a flower she could not bring herself to crush. Further, she understood that with Claudia's triumph that afternoon and Gracelyn's success with the play, the Cates women had taken up the reigns of leadership in their small community of women. The churchwomen's newfound sense of purpose opened the door for them to discover how limitless they were. Rebecca had gambled on their craving for leadership and she had won. But she would also lose.

XI

REBECCA STOOD OVER her laelias early Monday morning, watering them and slightly stirring the dirt in each pot. The blooms were coming on brilliantly, and she made a mental note to photograph them later in the week when they were at their peak. Steeling her mind against the possible loss of her lover, she wanted to preserve this memory of Leighton's gift. Despite her looming sadness, she reviewed the upcoming day. Gracelyn and Claudia were to sleep late, per her instructions, while Rebecca fed and bathed the men. Lucy Sims would be in by lunchtime and stay with Jake while the women traveled to Briney Memorial with Timothy and Herbert. Rebecca would return Wednesday afternoon in time to meet with the trustees that evening.

Rebecca hated worry. Her remedy was to refocus her mind and keep busy. Luckily, this morning she had more than enough to do. As soon as she left the greenhouse, she began making the men's oatmeal, keeping her ears alerted for any sounds coming from the second floor. Timothy, who had never eaten adequately, ate even less in the few weeks since Dr. Meyers provided Rebecca with his sedative. Under the new drug, he slept most of the time and didn't seem to mind being groggy. Rebecca told a relieved Claudia to no longer be involved with his care, and Rebecca kept him clean and fed. Carrying the breakfast tray up the stairs, she reflected that today was the last day Timothy would be in her household. After depositing him at Briney Memorial tomorrow, there would be only Jake left to settle at Sacred Lamb.

Following her chores with the men, Rebecca sat at the kitchen table drinking coffee. She decided to wait to eat until Claudia and Gracelyn woke up, so they could have breakfast together and go over plans for their trip. Hearing the front doorbell, Rebecca arose quickly, thinking that it must be Wayne, or that Lucy's husband may have needed to drop her off earlier than noon.

Rebecca opened the massive door and, to her complete astonishment, Julia Wilson stood on the front porch. She appeared hastily dressed, wearing a faded melon shift and beige cotton sweater tied by the sleeves around her neck. Her eyes were glassy, and her mouth was pursed above her tightly clenched jaw.

"May I come in, Rebecca?"

"Of course, Julia. What brings you here so early? Is everything all right?"

Rebecca had started to add, "with you and the pastor," but something kept her from mouthing the words.

"I've left him," Julia said simply, her voice trembling slightly.

"Lord help us. Please come in and sit down."

Rebecca gently ushered Julia to the kitchen, directing her to the table. She did so obediently, and Rebecca poured her a cup of coffee.

"How do you take your coffee, dear?"

"A little cream is fine. No sugar."

"Now, just relax. If you'd rather, we have some peppermint tea."

"No, Rebecca, thanks. I need the coffee. I think I'm more relaxed than I've been for a long time."

"That's good. You don't have to talk about it, but is there any way I can help?"

Julia Wilson spoke decidedly.

"I'm not going back. I've taken it for years. I've never complained. I've tried to do whatever he's wanted. But he's mean. He was mean to talk about that little girl like he did Sunday morning. I don't mind telling you he hates women. He hates us all. I don't know why, and right now, I don't care why. All I want is to get away."

Julia paused, sipping her coffee. Sensing she had more to say, Rebecca did not speak.

"He's done things to me, to my body. Things I should never have let him do. I have been so ashamed sometimes. I thought I needed to keep him happy, but nothing helped. I did whatever he asked. Nothing satisfied him. Our daughters, I'm glad they're both gone. They're good girls. One has her own family. One's in college. They couldn't wait to leave our home. They've always wanted me to leave him. Sometimes I couldn't look my girls in the eye. They've known everything. They've known about his appetites, his other women."

Julia paused again. Rebecca noticed she had begun crying, but she continued talking, her voice steady.

"I don't know how I kept lying to myself. I spoke to both my girls last night. They told me they loved me and not to blame myself. Can you believe that? They've suffered too. I said I've got to do this for me and for them. If they can be strong, I know I can."

Rebecca touched Julia's shoulder sympathetically, her heart touched by the woman's confession.

"What I need, Rebecca, is two hundred dollars for bus fare to Ohio. I have family there. I'll pay you back as soon as I find work. I want to leave right away. He was there when I left and he wouldn't let me take anything out of the house. But there's nothing there I want. He thinks I'm coming back. He doesn't know I'm with you. I promised him I wouldn't come by here yesterday for the tea. But he went to play golf, and I had one of the church sisters pick me up. He doesn't know what I've been doing or thinking for a few days. I want to keep it that way."

"That's wise," Rebecca answered her. "Julia, my sisters and I are leaving early tomorrow morning. We're heading north, up near Chicago. Why don't you spend the night here, and we'll drop you off at the airport so you can fly to Ohio. I can write you a check for your ticket, and I want you to take some cash. You can pay me back when you're comfortable, so don't worry about it. I'd feel better thinking you weren't alone on the bus all that time. You have enough to do getting yourself settled. I'm glad to help."

"I'm grateful, Rebecca."

"Good. Come on, I'll take you upstairs to our guest room. Would you mind if we packed you a travel bag? You look to be about Claudia's size."

Overcome by Rebecca's concern, Julia started to cry again.

"Right now, I just want to lie down."

"Fine, rest as long as you want. No one will know you are here. You'll be safe."

Rebecca showed Julia the third-floor room and brought her a towel and washcloth. Shortly after she returned to the kitchen, Claudia came downstairs, dressed and alert.

"Who was that at the door?" she asked Rebecca.

"Tina Turner."

Rebecca, still a bit stunned, did not explain her sarcasm. It turned out there was no need, as Claudia continued distractedly.

"Oh, I just thought it might be Wayne. I know he's not due here today. I guess I was just thinking about him. We had such a time this weekend. I couldn't have finished all that food without his help."

"Yes, dear. Did you hear Gracelyn stirring?"

Before Claudia could respond, Gracelyn walked into the kitchen, her face glowing.

"I sure got all the sleep I'll need for a while. I have a taste for pancakes. That all right with you all?"

"Fine with me. Gracelyn, I'm glad you feel rested. You deserve it. You did a wonderful job with that play. And, Claudia, whoever thought we'd have the First Lady under our roof. I'm proud of my sisters."

Rebecca regarded the two before continuing, her expression serious.

"You know we need to go over a few details for our travel tomorrow. But before we go into all that, I want both of you to take a deep breath."

Hearing Rebecca, Claudia's eyes widened while Gracelyn's narrowed. They were not used to hearing Rebecca, normally so matter-of-fact, speak with traces of emotion in her voice. Even Sunday, when she was incensed by Wilson and rising to address the congregation, her words had been measured, her tone barely inflected. But just now, they heard her sound slightly strained. Rebecca spoke again before Claudia or Gracelyn could speculate further on what was wrong.

"Julia Wilson is upstairs in the guest room. She has left her husband."

Rebecca let her remarks sink in before continuing. "She'll be leaving with us tomorrow morning, and we'll drop her at the airport. She's moving to Ohio to be with her family."

"Oh, I see," Claudia said knowingly. "You know, I'm not surprised."

Gracelyn, frantic, and immediately understanding the importance of this turn of affairs, was more vocal.

"Rebecca, are you serious? He's history! No, I mean it, he's really toast! Don't you see? We can really get rid of him now. Oh, I'm sorry. I should be more concerned about Julia. Is she all right?"

"She's fine. She just needed rest. And you're right, Gracelyn, this makes things a lot easier on us."

"Are you going to tell the trustees about this?"

"I'm still making up my mind. I have enough to tell them as it is."

Hearing this, Claudia reentered the conversation.

"Rebecca, you never told us what you planned to tell the trustees. I know you said it was confidential. Will we ever find out?"

"Honey, I imagine everyone will find out. I have to tell them about some money Pastor Wilson spent. Some church money. When I looked over the books, something didn't look right to me. So I looked into it further. He did something with some church money that he shouldn't have done. That's all I can say for now. Since Julia's leaving tomorrow, I don't suppose there's any harm in letting the trustees know that Pastor's marriage is over. The meeting's on Wednesday, and Julia will be in Ohio by then. But I feel like, to be fair, I should let her know I'm going to tell it. I'm thinking she won't mind. Between his taking the money and his wife leaving him, that should be enough for him to be terminated."

"Good Lord from heaven," Claudia said, mildly shocked.

"How much did he take?" Gracelyn asked.

"Only around three thousand dollars. But what he took it for, that's what's so bad."

"How do you know what he took it for?" Gracelyn went on.

"Honey, I made it my business to find out why. But I'd rather not say right at the moment. I don't want anyone else to be hurt."

Gracelyn zeroed in.

"Did he spend that money on a woman?"

"Yes and no," responded Rebecca. "Anyway, it's delicate. We'll talk about it again when this blows over. Julia deserves her privacy. She's had a hard time being with that man, and Lord knows, we all know about that."

"We certainly do," Claudia shot in. "I hope she'll be blessed in her new life. Rebecca, what you said was true. The universe brings us what we need if we open our hands. I hope Julia has that in mind."

Claudia paused, somewhat nervous.

"I have something to tell the two of you. You know, Wayne and I, we are getting really close. He's become more than a friend. I guess you can say he and I are courting. Now, I know I'm still married to Timothy, but it's not like he's going to be around. And Wayne says if I need time, he can wait for me to straighten things out. I didn't tell him I don't need any time at all, because it just sounded so brash to say that. But that marriage was over before it started. The only thing I need to do now is get it on paper. I know the Lord didn't send me this tender man for me to turn him away."

"No, I'm sure He didn't, Claudia," Rebecca soothed her.

"Claudia, what do you mean by 'tender'?" Gracelyn teased, her voice sugary.

Claudia, blushing, laughed. Rebecca rushed to her defense.

"Gracelyn, you leave your sister alone. Wayne has always been one of my favorite people, and we all need a tune-up periodically. He's has lots of character. Just leave Claudia alone."

"Rebecca, I don't mind Gracelyn's teasing me," Claudia said quietly. "I'm not ashamed, and he's not rushing me to do anything I'm not ready for. I always thought there had to be more to love-making between a man and a woman than I knew from being with Timothy. And now I know for certain."

She looked directly at Gracelyn.

"Honey, we all missed out on something. I missed out on feeling like I was going to die from pleasure, then the next minute knowing for certain I had gone to heaven."

"This sounds serious!" Gracelyn exploded.

"Darling, at my age, everything I do is serious."

"Well, just what have you done?" Gracelyn's tone was supercilious.

"Gracelyn, leave Claudia alone. If she wants to talk, she'll talk."

"Wayne has a really nice butt. I love men whose legs are the same length as their torsos. They look so strong. I like a tall man too, but only if he's filled out well. Otherwise, they get a little gangly when they're tall." Gracelyn looked sidelong at Claudia.

"Sounds to me like you took a good look at Wayne."

"I did. But don't worry. I would never stab my sister in the back. And I'm sure you've dazzled him, anyway. Any man who helps make tea sandwiches must really be whipped."

"I'm thankful you didn't use some awful language to say what you just said."

"She got pretty close, to my mind. Gracelyn, what's got into you?"

"Rebecca, I haven't really talked to anyone over fifteen for weeks, so you all should allow me some adult conversation. I'm younger than you, but I've been an adult woman for a long time."

"Yes, indeed. No arguing that," Rebecca replied to her. "And you're right, Wayne has a very nice build."

"A nice butt," Gracelyn said with emphasis. "Plus, he's a real nice color. Kind of a burnished tan. Have you looked at that man's arms? I love men's arms."

Rebecca shook her head, understanding Gracelyn was on a roll.

"Of course he's real lucky to have you, Claudia."

"I'm sure he knows that, dear," Claudia replied. "And, yes, I have looked at his arms. I think I told you all I was in his arms."

Gracelyn giggled, then went on.

"You know, I have a theory. Men of a certain age either stay looking good or they start to go down. Have you noticed that? Wayne is one of those men who is always going to be handsome. Partly because he has a good spirit. That shines through."

"You always amaze me, Gracelyn," Rebecca said thoughtfully. "Those are wise observations."

"I am a writer. I observe."

"Of course. That makes sense to me. What did you observe about Randall Leighton?"

"You mean that doctor? Rebecca, I'm glad you asked. He's quite a character. Sort of wild and refined at the same time. A lot of depth there, a lot of passion. Are you going to say why you asked about him?"

Claudia began speaking before Rebecca could answer Gracelyn's forthright probe.

"Rebecca, I didn't want to bring this up, but that night he stayed here during the storm, the whole time we were eating dessert, he kept turning his head to look at you, whether you were talking or not. Now, I didn't want to jump to conclusions, but it seemed to me there was something brewing, at least on his end."

"He keeps in touch."

"What kind of touch?"

"Gracelyn!" Rebecca playfully slapped Gracelyn's thigh. "I can see right now no one is safe from your questions. There's really not much to tell."

"Do you mean he isn't your type?" Claudia asked with sincerity.

"I'm not sure I have a 'type.' "

"Sure you do, Rebecca." Gracelyn challenged. "Just think about it. What do you notice most about a man? What makes a man attractive in your eyes?"

"I've been married so long, I haven't thought about it recently. I like large hands."

"Is that all?"

"Hands are important, Gracelyn. And long fingers."

"Rebecca, you're boring."

"I'll admit to that."

"Rebecca's not boring at all. She's just not as verbal about things as you are," Claudia protested.

"What you should say, Claudia, is I don't have Gracelyn's powers of description."

Rebecca's mind was somewhat eased, thinking that with the scandal brewing around the Wilsons, she might be able to keep her trip to Leighton's clinic to herself. She had rather not breach Julia's privacy, even after she left town.

Gracelyn's high-energy voice broke through her thoughts.

"He did seem very cerebral. That would be a good match for you, Rebecca, that is, if you're looking. I'm certainly not. I think I'm going to be on vacation from men for a long time."

"Well, you certainly can be if you wish. Give yourself time to heal. But then again, don't rule anything out."

"That's right, Gracelyn. Rebecca told me a few weeks ago to keep my hands open for the universe to drop something in it."

"Sometimes I hate men. They seem to be all the same."

"Believe me, Gracelyn, they're not, just like we're not. You'll find your soul mate after you find yourself again. You've just been offtrack for a while and Bernard is still not gone from your thoughts. Can you be a little patient? All that pain will ease in time, and you'll be a new person."

"Rebecca, it's so hard."

"Well, like anything else, take it a step at a time. You stay up in Chicago as long as you like. Claudia, are you planning to stay the week?"

"Yes, I want to take Herbert shopping. I thought he might like some new clothes. He's a handsome young man."

She cleared her throat.

"Did I mention that Wayne is going to drive his van up on Thursday and spend the night? He's offered to drive us all back Friday."

"That should work out well." Rebecca's mind was on what she would say at the trustee meeting two days from now.

"Claudia, I think Herbert has a crush on you. When we were rehearsing the play he asked me, 'How's Miss Claudia?' more than once."

"Oh, that's sweet. I'd love to have a son like him. He's so brave about his handicap, like he doesn't even notice it. And he's bright."

"Won't Herbert be jealous of Wayne?"

"Gracelyn, hush. I think they'll get on fine. You're just trying to torture me. Herbert's a boy, and remember, he's an orphan. He likes me because I mother him and he's grateful that I bought him new glasses. Raphaela has so many children over there, she can't get to them all."

"You know, that's true. Claudia," Rebecca traveled back from her disquieting reverie. "I think I'll see if Herbert can come over for a few weeks until school starts and take Jake outside for walks. He won't have much company with Timothy gone, and Herbert might enjoy making a little money."

"That's a wonderful idea, Rebecca. I like having him around."

"Claudia, you all right about tomorrow?" Gracelyn asked her sister, her tone shifting.

"I'm fine. There's a lot I don't understand. But I'm fine. I wonder how he's going to feel when he realizes where he is, and for the rest of his life, he'll be alone. I wonder if he will live long enough to face his demons. He's as much a stranger to himself as he is to me. I wonder if the people there can do anything for him. It's over for me. But for him, it may just be beginning."

"Girl, we'll just pray," Rebecca said softly. "We did as much as we could. We did our duty. Don't dwell on it too much."

"You know, this sounds terrible. But there are days when I don't even give Bernard a thought. It seems so far away when we were together, almost like another life. But then other times, I start crying and I can't stop. I don't know if I'm crying for something I lost, or because I'm afraid of what I have to do for myself. Most of the time, I'm betwixt and between."

"Gracelyn, that's growing pains. You and Claudia, the three of us, we know what's behind us, we know that pain. But we don't know what's ahead of us, and even if we think it can't be any worse, well, we can't be certain. It hurts to start over, it just seems like more pain. We have to keep telling ourselves everything's going to work out, and keep going. Sometime next week, we'll visit Bernard. He probably won't last long. So, Gracelyn, that will save you the trouble of explaining anything to anyone about your feelings for him. You'll be free to be with someone else or not. Remember, I always said the menfolk will see us on a regular basis once they're put away. But Claudia, since you're going to divorce Timothy, you can really let that go, and you and Wayne can continue to be out in the open. I don't think we'll hear anything back from the church-women, since as far as they're concerned, you walk on water. With Pastor having his troubles, I don't think we'll hear anything from the men. If there's a need, Gracelyn or I can run up to Briney Memorial and bring back a report to the congregation. After we take Jake to Sacred Lamb, I'll visit him often enough. I won't mind that."

"Will Randall mind?" Gracelyn was curious, realizing she knew very little about the workings of Rebecca's heart.

"Maybe not. I'll invite him to go with me. It's not like Jake will know the difference."

"That's true. Rebecca, will you divorce Jake?"

"I'm planning to. On paper, anyway."

"I see. He wasn't really a bad husband, was he, Rebecca? He didn't seem to be. It's just that he had that accident."

"Gracelyn, you're prying. Give Rebecca some privacy."

"I'm sorry, Rebecca."

"That's all right. Jake worked very hard. I know he wanted to make me happy."

"Don't you wonder why our lives weren't different? Why it had to be so hard for the three of us?"

"Gracelyn, it's harder for a lot of people than it's been for us. What we have to remember is, it won't be so hard now. It was just hard being wives."

The three sat silently, reflecting on Rebecca's last words.

"Good morning. I couldn't sleep."

The Cates sisters turned their heads around all at once to see Julia Wilson standing beneath the archway of the kitchen door.

"Come in, Julia. I just mentioned to Claudia and Gracelyn that you were here. Gracelyn promised us some pancakes, so I hope you can eat something."

Claudia sprang to her feet and pulled out a chair. Taking Julia by the hand, she spoke soothingly to her.

"Sit right here. Once you eat something, you'll probably sleep like a rock. Can I get you some coffee?"

"Oh, no thanks. Rebecca gave me coffee earlier. But I would love some warm milk if it's not too much trouble."

"No trouble at all." Claudia darted to fetch a large ceramic mug from an overhead cabinet and milk from the refrigerator.

"We're happy to have you with us this morning. I told my sisters you were headed to Ohio. So just relax, and don't think about anything except a nice hot bath and getting some rest." Rebecca smiled gently at their visitor. "Claudia, Julia told me she left everything behind, so I thought we'd pack a bag for her."

"That's a wonderful idea, Rebecca. Julia, you tell me if this is too hot. And I went ahead and sprinkled some nutmeg on top."

Julia tested the milk. "This is just fine." She sipped slowly from her mug.

"Right after we eat, I'll take you upstairs and you can go shopping in my closets. I love doing makeovers," Claudia said as she resettled herself at the table.

"Claudia, don't get carried away. Julia might not want a makeover, just a few things so she can travel fresh."

"Well, really, a makeover sounds kind of good."

"Great!" Claudia said happily. "Honey, looking good is always the best revenge."

Julia smiled. "I did want to talk," she said, looking directly at Rebecca.

"Just so long as you know everything you say stays in this room," Rebecca replied.

"That's right, Julia. We've all been there," Gracelyn said softly, turning from the counter and pausing from stirring pancake batter.

"I don't mind talking to all of you. I admire all of you a great deal. I've never been close to women who were really sure of themselves, who did spectacular things. When I came to this town two years ago, the first thing I noticed was the three of you sitting together in church service, so dignified. It wasn't just that you drove up in a Mercedes and lived in a fine house. It was how the three of you always were so easy talking with everybody, like you made up your own minds and didn't wait for a man to tell you what to say, and how everybody respected you. Even if people were envious of what you had, they respected you. Now, since Claudia started speaking out Sunday mornings and invited the church-women to her marvelous tea and Gracelyn did that play, you don't hear anything but good things. My husband, he's not the kind of man who would ever let a woman hold her head up."

"Do you have any sisters, Julia? That's meant a great deal to us."

"I do, yes. One sister and two daughters. They've wanted me to leave my marriage for a long time. I guess I'll have to figure out why I stayed so long."

"Don't be too hard on yourself. At least you're moving forward now," Rebecca said gently.

"I'm very happy being around my daughters. I know I'll see more of them away from their father. I should have protected them more. Things could have turned out very badly for them. I guess I'll have to figure that out too."

"Julia." Rebecca said firmly. "Do you realize how many women never do what you're doing? That says a lot. Please keep that in mind. It just so happens that the three of us always had more money than our husbands, so we didn't ever have to kowtow to them the way a lot of women do. None of us wanted to walk away from our marriages. The reason we can now is we've decided to let go of anything that doesn't bring us peace of mind. You're a lot stronger than you think, because you're starting out with nothing. Pretty soon, you're going to know yourself in a whole new way. You won't even recognize the new Julia."

Julia smiled. "I've been thinking about that a lot. I already feel different. I was trained as a nurse, but I think I might go back to school. I've always been interested in learning foreign languages. When I sat less than six feet away from Hillary Clinton, I just decided anything was possible."

"Anything is." Rebecca paused for a moment. "Gracelyn, do you need some help with the food?"

"No, I'm just keeping the pancakes warm while I scramble some eggs. You sound hungry, Rebecca."

"I am, at that. I waited to eat so we could all have breakfast together. Julia, you know I'll be at that trustee meeting tomorrow night. Is there anything you want me to say to them about your leaving?"

"I was just thinking about that. If you don't mind, I'd like to write a letter to the trustees. There are some things they need to know about church business. My husband stole money. Always a little at a time, but steady. He bought things for our house, expensive things, and wrote them down as expenditures for the sanctuary. I know exactly what those things are and I can list them. Also, he's had at least two girlfriends in the congregation since we've been here. I don't know how you feel about naming names, but at this point, I'll just write it all down and you do what you think best. One of the women left town. The reason he was so hard on that Bartleson girl was because her mother, Amelia, turned him down. When he doesn't get things his way, you can't put too much past him."

"My Lord." Rebecca shook her head.

"I don't know how you say this to a roomful of men, but maybe it needs to be said. I couldn't do some of the things he wanted me to do, things the Bible talks against. But I did agree to have breast surgery. I thought it would calm him down. It did for a minute, but then he was back to wanting me to do other things. I was too scared. I was worried about having problems with the implants. Thank God I saw a good doctor. But the main thing you need to know is that my husband used church money to pay for it. He told the trustees I needed surgery for 'women's problems.' "

"Uhm hum. I can understand that," Rebecca intoned. "That way, they'd feel too awkward to ask questions. I'll be certain to follow through, Julia. Thank you for letting me know all of this. I'll go over the books this evening and see what I can find. I think it's best that the church knows they're being cheated."

"Well, I'm grateful to you, and I know the church is important to your family. After I'm gone, it's not going to bother me who knows what my husband has been doing."

"As long as you're sure."

"Yes, Rebecca. I'm sure it's the right thing."

XII

REBECCA SAT ON the edge of her bed, slowly massaging her feet. Earlier that evening, she had heard Claudia down the hall rattling away to Julia as she pulled out items from her wardrobe for her trip to Ohio. Rebecca smiled, thinking how Claudia enjoyed this sort of thing, and wondering what sort of makeover she had given their pastor's departing wife. Though she couldn't hear Gracelyn up in her attic, her youngest sister would be writing, working well into the night. Gracelyn's discipline could be remarkable; her work made her happy.

Rebecca thought about her own happiness, her orchids, and how she enjoyed nurturing them into perfect bloom and showing them to vendors. And she thought of Randall Leighton. He would be hers now. She was out of danger. She did not feel like she was betraying Jake. She had in fact settled into a fondness for him, losing all bitterness about what he had done to cause difficulty in her life. She could regard him now as an old friend from her past, someone she would keep in touch with, but who would not be at the center of her life. Even if she divorced Jake, she knew she would still be a friend to him, and not leave him stranded at Sacred Lamb.

Rebecca felt at peace for the first time in many weeks. She decided she had better try sleeping again, since she, her sisters, and Julia would leave early in the morning, the Cates women for Chicago and Julia for the airport en route to Ohio. Rebecca was slightly baffled by the dream that awoke her. She was standing in the dining room holding a blue-and-white-patterned ceramic vase she had just filled with water. Somehow, she lost her grip on the vase and dropped it, the shards making a circle around her feet, imprisoning her. She was afraid to pick them up and afraid to walk forward. Then the front doorbell rang. As she was standing still, sunlight streaked through the window and fell onto Rebecca, covering the length of her. After that, the dream ended. Rebecca shook her head as if to dismiss it and lay down again.

The scene outside the Cates mansion the next morning was bustling, but orderly. Rebecca stood aside the Mercedes, which she had earlier driven midway down the driveway, and watched as Herbert steered the heavily sedated Timothy toward the car. Gracelyn appeared in the front doorway fully dressed, her energies high.

"Herbert!" she called out. "We've got muffins and sweet rolls. Do you want juice or some milk?"

"Milk's fine, Ms. Gracelyn. Thanks."

Gracelyn disappeared inside the house. A few moments later, she reappeared carrying a picnic basket, and went to sit in the backseat of the Mercedes, anchoring Timothy on one side.

Claudia and Julia Wilson, both outfitted in smart print dresses and prim hats with netting, appeared in the doorway next, smiling and chatting like old friends.

"Doesn't she look chic?" Claudia asked her sisters.

"She looks just grand," Rebecca replied. "Julia, now you remember, if Claudia goes into business, you have to send her some customers."

Rebecca directed the two women to climb into the front seat.

She waited for Herbert to descend the front porch steps with Timothy's suitcase, the ladies' garment bags, and his own tote. He arranged the luggage perfectly in the trunk of the car.

"Herbert, dear," Claudia called to him, "put Julia's bag on top, since she'll be getting out first. It's the green one."

"Yes, Ms. Claudia." Herbert busily did his rearranging.

"My, Herbert, everything just fit. You've done a good job."

"Thanks, Ms. Rebecca."

Herbert climbed in the car and sat next to Timothy, on the side opposite Gracelyn.

Rebecca remounted the porch steps and closed and locked the front door.

"Is everybody comfortable?" she asked, reentering the car. "I know we're a tight fit for a few miles."

"I'm just fine," Julia said.

"We're fine back here," Gracelyn responded.

"Herbert," Claudia said, turning, "Mr. Timothy looks like he's going to lean over on you any minute. I hope you won't mind."

"No, Ms. Claudia. I'll just let him sleep."

"Thanks, dear. You've been such a help."

"Yes, indeed," Rebecca restated the thought. "You've made all the difference this morning, Herbert, carrying all those bags."

Herbert beamed proudly at the women, oblivious to the weight of Timothy's head on his shoulder.

Arriving at the airport, the Cates women and Julia got out of the car. Inside the small airport lobby outside the gate entrance, they exchanged hugs. Julia thanked them tearfully for coming to her aid. Rebecca observed tacitly while Claudia patted her sympathetically on the back, and Gracelyn offered encouragement. She glanced the lone woman's way one last time as she walked toward the security apparatus. A solitary but elegant figure, Julia turned to blow a last kiss to her friends.

After they deposited Julia, Rebecca noticed that the car passengers were uncharacteristically quiet, until Gracelyn spoke heavily.

"We've all been there, haven't we?"

"Yes, indeed we have," Rebecca responded. Claudia also understood, without asking, their sister's meaning.

The three women could not continue this talk until they were alone together. Rebecca, enjoying a stretch of lush greens along the highway, did not regret the silence in the car. Though Timothy was heavily sedated, Claudia would not feel at ease talking in front of him about her future plans. Gracelyn might have, but she had already pulled out a book, and Herbert was too shy to initiate a conversation on his own.

Nearing the city, Rebecca spoke to Herbert.

"Now, Herbert, where we're taking Mr. Timothy is not in Chicago but just north of it. So when we double back and check into our hotel, you'll get to see those tall buildings and the lakeshore up close."

"Yes, Miss Rebecca. Miss Claudia told me we would be doing a lot over the week."

"Well, you just make sure you enjoy yourself."

"Yes ma'am." Herbert grinned.

After Claudia signed the papers the nurse handed her, the Cates women and Herbert left Timothy at Briney Memorial rather unceremoniously and set off for their Chicago adventure. Rebecca delivered Herbert and Claudia to Claudia's favorite day spa for facials and body packs. Later, Claudia would take the young man on a relentless shopping spree downtown.

"We'll go sight-seeing tomorrow, after I find you a new outfit," Claudia told Herbert as he was being led away by a heavily tipped attendant. "You'll be so handsome dressed up, I'll want to show you off."

"Claudia, you and Herbert meet Gracelyn and me for dinner at eight at the hotel," Rebecca announced.

"That sounds good. That will give us time to change into our clothes. Bye, dears."

"All that shopping should keep her mind off things," Gracelyn commented.

"Certainly will," Rebecca agreed. "She has her joy. She'll be fine. Let's get over to the beading exhibit you were talking about. I imagine the institute will be closing before long. Tomorrow morning, before I leave, I can take in one or two bookstores with you before I head back."

"Rebecca, I wish you could stay longer. It's fun having you to run around with."

"Oh, you'll have fun without me. Next trip, there'll be more time. Anyway, I'll be more relaxed after that trustee meeting is over."

"Does that have you worried?" Gracelyn asked immediately, not accustomed to hear Rebecca voice misgivings of any sort.

"I'm not sure what I'm feeling. I don't think there'll be a problem with removing Pastor Wilson. But it amazes me sometimes how much we all suffer in this life."

"You feel loss, Rebecca."

"Is that it?"

"Yes, that's it."

Rebecca looked at her pretty younger sister's face earnestly.

"Your fight is over, and now there'll be something missing in your life. Whenever something ends, it's like there's a big hole inside until something else fills it."

"Little girl, I think you're onto something. How did you get to be so wise?"

"You're wise, Rebecca. I try to be like you. You keep moving forward, you never get stuck."

"I don't know about never. But I do try to listen to myself. You know, that little voice that comes from somewhere. There's always some kind of choice that feels right."

"You're like our general, Rebecca. You see the big picture and you're focused. And you have a big heart. You make Claudia and me feel like we can do anything and that even if we fail, we can start over."

"That's the main thing, I think, starting over."

"You do too much for us."

"What makes you say that?"

"Because it's true. You put our happiness first, before your own."

"Well now, the two of you make me proud to lead you. So whatever I've done, I'm honored and happy to have done it. A leader's only as good as her followers."

The two walked close together down Michigan Avenue toward the Art Institute, Rebecca, utilitarian in khaki pants and tucked Oxford shirt, a single strand of pearls around her neck and her definite waistline suggesting an offhand femininity; Gracelyn's curves accentuated by a soft linen gold-colored skirt and a button-down turquoise blouse. Passersby thought them incongruously paired but close friends.

At noon on Wednesday, Rebecca arrived at the Cates mansion. Pulling halfway up the drive, she carried her small suitcase inside the front hallway. Reappearing on the front porch, she retrieved the last two days' mail. Her heartbeat quickened as she picked up a letter addressed to her, airmail from France. She knew at once it was Leighton's handwriting.

"I have just arrived here, and am ready to hold you to your promise to join me. I must see you, Rebecca. It would be wrong of you to deprive me of your warmth in this magical city. Let me know how soon you can leave. I will make all arrangements."

Rebecca, smiling at the passion in Leighton's communiqué, looked forward to savoring the intimacy of reading it over and over. She knew her trip abroad would have to wait until she had committed Jake to Sacred Lamb, and having just taken Timothy to Briney Memorial, she felt decorum dictated that she and her sisters wait at least a month before embarking on this last spousal duty. She was glad Leighton longed to see her, but she also suspected he was testing her. Typical, she thought, for a man to see if she would drop everything and run to him. Rebecca, arriving at this thought, tilted her head, astonished. Drop everything and run to him is exactly what she wanted to do.

Questions thronged Rebecca's mind. Did Leighton not know how she planned everything, thought through every detail, reviewed tactics repeatedly, and never revealed strategy, very much like the general Gracelyn had termed her? She had met Leighton while in fight mode. Did he long to see her always as she was after their lovemaking, defenses down, tender toward him? Or, had he espied both the warrior and the lover? Rebecca knew she had reached him without pretense. Their passion was not something she was looking for, not something she had chosen. It came at a moment when her mind was totally involved in another matter. But now, in her mind and heart, she knew being with him was more important to her than anything else, the thing she was supposed to do now.

As if on cue, she heard Jake ranting as Lucy Sims came down the front stairs.

"Hello, Sister Rebecca. I sure prayed everything went well with Mr. Timothy."

"Everything went fine, Lucy. Why is Jake hollering?"

"He's gotten worse, Sister Rebecca. He wants somebody with him all the time. It's like leaving a baby."

"Oh, I see. Lucy, did I tell you I needed to be at the trustee meeting this evening?"

Lucy's head jerked up.

"Oh, yes, Rebecca. I planned to stay until you got back. I just came down to get some dinner started, so don't worry about that."

Lucy gave a quick wave and headed for the kitchen. Immediately, Rebecca walked to the library and dialed Dr. Meyers's office.

"Dr. Meyers, this is Rebecca Cates. Yes, Timothy's all settled. We'll be going up to visit him in a week or two. But I'm afraid Jake has taken a turn; he's quite overexcited. Can you prescribe a sedative for him? Nothing too strong, just to calm him down a bit so he's not liable to wander around and hurt himself. Thank you. I'm here alone for a few days, so please arrange for a delivery. Of course. I'll call if anything else develops, but I think we'll be fine."

Climbing the stairs to go check on Jake personally, Rebecca knew that nothing would prevent her from going to meet her lover. She determined to be ready as soon as Claudia and Gracelyn returned from Chicago. Tonight, after the trustee meeting, she would contact Leighton and tell him she could leave Sunday evening. Tomorrow, she would be on the phone with Sacred Lamb, rescheduling Jake's commitment for this coming weekend. She hoped to see her sisters before leaving town so suddenly, but that wasn't going to stop her either.

"Jake, Lucy tells me you're upset. I want you to lie down and try to relax. It's not good for your blood pressure to get so wound up."

"Yes, Rebecca," Jake replied obediently.

"Good. Now, we'll have some dinner ready later, but if you get hungry, you call or come downstairs and I'll fix you some peanut butter and crackers."

"Not hungry now, Rebecca. Just sleepy. A little sleepy." Jake smiled sweetly as he drifted off.

"All right, then. I'll check on you in a little while." Rebecca smiled at him, again realizing she bore him no ill will for their life together.

That evening, Rebecca bathed and dressed for the trustee meeting, wearing a tailored pale gray summer-weight suit. Her only accessory was a blue-and-pink paisley scarf around her neck, the ends meeting pertly in a cross-tie. Reading Leighton's letter earlier, she had had such a pleasurable feeling she wasn't sure she could do battle. But understanding that tonight was the opportunity to clinch her strategy, she regained focus. Looking at herself in the mirror, she knew that being with Leighton was all she needed to bring back her softness. She reminded herself to travel in this suit, recalling that Claudia had once pointed out that it perfectly matched her eyes. Claudia also advised her to keep her accessories minimal, but to complete the subdued outfit with bright pink lipstick.

Rebecca thought for a moment. Impulsively she rummaged in her dresser drawer and drew out a cosmetics bag. An unopened Guerlain lipstick read ROUGE AZALÉE. Rebecca opened the gold filigree case and gave her lips a quick swipe. Looking at her face again, she thought it just enough color to keep her thinking about her Paris destination without distracting the trustees from the seriousness of her mission.

She realized things could get ugly between her and Wilson. Her words during their exchange the previous Sunday during service were strained and, she was sure, noticeable. She wanted to present her information to the trustees with total composure. But something fierce was brewing inside her. In her mind, she saw Julia walking bravely toward her new life, and she remembered the pain of her tell-all confession at the Cates kitchen table. Rebecca rarely displayed anger in an uncontrolled way and she wasn't vengeful. But in this moment, she knew what she was feeling was rage, and she was tempted to respond in true warrior fashion, aiming for the total destruction of her enemy. She realized this would not do. It would not serve her purposes. Julia had come through, no longer helpless, and looking toward the future. The years she and her sisters had lost in their abusive marriages had yielded to ones of promise. They had all been blessed with courage and hope, and with each other. Rebecca determined to honor those blessings.

"Lord, the Devil is busy," Rebecca reminded herself. She went downstairs, left the house, and headed for the church.

"Sister Cates."

Deacon Smitherson stood and pulled out the chair next to his from the conference table in the church's downstairs meeting room. The five other trustees, including Deacon Johnson, were already seated on either side of the table. The head chair was empty.

"I reckon we're all a bit early, except for the pastor. We were pretty concerned, hearing your announcement. You speak in church so seldom, and it sounded serious."

"Thank you, Deacon Smitherson."

Rebecca took the seat offered her, then nodded her head in a general greeting to the others present.

"I hope the trustees will take the matter seriously. I'm sorry to say, it's pretty unpleasant business."

Rebecca paused briefly before continuing.

"Shall I go into it, or wait for the pastor's arrival?"

"That would be up to you. Deacon Johnson can chair our meeting until Pastor arrives, and we can repeat your information so you won't have to be here the whole time. We're a pretty dull bunch."

Rebecca smiled, grateful for Deacon Smitherson's humor and thoughtfulness.

"Well then, I see no point in delay."

Rebecca unzipped her small handbag and removed Julia Wilson's letter.

"I am so sorry to have to report a crisis in our midst. Julia Wilson was at my home two days ago and entrusted me with this letter for the church leadership. I did not open it, but she made me aware of its contents. She described some rather unseemly situations in her household and has apparently left her marriage. I believe she felt more comfortable expressing these things to a woman. You understand?"

"Of course," Deacon Johnson responded quickly, then made

brief eye contact with the other trustees, whose concern had registered vividly on their faces.

"I'll try and be brief. I will leave the letter in your possession, as you are the most trusted members of our congregation, and I would prefer not to go into detail."

"Do not do anything that will make you uncomfortable," Deacon Johnson soothed.

"Aside from the marriage breaking up, which is really to my mind a personal matter, and what is more important for our purposes, Julia has indicated several instances of misappropriation of church monies by Pastor Wilson. I ask that you give serious attention to this, and get back to me as soon as you can. I have done my own preliminary review of the church budget and have identified some discrepancies. I would be happy to have these explained following your own review. You know, my family has always been honored to give whatever financial support we could to the church, and we have no plans to abandon that tradition. But if there is a rotten apple somewhere, we truly will not be comfortable until it is rooted out."

Rebecca finished speaking, and for several minutes the room was silent.

"Well, I'll be," Deacon Smitherson said, slowly shaking his head.

"You know, you hear things and just let them go right by you. People are always ready to gossip. But this sounds like more than a notion," Deacon Johnson commented.

As Rebecca stood to leave, the roomful of men stood up. Touched by the respect they showed her, she felt satisfied they would follow up, particularly with regard to any funds embezzled. She left the meeting happy that they had accepted what she brought before them without resistance, and that Wilson hadn't been there. She knew she had Julia's courage to thank for this smooth sailing.

XIII

THOUGH EXHAUSTED FROM her drive back from Chicago and the gravity of her meeting with the trustees, Rebecca stayed up a few hours after Lucy left. She was anxious to contact Leighton so they could complete her travel arrangements for Sunday evening. She was eager as well to hear his voice.

When she did awaken Thursday morning at her usual time, she felt relieved, as if a weight had been lifted from her, as indeed it had. She showered and dressed so she could begin preparation for Jake's breakfast. It was strange thinking the two were alone in the house together. Though she was still legally his wife, Rebecca's feelings toward Jake were like those one has toward a distant, ailing relative needing assistance, for whom she felt a degree of compassion. Rebecca felt rested and happily thought of being with Leighton in less than a week. She was puzzled at having the same dream she had had a few days ago, but it did not invade her sense of well-being.

For the next half hour, Rebecca cooed over her orchids. Back inside the kitchen, she boiled water for Jake's oatmeal, started her coffee, and downed a glass of juice. Her feeling of loss had diminished, and her thoughts shifted to the new beginning she would make with Leighton next week. She was sure of him, of his devotion. The way he had kissed her and made love to her the last time was just as feral as it had always been, but also tender, and she felt anchored in the plans he spoke of about blending their lives. She knew he wanted to marry, but she also knew he would wait until she felt she wanted to be a wife. The important thing was that their bonding was so intense, and that she trusted him. He seemed to understand and accept her closeness with her sisters, though his own family connections appeared less central in his life. Rebecca was joyful, thinking what they could give each other over time.

The front doorbell rang, interrupting her reverie. Rebecca turned off the stove, then went to see who was visiting.

"Just a minute," she called, walking swiftly through the hallway.

Expecting to see Wayne, she was surprised to see Reverend Wilson standing outside her door. Some instinct told her that rather than let him inside, she should speak to him on the front porch.

"Good morning, Reverend Wilson. How can I help you?"

Rebecca's tone was neutral as she shut the door behind her.

"Oh, I believe you know full well how you can help me, Sister Cates."

Rebecca tilted her head slightly, regarded him evenly, but did not answer. Understanding that he would have to move things forward, Wilson bellowed at her, "Where is my wife?"

"Do you realize you are yelling, Pastor?" Rebecca asked, not expecting an answer. "Since I cannot answer your question, we really have nothing to discuss. I suggest you leave my home."

"You cannot or you will not!" Wilson was furious. "Is she in there?"

Leaning to the side, he curved his head around Rebecca's tall figure, in an attempt to see inside the mansion.

Rebecca, surprised, decided she just wanted to get rid of her visitor and go on and get Jake fed.

"Julia is not here. Now, please leave."

Wilson, irrational, was not leaving. He unleashed a tirade against Rebecca and women in cahoots with other women, scheming to break up marriages. Rebecca, unafraid, listened without flinching, hoping that he would complete his tantrum quickly and leave her to her tasks. She watched, totally disengaged, as though she were looking at him from afar. This enemy who underestimated her and whom she had conquered still had no inkling of what he was dealing with. He could not have imagined her discipline or tactical skills, or allowed that any woman could think in a straight line. Rebecca was to him no different from other women, an outline onto which he projected primal fears and his grossest fantasies.

Mattie had once told Rebecca that there were two types of men. "The ones who like women and the ones who don't." She stressed that, once the mold had been set, there was little any woman could do with the latter variety. She told her daughter she was sorry they hadn't come up with a name for this category, because it would make it a lot easier for women to distinguish one sort from the other.

Rebecca was impatient after several minutes of watching Wilson flail his arms and rage at her. But she calculated that despite her relative strength, she could not force him to leave her property without his violent response, and she wasn't sure a physical fight was one she could win. She considered calling the police, and wondered, if she tried to reenter the house, whether he would force his way inside, do some damage, or even accost her. Wilson could not defeat her psychologically, but in his state of desperation, she thought it possible he might attack her. She certainly did not want to travel to Paris with any bruises or injury. Rebecca decided her best option would be to let Wilson wear himself out, though the thought of standing passively outside her own front door suffering verbal abuse from someone she did not respect was anathema to her. *So here I am,* Rebecca thought, *rope-a-dope.*

At the point she began to consider whether she should be afraid, she glimpsed someone crossing the yard. In a few moments she realized it was Wayne's long arm that yanked Wilson backward and away from her. Turning to see Wayne, Wilson, in total surprise, pointed his finger at Rebecca and began to sputter.

"She . . . they . . . I won't have it!"

"Get off this property," Wayne said simply.

Wilson sized up the stranger and realized, as Rebecca had before, that he was now the one unsure of what he was dealing with. He hadn't reckoned on a brawny male presence at the Cates home, a man without any infirmity.

Angry still, but deflated, Wilson turned to descend the front porch stairs. As he walked away swiftly, he glared at Rebecca over his shoulder.

"My Lord. Wayne, I wasn't sure what he was going to do."

"Never mind him, Rebecca. Are you okay?"

"I'm fine, thanks to you. We let his wife stay here before she left him," she said, feeling the need to clarify the situation.

"That's no excuse to come on your property and threaten you. Any man who threatens a woman has some serious issues."

"That would be true of Pastor Wilson."

"Pastor? You mean he's a pastor? Your pastor?"

"Well, I don't think he'll be our pastor much longer. One of the reasons his wife left him is he's been stealing from the church. He was also abusing her for a long time."

"Uhm uhm. Sounds like you all had a lemon."

"We did that. Wayne—" Rebecca paused. "I have to feed Jake so he can take his medicine. Why don't you come inside for some coffee?"

"I will, Rebecca. Just to make sure he doesn't come back, I'd like you to make a police report, get a restraining order."

"I guess I can do that. But Claudia and Gracelyn will be back tomorrow, so I won't be alone here. Claudia told me you were bringing them home."

"Yes, I was. But under the circumstances, I believe they will probably want to come back as soon as they can. I have Claudia's hotel number. I'll go ahead and call her, if that's all right with you."

"I don't want to worry them."

"Rebecca, I know they would want to be here with you. Chicago's close enough, they can always go back. It's not like they're in France."

"No, I guess not. They're not in France."

Rebecca busied herself with Jake's light breakfast, realizing she was somewhat dazed by the morning's encounter. She made certain he ate most of his oatmeal, then came back downstairs to put the kitchen in order. She was surprised to find that Wayne had already cleaned the pot and was wiping down the counters. He turned to see her standing with Jake's tray.

"Just give me that, Rebecca. I want you to sit down and put your feet up. Do you think you can totally relax for a while?"

"I may need to, Wayne. Is there coffee left?"

"I'll make a fresh pot and bring you some. Sit in there," Wayne pointed toward the living room, "and put your feet up. I already spoke to Claudia. She and Gracelyn are on their way."

"I was about to ask."

"It might help for you to have a little brandy in your coffee. Just tell me where to find it. I won't make it too strong."

"Oh, that sounds good, Wayne. There's a liquor cabinet in the library. I think there's some brandy."

Rebecca did as she was bid and sat quietly in an overstuffed chair, her feet perched atop the matching ottoman. Stopping to rest, she thought of how quickly things were developing. Wayne carried in her coffee and brandy, placing the tray on a side table.

"Rebecca, if you want, I can call the police a little later on. I think you need to catch your breath."

"Thanks, Wayne. I think I do."

"Now, I can go outside and start my work, or I can stay in here with you. Whichever you prefer."

"Oh, I don't mind being alone. I'll probably doze off after this alcohol."

The doorbell rang.

"Looks like you have some more company. Don't worry, it's not Wilson."

Wayne went to the door, opening it to let Lucy Sims enter.

"Good morning, Wayne. I came to see about Rebecca. I know our pastor was over here looking for his wife. He has been going around to some of our women's homes, accusing them of hiding her. It's been horrible. I knew Rebecca was here by herself. But I see she's not."

"No. I got rid of your pastor about a half hour ago, at least for the time being. But I want Rebecca to make a report with the police to make sure he doesn't come back on the property."

"Oh yes, indeed. When a man like that is that upset, he's not safe for a woman to be around. Could I speak with Rebecca?"

"Wayne, is that for me?" Rebecca called from the living room.

At Wayne's nod, Lucy moved forward.

"Rebecca, it's Lucy. I came to make sure you were all right. I heard what happened here this morning. It's a shame. He was over to Annie Turner's and Martha Davis's too. Last I heard, anywhere there was a woman alone, he showed up."

"Where is he now?"

"Honey, I really can't say. But you go on and let the police know he's not welcome here. I don't see how he is going to show his face at church anymore."

"Rebecca, I'm heading outside," Wayne called from the hallway.

"That's fine, Wayne. Thank you."

"Can I get you anything?" Lucy looked concerned.

"No, I'm a lot calmer now. Wayne put a little brandy in my coffee."

"That was a good idea. You rest. I can stay at least long enough to get Mr. Jake his lunch."

"Thank you, Lucy. Please don't let us be a burden to you over here."

"I don't mind, Rebecca. I needed to come and make sure you were okay. You're a fine person, and you don't deserve this kind of confusion. That man messed up his marriage on his own and he'll have to face himself. All anybody else can do for him is pray."

"Lucy, you know, I think we're all in process."

"Yes, that's true, Rebecca. Now, my Earl's a good man, but we have our moments when we don't seem to be talking the same language. But he's never raised his hand to me, or sworn at me, or called me a name. And if he did, he knows he better pack his bags. Even so, I don't think he has it in him to be mean to me. I know I have his heart, and I know I'm a lucky woman."

"I'm sure he feels lucky too."

"Oh, he does. It's my life's chief blessing that we found each other."

Neither woman spoke for a long moment.

"Rebecca, could I say something personal to you?"

"I'm sure I won't mind."

"It's about that Randall Leighton. I only met him one time, but that man's heart is on his sleeve when he looks at you. Now, you are a beautiful woman and you will most likely have your health for a long time. Mr. Jake can't do a thing for you. So, if that doctor is trying to court you, don't you put him off. I know he's been here a few times, and I hope you didn't discourage him from keeping in contact."

"Lucy, I'm amazed. Is it that obvious?"

"It's obvious to anyone with sense."

"I tried to resist, but that didn't last long."

"Good. I'm glad to hear it. I know what your plans are for your husband, and I believe you're doing the right thing by him. You're in your prime, and it's time for you to move on. And, Rebecca, you know I'm not one to talk your business."

"Lucy, you are something."

"Any fool would do what I'm telling you to do. The sooner the better. And you know, the Lord moves in mysterious ways. We won't have Pastor Wilson hollering and screaming from the pulpit any longer. So I take all that as a sign for you to find some happiness for yourself. Julia Wilson did everybody a favor."

"I feel the same way, Lucy. Thank you for being so honest with me."

"Maybe our new preacher will have some sense. If Wilson had quoted one more verse about Jezebel or Bathsheba or the like, I believe I would have gone upside that man's head with my very own King James."

Rebecca laughed loudly at Lucy's remark. The doorbell rang again.

"You don't move, I'll get that."

Standing outside the door was Amelia Bartleson, armed with a bat and breathing heavily, her cheeks flushed.

"Amelia, what on earth?" Lucy said, astonished.

"Has he been over here? I heard he came over here and was yelling at Rebecca. I came to see for myself and give him a piece of my mind and whack him a few times if he acted like he didn't care for it!"

"Amelia, he's been here and gone. Rebecca's workman got rid of him. Rebecca's fine; she's resting. Why don't you come on in and see for yourself."

Amelia entered and placed her bat against the wall, then followed Lucy to the living room.

"Rebecca, I'm here to check on you. Is everything all right?"

"Everything's fine, Amelia, and thank you so much. How on earth did you know that Pastor Wilson had been by here?"

"Raphaela called me. You know that woman knows everybody's business. The CIA should hire her to teach their people how to dig up dirt. But she means well. Anyway, if that evil man thought he was going to come over here and raise hell—sorry—raise Cain with you, I figured I'd see how long he could talk with a bat going upside his head."

"Truly, Rebecca, Amelia carried her bat over here," Lucy explained.

"Amelia, I always thought of you as the quiet type."

"Well now, Rebecca, I'm generally quiet. But I have a fighting spirit when I need to. That man got on my last nerve when he berated my daughter. Upset me so bad. I've been looking for a reason to get in his face ever since. Not that I didn't think you could stand up to him, but two can be better than one to drive home a point."

"Word sure gets around. Well, thank you for thinking of me. How are all your children?"

Amelia calmed and began to lovingly recount the exploits of her rowdy offspring.

"But you know, Rebecca, my real problem is I'm raising three children plus raising a grown man. He's no help to me at all. I believe I'd be better off just putting him out once and for all. The children love their father. That's the only thing stopping me."

"I hope you can work everything out. I will certainly keep you in my prayers."

"I'll do the same," Lucy added. "Rebecca, why don't I fix us some sandwiches. After all this excitement, we need sustenance."

"Oh, fine, Lucy. I am sort of hungry. Amelia, will you stay to eat?"

"I can stay a little while. James is at home today. Of course that doesn't mean my house won't be a total wreck by the time I get back."

Rebecca and her guests spent most of the afternoon chatting

and laughing. The phone rang frequently, as several of the church-women called the house to ask about Rebecca, having heard that Wilson was heading to the mansion. Lucy and Amelia alternated answering the phone, briefly reassuring each caller that Rebecca was fine and that there would be police follow-up.

"And you know, if he shows up again, I came over here with a bat, which I'm perfectly ready to use," Amelia informed some of the callers.

Claudia, Gracelyn, and Herbert arrived early evening. By this time, Amelia had departed, and Lucy was tidying up in the kitchen. The two younger Cates sisters walked in hurriedly, look-ing frantically for Rebecca, who had gone upstairs to do some packing for her trip.

"Hello, dears," she said to her sisters, opening her bedroom door to let them in. "What a day. I feel bad you had to cut short your week."

"We wanted to come home as soon as we heard what hap-pened," Claudia said, walking over to hug Rebecca.

"Rebecca, I wish I had been here when he came." Gracelyn's face was tense as she followed behind Claudia. "How dare he come to our home and threaten you!"

"It's over now, and it could have been a lot worse. I believe Pas-tor's world just crashed down on his head, and he couldn't really do anything to stop it. Wayne, Lucy, and Amelia took good care of me. I didn't have to lift a finger all day. Get yourselves settled. There's something I need to tell you."

Still looking worried, Claudia and Gracelyn spaced themselves at the foot of Rebecca's bed across from where she sat cross-legged at the head, facing them.

"Sunday, I'm going away. It will be for a while, I don't know how long."

"Is it business, Rebecca?" Claudia asked.

"I may do some business, but it's mainly personal."

Rebecca took a long pause.

"I'm going to be traveling with Randall Leighton." Waiting for a response that did not come, Rebecca continued. "We're going to Paris for a few weeks, then Senegal. Will you all be okay with Jake until I get back?"

"Oh, Rebecca, that's wonderful," Claudia said, emotion heavy in her voice. "We'll be fine with Jake. Herbert will be around all summer, so we'll have extra help. You go, and stay as long as you wish. I'm so happy for you."

Claudia stopped speaking and began to cry. Rebecca squeezed her hand.

Gracelyn, once Rebecca's announcement had sunk in, bounced excitedly on the bed.

"What in hell's name are you doing still here?"

"Shush, Gracelyn," Claudia immediately remonstrated. "No need to be coarse."

"You should have been gone with that fine man. Claudia and I can clap Jake's behind in Sacred Lamb. By this time, we know how to put a man away."

"Gracelyn, honey, I need to do that myself. He's my husband, and at least until we're divorced I need to do my duty."

"I knew you were going to say that. But just get packed and go. We'll take good care of Jake for however long. And we'll visit Timothy and Bernard like you planned. We'll take your car whenever we go, so all the gossips will know we're doing it. I don't suppose anyone really cares, though, at this point."

"Rebecca, Gracelyn's just talking. We'll do everything just like you wanted. Don't worry about a thing, including those orchids. If you write down some instructions, I'll follow your routine. I'll ask Wayne to help."

"I'll help too," Gracelyn said, alerting Rebecca that she would have to think quickly of a way to keep her youngest sister's energies occupied.

"Gracelyn, you leave the orchids to Claudia. I want to see some manuscripts from you when I get back."

"You're right, Rebecca. I should be able to finish all those poems and get started on a screenplay I've had in mind. With only Jake here, there won't be much to do around the house. Oh, I'm going to miss you, though!"

"I won't be gone too long, and if I am, I'll just bring the two of you over. I'm sure Randall and I will want to see new faces after a point."

"Well, you just see how it goes," Claudia said, wiping her eyes.

"Are you going to marry him?" Gracelyn asked.

"I have no idea," Rebecca answered honestly. "First, I have to figure out why people get married."

"I know just what you mean," Claudia replied.

"Well, when either of you find out, be sure and let me know," Gracelyn said, shaking her head.

"I think we'll all find out for ourselves in our own way, before long," Rebecca said encouragingly. "Right now, it's just nice to be loved. Anyway, I usually feel like I'm married to the two of you."

"Loved?" Gracelyn said, right on cue. "Rebecca, are you saying you've made love with him? When was all that going on?"

"Why do you need to know?" Rebecca replied with mock indignation.

"I tell you, Gracelyn, you have the biggest nose of anyone I know." Claudia rolled her eyes.

"Rebecca, tell me."

When Rebecca didn't respond, Gracelyn yelled excitedly, "You have, I can tell you have!"

"Gracelyn, calm down." This time it was Rebecca remonstrating with her. "I don't think I have to tell you everything I do or don't do. I'm just going to let you wonder."

"That's mean, Rebecca."

"No it's not," Claudia answered for Rebecca. "Have you ever

heard of privacy? We don't want you writing about our affairs in one of your books."

"It's still mean."

"Would you all mind if I finished packing so I can go to bed? I want to be up early, and today was kind of tiring."

"Of course, Rebecca." Claudia leaned over to hug her.

Gracelyn clambered down from the bed and went over to kiss Rebecca on the cheek and wrap her arms around her neck.

"I love you so much. I love you too," she said, next enfolding Claudia.

XIV

Rebecca completed her perfunctory packing well before midnight. She fell asleep thinking of her sisters and their lives. Largely through their own efforts, the deck was no longer stacked against their happiness. She believed they would all do well defining themselves in a way they couldn't have as younger women, and she was confident they would never relinquish their importance to each other, that they would continue to share in the chapters of their lives to come. She realized they had all missed out on something, but that in their devotion to each other, they had something that other people were without. They would undertake their new journey with their love for each other and with courage, but without the heartache each had carried over the years. They had cemented their community profile and they would never be alone. They were Cates women, brilliant, estimable, strong.

Rebecca awoke as usual predawn. The recurring dream had come back to her during the night. Still, she had a new excitement over everything she planned to do. Going out to her orchids, she compiled notes for Claudia while walking through the greenhouse. Claudia, she knew, would follow her instructions precisely. She decided to bring in some blooms for an arrangement at the breakfast table, to keep up a mood of celebration. She wondered how her sisters would feel when they woke up, and whether they would have the same feeling of starting over.

Gracelyn immediately noticed the flower arrangement and decided to go all out for breakfast, fixing Rebecca's favorite duck sausage, cheese grits, and plain croissants with plum preserves. She sprinkled nutmeg in a pitcher brimming with milk, added some shaved almonds, and put the entire concoction in a blender on high speed. Claudia entered the kitchen talking, telling Rebecca what she should wear when Randall took her to dinner.

"I'm glad you're packing that gray suit, but I want you to be a little daring. You will be in Paris, after all. No point in announcing to the world that you don't attend too often to style."

"Yes, Claudia. What do you have in mind?"

"It's a little cooler over there, so don't take any of those loose muslin dresses you wear around here. I don't want you looking like a flower child."

Rebecca looked blankly at Claudia. Claudia went on.

"I know you won't bother with linen, but a lightweight jersey dress or two would be a good compromise. And do some shopping, please, Rebecca. Those European cuts are heavenly the way they fit anybody's figure, and the fabrics are not only chic, they're indestructible. There's a lot to be said for natural, I know, but everything you put on doesn't have to be biodegradable."

"Yes, Claudia."

"I'm getting a vision of you in red, or magenta; something pink. That would be exquisite with your eyes. If I could just get you out of those khakis for one day!"

"I promise, I won't wear them every day."

"Claudia," Gracelyn cut in, "just who is Rebecca doing all this for? Is she dressing for Randall or for you?"

"Lady bird, I have news for you. Women dress for each other. How many men do you know who read *Harper's Bazaar?*"

"Claudia, you know I'm not going to read that," Rebecca informed her. "But I will try to be a little more adventurous in my dress. I'll pack whatever fancy items you bring back. Randall seems to like silk, so if you have time, run out and see if you can find a dress or a pantsuit in a nice color for me."

"Rebecca, that is right up my alley. I have waited years—no, decades—to give you a makeover."

"One outfit is not a makeover, so don't get carried away. But I'm willing to make a small step, if it's not too extreme. Oh, yes. Randall also likes lace."

"Lace!" Gracelyn's eyes bugged. "Rebecca, this is a real romance!"

"Well, I hope so, honey child. I think I could use some."

"Rebecca," Claudia continued, not hearing the other two chat, totally off on her fashion tangent, "what we'll do is subtle main pieces and dramatic accessories. That should make you comfortable and give Randall some titillation. But I do want you to have a red or fuchsia silk dress as a staple. It can be long-sleeved and demure, everything but the color. I know you never want to be flashy. But it will be a nice staple, and you can dress it down with some quiet gold jewelry."

"Yes, Claudia. Gracelyn, are there any more of those cheese grits?"

"Coming right up. But you know, you won't have any cheese grits in Paris."

"I guess it's foie gras, then."

"Rebecca," Claudia was unrelenting, "now shoes. You don't have to wear heels, but there are some very sexy flats out this year. It's the Audrey Hepburn *Breakfast at Tiffany's* kitten heel, and they are smashing."

"Tiffany's is in New York."

If Claudia caught Rebecca's sarcasm, she didn't let on.

"Your hair."

"My hair?"

"If you insist on wearing that bun, at least braid it and coil it lower at the nape, sort of chignonlike. You really need to think about getting it cut and styled. A simple pageboy would be really elegant with your features."

"Claudia, please. Enough! Let me get used to the red dress before you turn me into Jackie Onassis."

"I was really thinking more Barbara McNair or Anne Bancroft."

"How do you keep all this stuff in your head?"

"We owe the world glamour."

"Well then, I am deeply in debt."

Claudia's tone softened. "Rebecca, you know I think you are beautiful whatever you do."

"Thanks, dear."

"Rebecca, I want to do something special for your trip," Gracelyn whined.

"You're doing this wonderful cooking. Do you think I'm going to eat what those French people eat? I may come back here looking like Twiggy, unless I stick to pastry. I don't plan to eat anybody's rabbit or horse, and I'm definitely not eating gallstones."

"Whose gallstones?" Claudia asked, her fashion fixation broken.

"That I can't say. Maybe yours and mine, should we have occasion to pass any."

"Gross!" Gracelyn made clear her distaste. "Isn't that cannibalism?"

"Damn close, I would say."

That afternoon, Rebecca heard from Deacon Smitherson.

"Rebecca, we've relieved Wilson of his duties. But I want you to know, we're giving him a chance to return a portion of the funds he embezzled. We'd just as soon avoid a scandal and not have him prosecuted."

"I understand fully. I'm so glad you got back to me. I'll be out of the country on business for several weeks."

"My stars. Best of luck to you. Was this a sudden decision?"

"No, actually I've put this trip off for a long time. But it looks like now I can get away for a while."

"Well, good luck to you. I know you'll represent us well abroad."

"I'm proud to do so, Deacon Smitherson."

"I hope it turns out to be a profitable trip."

"You're very kind. Thank you."

Rebecca spent the afternoon in the library reading travel books on France and Senegal, humming as she noted references to restaurants with a quasi-American cuisine. She was sure Leighton would know enough places where she would be comfortable, so her activity was really to occupy herself. She noted several exhibits that interested her, but they had already both decided to start their viewing at the Louvre. Rebecca had traveled to Paris a few years earlier, and knew that traversing the vast museum was nearly impossible during a short stay. She was thrilled she would be able to take her time this trip and savor many more of the salons.

Rebecca heard the front doorbell right before dinnertime. She knew Claudia was still out shopping, and Gracelyn was bustling in the kitchen preparing a surprise for dinner, so she went herself to answer it. She saw with relief that it was a woman standing there, a young woman perhaps in her late twenties, quite petite, and wearing shades. "Hello, I'm Lydia Ellington. You're Mrs. Furness, I know. May I come in?"

"Please." Rebecca stepped back to allow the young woman entry. "What can I do for you, Ms. Ellington?"

"Please call me Lydia."

Lydia, standing in the hallway facing Rebecca, shuffled nervously back and forth on her feet. In these few seconds, Rebecca took note of her tasteful dress. The young woman wore a beige cardigan over a deep brown turtleneck, a knee-length brown suede skirt, and flat shoes.

"Fine, Lydia." Seeing how tense she was, Rebecca said, "Let's go sit in the library."

The tiny woman, still wearing shades, accompanied Rebecca across the hall. They sat facing each other, Lydia on the leather sofa, which dwarfed her, Rebecca, feeling comfortable but curious, settled into one of the club chairs.

"I was here a few weeks ago, but no one was home, I don't think. I didn't stay around long." Feeling a need to confess, Lydia continued, "I looked in your greenhouse. It is so lovely. I was really sorry I missed meeting you, the person who could grow all those flowers."

"Thanks, Lydia. I'm glad we're meeting now." Rebecca waited patiently for an explanation of her visitor's business.

Rebecca watched, puzzled, as Lydia hung her head.

"I think most of them were orchids?" Lydia's words were hard to hear, aimed as they were at the floor.

"Yes, I breed different varieties. My favorite type are laelias, but I've been lucky with dendrobium and phalaenopsis too. I like the mix of colors, from white to pale to really deep purples, oranges, reds, and fuchsias. Most people don't know that orchids are the largest plant family in the world. What's so fascinating, Lydia, is their evolution. I mean, you can crossbreed a species on your own and find that what you've done duplicates exactly a natural hybridization. Do you know what I mean by less hybridization?" Rebecca thought talking casually would draw the young woman out.

"Oh, yes! I know." Lydia's head shot up. "Laelia. That has a nice sound."

"Laelia was one of the Roman vestal virgins, so it is a woman's name. I think of all my flowers as friends or sisters. I'm very attached to them, as you can see." Rebecca was happy to share her knowledge.

"You're so kind. You're so very kind to share all this with me." Lydia paused and breathed deeply.

Rebecca waited for her to begin speaking again.

"I have to tell you why I've come here. Why I came before."

Lydia removed her glasses and raised her head, her eyes level with Rebecca's. The young woman had a face very familiar to Rebecca. It was Jake's face. There was no doubt in Rebecca's mind that the small, dark, intense eyes, pointed chin, and delicate cheekbones came straight from her husband's gene pool. For several moments, Rebecca, staring, could say nothing. Finally, she spoke evenly.

"Lydia, you are apparently related to my husband."

"Yes, I'm his daughter. I'm looking for him. We've never met. I hope it was all right for me to come here."

"The resemblance is very strong. I didn't know Jake had a daughter."

"Oh, dear."

Lydia bowed her head before speaking again.

"Then, I come as a complete surprise. I don't really know what to say to you."

"Who is your mother?"

"My mother was Janie Burgess. She died several years ago in St. Louis. I believe she met my father in Los Angeles. I didn't know my mother."

"I see." Rebecca felt a little like screaming, but she wanted to be kind to the girl. "Lydia, will you excuse me for a few moments? I'm going to fix some tea. I'll fix us both some. Some nice peppermint tea. You just sit and be comfortable while I do that."

Rebecca stood up, shaking her head slightly as she tried to focus her thoughts. Tea, that would be simple enough. Suddenly, nothing was simple. Rebecca started down the hall to the kitchen, then turned around again to slide the library doors closed. Rebecca had to absorb what she had just learned before Claudia or Gracelyn discovered their visitor and saw the girl's startling face.

Thankfully, Gracelyn had gone upstairs for the few minutes it took Rebecca to boil some water. In her confusion, not finding a teapot, she placed the tea leaves in a large glass bowl and poured the water over them. She set up a tray with two mugs and a honey dish, sat down at the table, and waited for the leaves to steep. After a few minutes, Rebecca went back down the hall to the library.

Lydia bounded to her feet to help when she saw Rebecca trying to maneuver the tray with one hand while she reopened the heavy doors with the other.

"I hope I haven't upset you by coming here," Lydia said to Rebecca when they were again seated facing each other. "I took a chance coming. I wasn't sure you would let me in the door."

"I'm not upset." Rebecca spoke slowly.

"I suppose you didn't know anything about me."

"No. Nothing. But I guess that may have been for the best. You look to be pregnant, Lydia."

"Yes, I am four months now."

"Are you alone?"

"No, Ms. Rebecca, I'm not. My husband is in the army. We're on our way to Berlin. He'll be stationed there for two years."

"I see."

"I've looked for my father for ten years. You see, I was raised in foster homes, and I didn't know who either of my parents were for a long time. Sometimes, they don't want to give you the information. But I kept on digging and writing letters and reviewing records, anything I could find to figure this out."

"And you succeeded."

"Yes, in a way. I found out my mother was dead. I am sorry to have to say she was a prostitute during the time she was in California. I believe when she moved to St. Louis, she spent some time in prison for shoplifting, but I think for her last few years she led a decent life. She lived with a cousin, an elderly woman, until she died and she kept house for her. I found out she started school later in life, and was working on an Associate's Degree. I'm very proud of that."

Rebecca listened carefully to the delicate girl.

"Ms. Rebecca, will I be able to meet my father?"

"You have every right to, Lydia. But there is something I have to tell you first. Your father has been brain damaged for a number of years, and I have decided to commit him to a rest home very shortly."

"Have you had to take care of him?"

"Yes, my sisters and I. In the state he's in, Jake won't be able to tell you much about his life, so I will fill you in. He majored in business in college and ran our family department store after we married. I guess I don't have to tell you he wasn't the perfect husband. But we had some good years together. He was very smart and very ambitious. Jake was injured at work, very tragically. A shelf collapsed while he stood underneath, and a heavy carton fell on his head and cracked his skull. It was very unfortunate."

Rebecca stopped speaking, watching for Lydia's response. Lydia looked serious, but she said nothing.

Rebecca continued. "I can tell you, Jake would have loved knowing you and been proud of you. He wanted children very much."

"I'm glad," Lydia said finally. "Since I'm leaving the country, I wanted him to know about his grandchild."

"I understand. Lydia, he won't grasp anything you say to him. He can only make sense of things that happened long ago, nothing new, as you will be to him. But I have no objection to your meeting him."

"Thank you. I came a long way to do that."

"It seems to me you've come a long way, in general. Thank you for sharing so much with me."

"You are so very kind. I can't believe you are so very kind."

"You weren't responsible for how you got here, and I admire anyone who has borne up under rough circumstances. I see that you are determined and honest. That always counts for a great deal. Wait here, I'll bring Jake downstairs. Afterward, I'll tell my sister Gracelyn you are here so she can meet you. I hope that won't be too awkward."

As was his habit, Jake wore a tie and sports jacket, as if he were going out to work for the day. Rebecca led him from his room and down the front stairs, saying gently, "Come with me, Jake. You have to meet someone."

"I have his face," Lydia said, covering her mouth in surprise as soon as Jake and Rebecca entered the library.

Rebecca sat Jake down in one of the club chairs so he would be across from Lydia. She sat in the chair next to him.

"Hello, I'm Lydia. I'm your daughter." Lydia turned to Rebecca. "Does he understand any of that?"

"Not really. He goes in and out, but he never does well with short-term memory. What he does remember is from the time before his accident. Anything after, he doesn't."

Rebecca paused, her head turning, hearing Claudia enter the front door and walk through the hallway.

"I need to prepare my sisters before they meet you. But don't worry about anything. You sit here with Jake while I speak to Claudia and Gracelyn. He should be pretty peaceful. Lydia, before you leave, I want to give you some flowers."

Claudia had gone into the kitchen with her packages, thinking she would find both of her sisters there. Standing and talking rapid-fire to Gracelyn about her purchases, her back to the entrance, she turned when Rebecca entered.

"Rebecca, what's wrong?" Claudia noticed Rebecca's queer expression.

"I don't suppose anything is really wrong, but we do need to talk. Gracelyn, could you pour me some water?"

"Of course, Rebecca." Gracelyn exchanged an anxious look with Claudia.

Rebecca took several deep breaths.

"What I have to tell you is Jake has a daughter. Her name is Lydia. She's a young woman in her twenties. She's up front, sitting in the library. I want you to come meet her."

"What?" Gracelyn blurted out without thinking.

"Oh, Rebecca, I'm so sorry," Claudia said.

"No, please. She's actually lovely. She's had a difficult life, not much support. But she's married to a soldier, and they're expecting their first child. She came here to let Jake know before they left the country."

"Rebecca, you don't deserve this. I had no idea Jake was like that. I know it's not the girl's fault, but isn't this hard for you?"

"It was hard before his accident. He was unfaithful several times. But now, everything Jake did to me, I've let it go. My life is very different from when all that happened, and I'm stronger. I built my business, I have the two of you, and now I have Randall. I want you both to hear what I'm saying. The only power we have, really, is to let things go. There's no reason to hold on to all that pain."

"Oh, Rebecca," Claudia said earnestly, "I never thought you suffered like I did, like Gracelyn and I both did. I told you all my problems and you never once mentioned your own. I feel very bad that I didn't comfort you."

"You couldn't have, because I didn't let you know I needed comfort. And maybe I didn't, in the same way. But you both are so precious to me that I haven't needed much more than your being in my life. Never forget that."

"Things are just never fair, are they?" Gracelyn said, still distressed.

"Things are what they are, Gracelyn. But they can always get better. Look what's happened to me. I'll be in Paris next week with a wonderful man."

The three sisters sat registering what had happened in Rebecca's life and what was about to happen.

"And don't forget, Wilson's gone. Deacon Smitherson called me this morning."

"That's fantastic!" Gracelyn instantly shifted gears.

"So, I want you both to meet this young lady and put her at ease. Her life has been harder than any of ours, and she's not bitter. Don't you see the lesson in all this?"

"Lord, have mercy," Claudia said, shaking her head. "I do, Rebecca. But I don't want any more of these lessons for a while. I shouldn't say such, but it's true."

"We all need to rest for a minute. It will be good for me, going away. Now, you all won't be mean to Jake, will you?"

"No, we won't."

"Gracelyn, I didn't hear you say anything."

"I promise I won't be mean. I promise you, Rebecca. But only for you."

"That's a good girl. After all, the man is defenseless." Rebecca smiled. "Come along, now. I don't want Lydia sitting alone with her father if he starts getting wound up. She won't know what to do."

Claudia and Gracelyn followed behind Rebecca down the hall to the library. Stopping at the door, they both stared at Lydia, transfixed by her resemblance to Jake.

"I'm sorry for staring, but it's amazing how much you look like Jake . . . your father," Claudia spoke kindly. "I'm Claudia," she extended her hand. "It's good to meet you."

Gracelyn followed suit. "I'm Gracelyn, Lydia. This is a little unreal, but I'm glad to meet you too."

"I know it must be strange for all of you, especially for Rebecca. But I'm grateful she let me in."

"Oh well, dear. Stranger things have happened," Rebecca replied. "It's probably best to take Jake back upstairs now. Grace-lyn, would you mind?"

Gracelyn complied without answering, taking Jake's hand and leading him back into the hallway and up the front stairs. When she returned, she joined her sisters and Lydia, who were talking calmly together.

"I suppose there are a lot of things to know when you meet a person," Rebecca said. "I'll send you a scrapbook once you get to Berlin. I have lots of pictures of Jake. I'll send the address for Sacred Lamb too, in case you get back this way. Do you think you will be coming back stateside this year?"

"We hadn't planned to. But I'll certainly be in touch."

"That will be good."

"Did Rebecca tell you she's leaving for France on Sunday?" Claudia asked.

"You are? That's a coincidence."

"It is, isn't it? The trip came up kind of suddenly, but I'm really looking forward to being away. Jake will be in good hands with my sisters until I get back."

"I wasn't worried, Rebecca. I can tell you care about him."

"I do. I'm not in love with him, but he's a family member, a part of my history." Rebecca paused. "I'll be traveling with a male companion, a wonderful man. Maybe we'll get a chance to meet your husband overseas."

"I would like that, Rebecca."

"Will you stay in touch with us here, Lydia?" Claudia asked, still damp-eyed. "At least let us know if you need anything."

"Oh, yes. If you want me to. I would be delighted. Outside of my husband I don't have any other family."

"You have family now, dear," Claudia told her.

"Claudia, will you go and see what Gracelyn is doing about dinner?" said Rebecca. "Lydia, I hope you'll join us," she added, realizing the girl was probably hungry.

"I'd love to, but I can't. I promised Robert I would get back to the base before late, since I'm driving alone. But I would very much like to visit again."

"We look forward to it. You're a very sweet girl. We should get your flowers now, so you'll stay on schedule."

"Rebecca, I brought back some wonderful tangelos from the market," Claudia said, as the three stood up to leave the library. "I'll fix Lydia a bag of those and wrap up some bread and cheese so she won't get faint during her drive."

"That sounds fine, Claudia. But I hope tangelos are not what Gracelyn's serving for dinner tonight." Rebecca's remark made them all laugh.

Claudia gave Lydia a quick hug, then left her and Rebecca to gather up a bouquet from the greenhouse and say their temporary farewells.

After Claudia walked away, Rebecca turned back to Lydia.

"Lydia, don't take this the wrong way, but do you have your own money?"

"Yes, Rebecca. I have some savings and I plan to work, once I learn the language."

"You let me know if ever you don't. That's one thing we don't mind doing. A man always holds some cards. It won't hurt for you to be holding a few."